D1098664

Leadership Masterclass

John Adair is currently visiting Professor in Leadership
Studies at the University of Exeter and an international
consultant to a wide variety of organizations in business,
government, the voluntary sector, education and health. He
has been named as one of the forty people worldwide who
have contributed most to the development of management
thought and practice.

Educated at St Paul's School, John Adair has enjoyed a
varied and colourful career. He has served in the Arab
Legion, worked as a deckhand on an Arctic trawler and had
a spell as an orderly in a hospital operating theatre. After
Cambridge he became Senior Lecturer in Military History
and Leadership Training Adviser at the Royal Military
Academy, Sandhurst before becoming Director of Studies at
St George's House in Windsor Castle and then Assistant
Director of the Industrial Society. He writes extensively on
both management and history.

John Adair is married with three children. He lives near
Guildford in Surrey.

JOHN ADAIR

EFFECTIVE

Leadership Masterclass

What every
manager can
learn from the
great leaders

PAN BOOKS

First published 1997 by Pan Books

an imprint of Macmillan Publishers Ltd
25 Eccleston Place London SW1W 9NF
and Basingstoke

Associated companies throughout the world

ISBN 0 330 34785 3

Copyright © John Adair 1997

The right of John Adair to be identified as the
author of this work has been asserted by him in accordance
with the Copyright, Designs and Patents Act 1988.

9 8 7 6 5 4 3 2 1

A CIP catalogue record for this book is available from
the British Library

Typeset by CentraCet Limited, Cambridge
Printed and bound in Great Britain by
Mackays of Chatham plc, Chatham, Kent

CONTENTS

Introduction   1
How to Get the Best Out of This book   3

1 LEADERSHIP THROUGH KNOWLEDGE

Socrates – A Leader of Ideas   10
The Case of the Aspiring General   12
The Case of the Young Cavalry Commander   14
Knowledge – The Key to Leadership   15
Are Knowledge and Experience Enough?   18
A Leader in Action   21
Key Points   25
Points to Ponder   26

2 LEADERSHIP SKILLS

The Case of Nicomachides   29
Human Needs and Leadership Functions   32
A Leader in Management   35

Are Leaders Born or Made? 38
Key Points 39
Points to Ponder 41

3 A LEADER OF LEADERS

In the Gedrosian Desert 44
Creating Unity and Teamwork 46
Caring for Individuals 48
Key Points 49
Points to Ponder 50

4 CHARISMA

The Divine Gift 51
Evocation and Invocation 54
Alexander as Charismatic Leader 57
The Persian Method 61
Key Points 66
Points to Ponder 67

5 THE SERVANT-LEADER

The Teaching of Lao Tzu 72
The Tao of Leadership 74
Jesus and His Disciples 79
Servant–Leadership in Perspective 81
The Japanese Contribution 86
Key Points 88
Points to Ponder 89

6 NELSON

Early Life   92
The Man and the Legend   93
Achieving the Task   98
Bringer of Harmony   100
Meeting Individual Needs   102
The Sailors' Response   103
Nelson's Legacy   107
Key Points   109
Points to Ponder   110

7 MAKING THE RIGHT DECISIONS

Thinking to Some Purpose   112
From Ideas to Responsible and Decisive Action   117
Case Study: Chairing the Cabinet   122
Intuition and Imagination   124
Calmness under Pressure   131
The Value of Humour   134
Key Points   136
Points to Ponder   138

8 THE ART OF INSPIRING WHILE INFORMING

The Effective Communicator   140
The Art of Inspiring Others   142
The Relevance of the Second World War   146
Case Study: The Forgotten Army   148
Case Study: Montgomery   157
The Effects of Telecommunication   160

Key Points   161
Points to Ponder   162

9   LEADERSHIP IN A CHANGING WORLD

Captains of Industry   165
Case Study: Gino Watkins   170
Management Through Leadership   172
Slim on Leadership   173
Key Points   178
Points to Ponder   179

10   WOMEN AS LEADERS

The Western Tradition   181
Leadership in Marriage   188
Great Social Reformers   192
Women as Leader–Managers   195
Case Study: Margaret Thatcher   198
Key Points   205
Points to Ponder   207

11   STYLES OF LEADERSHIP

On Greatness   209
Abraham Lincoln   211
Charles de Gaulle   214
Adolf Hitler   221
Mahatma Gandhi   228
Nelson Mandela   234

Key Points   238
Points to Ponder   239

12   LEADERS FOR TOMORROW

Not Followers but Companions   244
An Invitation to Greatness   246
Key Points   246

Further Reading   251
Index   254

INTRODUCTION

'If you wish to be great, then keep company with the great.'

So says an old proverb.

This book is an abridged and revised version of *Great Leaders* (1989). My object in writing *Great Leaders* was to trace for the first time the history of leadership as a concept, and to identify some of its significant and great practitioners. Here I am drawing those great leaders out from its pages to serve as teachers in a kind of leadership masterclass. For pre-eminence projects the strengths and shortcomings of leadership on to a very large screen. The invitation to take part in it extends to all those who are already leaders, or who aspire to be leaders, or indeed have a professional or personal interest in leadership. I hope that includes you!

Imagine the feelings of an artist invited to a lesson with Leonardo da Vinci, or a musician with the opportunity of instruction by Mozart. Yet in these pages, you will find their leadership equivalents, men and women of genius, ready to instruct you in the art of leadership, both by their words and, more importantly, by their examples. For actions often speak louder than words. You can, of course, learn all that is in this book by your own experience, but you may be too old by the time you graduate from that school – and the fees you pay will be higher!

By the time you have read this book you should have an idea about:

- the essential leadership philosophy common to great leaders as revealed in their actions
- how these enduring universal principles might transfer to the field of human enterprise in which you find yourself
- your own role as a leader, together with your strengths and areas for improvement.

HOW TO GET THE BEST OUT
OF THIS BOOK

In order to get the most from this book I suggest you read it once through to get a general understanding. Then go back – perhaps on another occasion – and spend some more time on the KEY POINTS at the end of each chapter, using them like checklists to assess your own performance as a leader. Use paper and pencil to list your own strengths, together with areas for improvement. Then add these points up to serve as your own action plan for self-development. For leadership cannot be taught, it can only be learned by YOU.

The POINTS TO PONDER sections provide you with further learning opportunities. They include both some more general reflections, inviting you to relate what has been said to issues or questions of our own day and to your own field. They also include some specific guidelines and exercises designed to help you to apply the lessons of the leadership masters in this way.

You will notice that each chapter in the book centres around a MAIN IDEA, although some – like musical compositions – have minor themes as well. Therefore there is no need to start at the beginning and read through to the end, unless you want to. You may prefer to choose a subject or theme that interests you, and then broaden out your coverage of the book as time and inclination allow. To help you identify at a glance the main ideas in each chapter, here is a condensed list of themes:

MAIN IDEA		NOTES
1	Knowledge	What leaders need to *know* and *be*
2	Skills	What leaders need to *do*: the functions of leadership and the three circles concept
3	Example	A leader of leaders, Alexander the Great, in action, meeting the three circles at strategic or organizational level
4	Charisma	The nature of charisma and how some people create the illusion of it
5	Humility	An unlikely leadership quality, the core of servant–leadership
6	Nelson	Drawing the threads together – a model of an inspirational, three circle leader
7	Decisions	Leadership is not only giving direction but going in the *right* direction!

MAIN IDEA		NOTES
8	Communication	Imparting and receiving information and ideas, but more – communicating purpose and inspiring vision
8	Change	Change throws up the need for leaders; leaders bring about change. How leadership spread from the military and political fields into business management
10	Women	The story of women as leaders, one of the great new factors in the picture of leadership
11	Styles	Five case studies suggesting that different styles of leadership can be very effective given their appropriateness to their context
12	Tomorrow	Where is leadership going? What will the world expect from its leaders tomorrow?

You will notice that there are passages in BOXES. These are supplementary, and can be missed if you are pushed for time and want to skim through the book. Later, you can return to them if you want more illustrations of the themes or sub-themes in that particular chapter.

HOW WE LEARN

Within the themes, see if you can identify the *principles* behind the examples or case studies, for they are the bridges which enable you to see the relevance of one situation — distance in time or field of work — to your own circumstances. It is when sparks jump both ways between those two poles — principles or theory and experience or practice — that learning occurs.

It is essential to remember that people learn by the interaction of

PRINCIPLES   EXPERIENCE

or   **and**   or

THEORY   PRACTICE

It is when sparks jump between two poles — the general and the actual — that learning occurs. So you need both. The various case studies, stories and examples that crowd this book are designed as *stepping stones*:

PRINCIPLES ⇨   ⇨   *YOUR*

or   HISTORICAL   EXPERIENCE

THEORY ⇦   EXAMPLES   ⇦   or

PRACTICE

The arrows are drawn in both directions because the process must work in reverse as well. Your practical experience, gathered from working for leaders good, bad or indifferent, coupled with what you have learnt by practising leadership yourself, must be brought to bear in a *constructively critical* way on the ideas presented in this book.

With the significant exception of the three circles model (p.33) I have not introduced any modern academic theories or ideas into the book because I know of none that will help you to get more out of this book than you can glean by commonsense. All the principles or theory you need – like vitamins – are implicit – and occasionally explicit – in history, as this book demonstrates. The three circles model is the exception, partly because it is globally accepted and has proved to be of such practical value in developing leaders. Even that, however, is only introduced because it tidies up the rough idea of functional leadership that occurred to Xenophon some 400 years before the Christian era.

As you accumulate knowledge of principles, attitudes, skills and qualities, so you will begin to forge your own personal *philosophy* of good leadership – and leadership for good. Then you will find it hard not to do what you know belongs to your own framework of values. That is the objective or the end-product of this journey together through the pages of history.

Lastly, I do hope that you will enjoy this book as much as I have enjoyed writing it. Perhaps through this book you will fall in love with leadership and commit yourself to it. You will find – if you haven't done so already – that leadership, like love, isn't always fun. But, as someone once said of married love, 'No other pleasures are worth its pains.' The path of leadership before you is steep and thorny, and as you journey onwards you need to find wells of inspiration by the wayside to refresh you. May this book be such a source for you.

John Adair

1

LEADERSHIP THROUGH KNOWLEDGE

'Authority flows from the one who knows.'
A modern proverb

Xenophon lived in the fourth century BC, a fascinating period of Greek history. It began with Sparta triumphant over Athens and ended with all Greece subject to Macedon. Like our own, it was an age of turmoil, uncertainty and change – the seedbeds of leadership.

Born in Athens in the early years of the long struggle against Sparta, Xenophon belonged to a family ranked in the class of knights, those wealthy enough to maintain a horse and so render mounted military service. Those eligible for the cavalry in those days numbered about 1200, compared to near 30,000 men of military age in the armoured infantry or *hoplite* class and to the uncounted mass liable for service in the fleet or in the lightly armed forces. Although Xenophon probably served in the cavalry against Sparta he had neither enthusiasm for continuing the war nor any animosity towards the Spartans.

Quite when Xenophon first met Socrates or how long their association lasted, we do not know, but Xenophon was deeply influenced by his encounter with this remarkable man. The first thought about the nature and practice of leadership can be traced to their days together in the market-place, streets and houses of Athens, under the shadow of the Parthenon. For Xenophon joined one of the circles of young men who gathered for instruction from the foremost Athenian philosopher of his day – and perhaps of all time.

SOCRATES – A LEADER OF IDEAS

In early life, Socrates is said to have been a sculptor or stonemason, the trade of his father. As a citizen-in-arms he served in the ranks of *hoplites* in at least three campaigns, gaining a reputation for great courage. He was a man of strong physique and remarkable powers of endurance, completely indifferent to comfort or luxury. With his unflinching courage, both moral and physical, and his strong sense of duty, went an extremely genial and kindly temperament with a keen sense of humour. Above all, he was a man of the greatest intellectual ability.

The greater part of his life Socrates devoted to philosophical discussion and therefore he spent it in comparative poverty. He set himself the task of clarifying for himself and other men the key issues of the right conduct of life. The method he used was so distinctive of him that we still describe it as 'Socratic'. Briefly, Socrates pretended ignorance in order to encourage others to express their views fully. When he had drawn them out by cross-examination he gently exposed their inconsistencies by the same process. It was not an approach that made him popular in all quarters – Socrates was no respector either of persons or of hallowed beliefs in his quest for truth. He showed considerate integrity, for example, when he found himself one of the Presidents of the Assembly at the time of the trial of some unpopular generals: he courageously refused to put the illegal motion to the vote in spite of the fury of the multitude. In 399 BC Socrates' enemies accused him, quite wrongly, of impiety and of corrupting the young. In spite of an eloquent self-defence at his trial, they condemned him to death by forcing him to drink hemlock.

Socrates wrote no books. Our main sources of information about him are Plato's *Dialogues*, Xenophon's *Memorabilia* and Aristophanes' satirical picture in *The Clouds*. It is uncertain how far Plato and Xenophon attributed their own opinions to their common master. When it comes to the theme of leadership it is especially difficult to determine how much goes back to Socrates. Xenophon himself was both a leader and a thinker about leadership. Did he put his own views into the mouth of Socrates? He certainly wrote in the form of Socratic dialogues, with Socrates as one of the speakers. Or when as a young man he heard Socrates cross-examining various would-be leaders, did he take notes which he used much later in his life when he wrote his various books? These questions cannot be answered with any degree of confidence, but at least we know of one core idea in Xenophon which does go back to Socrates – that leadership is tied to situations and depends largely upon the leader having the appropriate knowledge; we know this because Plato also takes up that theme.

THE PARABLE OF THE SHIP'S CAPTAIN

The sailors were quarrelling over the control of the helm . . . They do not understand that the genuine navigator can only

> make himself fit to command a ship by studying the seasons of
> the year, sky, stars, and winds, and all that belongs to his craft;
> and they have no idea that, along with the science of naviga-
> tion, it is possible for him to gain, by instruction or practice, the
> skill to keep control of the helm whether some of them like it or
> not.

But Xenophon's own experience and reflections must
have led him to develop the seeds of ideas thrown out by
'The Thinker' (as he and his fellow students nicknamed
Socrates). Xenophon's own military interest, for example,
comes over clearly in the two following dialogues.

THE CASE OF THE ASPIRING GENERAL

One of the young Athenians around Socrates announced
that he wished to stand in the annual election of ten
generals in the city's army. Socrates encouraged him to
attend the classes of an itinerant teacher called Dionysodurus, who had recently arrived in Athens and advertised a
course in generalship. When the young man returned he
had to endure some good-humoured banter from Socrates
and his friends.

'Don't you think, gentlemen,' said Socrates, 'that our
friend looks more "majestic" as Homer calls Agamemnon,
now that he has learned generalship? For just as he who has
learned to play the harp is a harper even when he does not
play, and he who has studied medicine is a doctor even
though he does not practise, so our friend will be a general
for ever, even if no one votes for him. But an ignoramus is
neither general nor doctor, even if he gets every vote. Now,'

he continued, turning to the young Athenian, 'in order that any one of us who may happen to command a regiment or company under you may have a better knowledge of warfare, tell us the first lesson he gave you in leadership.'

'The first was like the last,' the young man replied: 'he taught me tactics – nothing else.'

'But that is only a small part of generalship,' replied Socrates. By question and answer he then led the young man into a much fuller understanding of the knowledge and abilities required for a successful military leader. A general must be good at administration, so that the army is properly supplied with military equipment and provisions. Moreover, as Xenophon knew from his own experience, a general should ideally possess a number of personal qualities and skills:

> He must be resourceful, active, careful, hardy and quick witted; he must be both gentle and brutal, at one straightforward and designing, capable of both caution and surprise, lavish and rapacious, generous and mean, skilful in defence and attack; and there are many other qualifications, some natural, some acquired, that are necessary to one as a general.

Even on the all-important subject of tactics, Socrates found the instruction given to his young friend by Dionysodurus to be deficient. Did Dionysodurus give *no* advice on where and how to use each formation? Was *no* guidance given on when to modify deployments and tactics according to the needs of the many different kinds of situations one encounters in war? The young man insisted that this was the case. 'Then you must return and ask for your money back,' said Socrates. 'For if Dionysodurus knows the answers to these questions and has a conscience, he will be ashamed to send you home ill-taught.'

THE CASE OF THE YOUNG CAVALRY COMMANDER

One day Socrates met a newly elected cavalry commander – perhaps it was Xenophon himself. Socrates asked him first why he had sought that office. The young man agreed that it could not have been because he wanted to be first in the cavalry charge, for the mounted archers usually rode ahead of the commander into battle, nor could it have been simply in order to get himself known to everyone – even madmen achieve that. He accepted Socrates' suggestion that it must be to leave the Athenian cavalry in better condition than when he found it. Xenophon, who later became both a renowned authority on horsemanship and the author of a textbook on commanding cavalry, had no difficulty in explaining what needs to be done to achieve that end. The young commander, for example, must improve the quality of the cavalry mounts; he must school new recruits – both horses and men – in equestrian skills and then teach the troopers their cavalry tactics.

'And have you considered how to make the men obey you?' continued Socrates. 'Because without that horses and men, however good and gallant, are of no use.

'Well, I suppose you know that under all conditions human beings are most willing to obey those whom they believe to be the best. Thus in sickness they most readily obey the doctor, on board ship the pilot, on a farm the farmer, whom they think to be most skilled in his business.'

'Yes, certainly,' said his student.

'Then it is likely that in horsemanship too, one who clearly knows best what ought to be done will most easily gain the obedience of the others.' Xenophon captures here a very distinct theme in Socrates' teaching on leadership. In harmony with the rest of the doctrine of Socrates (for, despite his pose of ignorance, Socrates had ideas of his own), it emphasizes the importance of *knowledge* in leadership. People will obey willingly only those whom they perceive to be better qualified or more knowledgeable than they are in a particular situation.

KNOWLEDGE – THE KEY TO LEADERSHIP

Socrates clearly taught that professional or technical competence should be a prerequisite for holding a position of leadership responsibility. 'You must have noticed,' said Socrates to another man, 'that if he is incompetent, no one attempts to exercise authority over our harpists, choristers and dancers, nor over wrestlers? All who have authority over them can tell you where they learned their business.'

The tendency of people to follow a leader who knows what to do is strengthened in a time of crisis. In a discussion with Pericles, son of the famous statesman, which took place when an army from the Greek state of Boeotia was threatening Athens, Socrates made the additional point that such a crisis should be more to an effective leader's liking than a period of ease and prosperity, for it is easier to make things happen. He illustrated this point with a favourite analogy, the behaviour of sailors at sea:

> For confidence breeds carelessness, slackness, disobedience: fear makes men more attentive, more obedient, more amenable to discipline. The behaviour of sailors is a case in point. So long as they have nothing to fear, they are, I believe, an unruly lot, but when they expect a storm or an attack, they not only carry out all orders, but watch in silence for the word of command like choristers.

There are three main forms of authority in human affairs: the authority of position or rank, the authority of personality, and the authority of knowledge. Socrates clearly emphasized the latter. It is the man or woman who knows what to do and how to do it who will be

---

A MAN OF THE MOMENT

Apparently against the advice of Socrates, Xenophon enlisted in a Greek army which the Persian prince Cyrus the Younger hired in a bid to replace his brother Artaxerxes II on the throne of Persia. In 401 BC a decisive battle was fought at Cunaxa, not far from ancient Babylon. The 10,400 Greek *hoplites* – heavily armed spearmen – acquitted themselves well on the day, but Cyrus lost both the battle and his life.

After the battle of Cunaxa, the Persians offered the Ten Thousand (as the Greeks were later known) surrender terms if they stayed where they were, but threatened to attack if they moved from their camp. One of their six generals, a Spartan named Clearchus, took it upon himself to act as spokesman for his fellow generals to the Persian emissaries, but gave no indication to anyone what he was going to say. After sunset he summoned a meeting of the officers, briefly reviewed the options and then told them what they must do. They must head northwards that very night on the first stage of a long march to safety on the shores of the Black Sea, which lay some 800 miles away. As Xenophon records in *The Persian Expedition*, everyone sensed that only Clearchus would lead them out of mortal danger:

> On receiving their instructions the generals and captains went away and carried them out; and from then on Clearchus was in command, and they were his subordinates. This was not the result of an election, but because

they realized that he was the one man who had the right sort of mind for a commander, while the rest of them were inexperienced.

obeyed, especially in times of crisis. Now, if that were the *whole* story about leaders, then the right to lead would be acquired with technical or professional knowledge. When the soldier learns tactics, the doctor studies medicine, the sailor acquires knowledge of navigation and the farmer becomes experienced in agriculture, then they would also be qualifying as leaders. For they are accumulating the necessary knowledge and experience which will incline those more ignorant than themselves to obey, at least in their own field. For Socrates and his school, as exemplified by Plato, knowledge is the main gateway to leadership. We can trace here the beginnings of a major theme in the world's tradition of leadership. The desire for educated rulers, governors or leaders — men and women with an authority based on knowledge and experience rather than those who relied upon birth, title or position — would encourage the establishment of schools and universities. It was a rivulet in the tradition which the Renaissance transformed into a mighty river.

But is having relevant knowledge and experience to the situation — the general working field or the particular situation of crisis — the *whole* of leadership? Xenophon knew that it was not so. From his close observation of men in action, he made a distinction between those leaders who won *willing* obedience from their subordinates and colleagues, as compared to those who merely extracted compliance from them either out of fear or a grudging acceptance of the authority of knowledge.

ARE KNOWLEDGE AND EXPERIENCE ENOUGH?

Clearchus, the Spartan general who saved the day after Cunaxa, is a good example of such a limited leader. We can recognize men of his stamp again and again in military history. The Roman army depended upon men such as he. Their type would resurface in later armed forces: the Prussians of Frederick the Great, the British Royal Navy in Georgian times, the German *Wehrmacht* in the Second World War, and the American Army in Vietnam.

Clearchus was about fifty at the time of his death. He had spent much of his life at war, acquiring by hard experience a sound knowledge of his profession. But, as Xenophon noted, Clearchus never won the hearts of men. He had no followers who were there because of friendship or good feeling towards him. Xenophon continued:

> As for his great qualities as a soldier, they appear in the facts that he was fond of adventure, ready to lead an attack on the enemy by day or night, and that, when he was in an awkward position, he kept his head, as everyone agrees who was with him anywhere. It was said that he had all the qualities of leadership which a man of his sort could have.
>
> He had an outstanding ability for planning means by which an army could get supplies, and seeing that they appeared; and he was also well able to impress on those who were with him that Clearchus was a man to be obeyed. He achieved this result by his toughness. He had a forbidding appearance and a harsh voice. His punishments were severe ones and were sometimes inflicted in anger, so that there were times when he was sorry himself for what he had done. With him punishment was a matter of principle, for he thought that an army without discipline was

good for nothing; indeed, it is reported that he said that a soldier ought to be more frightened of his own commander than of the enemy if he was going to turn out one who could keep a good guard, or abstain from doing harm to his own side, or go into battle without second thoughts.

So it happened that in difficult positions the soldiers would give him complete confidence and wished for no one better. On these occasions, they said that his forbidding look seemed positively cheerful, and his toughness appeared as confidence in the face of the enemy, so that it was no longer toughness to them but something to make them feel safe. On the other hand, when the danger was over and there was a chance of going away to take service under someone else, many of them deserted him, since he was invariably tough and savage, so that the relations between his soldiers and him were like those of boys to a schoolmaster.

It is tempting to conclude that while Clearchus had great abilities as a soldier, and also as what we would now call a manager (planning and controlling), he fell far short as a leader. One reason why people today often react so negatively to the idea of military leadership is because they assume that all military leaders are cast from the same mould as Clearchus. This is certainly not the case.

Xenophon's last point, that Clearchus treated his soldiers like a *pedagogue* (literally in Greek a 'leader of children') is illuminating. The Greeks prided themselves on the belief that they were the most intelligent people on the face of the earth; they were deeply conscious, too, of their tradition of equality and democracy. They did not like being bullied or treated as children.

Xenophon, aged twenty-six, was elected as one of the successors to Clearchus and the other five Greek generals whom the Persians butchered in an act of treachery not long after Cunaxa. Having been taught leadership by Socrates, what style of leadership would Xenophon display? Doubtless he thought hard about that question. Obviously he did not want to be another Clearchus, not did he want to err too far in the opposite direction of courting popularity and appearing weak. Xenophon tells us that Proxenus the Boeotian, one of the other murdered generals, had made that mistake. It was he, incidentally, who had first invited Xenophon to go on the Persian expedition, and so they were probably friends. Proxenus was a very ambitious young man and had spent much money on being educated by a celebrated teacher called Gorgias of Leontini. 'After he had been with him for a time,' wrote Xenophon, 'he came to the conclusion that he was now capable of commanding an army and, if he became friends with the great, of doing them no less good than they did him; so he joined in this adventure planned by Cyrus, imagining that he would gain from it a great name, and great power, and plenty of money.' Yet, with all these ambitions, Proxenus made it clear to all that he wanted to get these things in a fair and honourable way or not at all. He liked to be liked, however, which led him into the mistakes of appearing soft and of courting popularity for its own sake:

> He was a good commander for people of a gentlemanly type, but he was not capable of impressing his soldiers with a feeling of respect or fear for him. Indeed, he showed more diffidence in front of his soldiers than his subordinates showed in front of him, and it was obvious that he was more afraid of being unpopular with his troops than his troops were afraid of disobeying his orders. He imagined that to be a good general, and to gain the name for being one, it was enough to give praise to those who

did well and to withhold it from those who did badly. The result was that decent people in his entourage liked him, but unprincipled people undermined his position, since they thought he was easily managed. At the time of his death he was about thirty years old.

It could be said that Proxenus was not right for the military situation, and he could not establish the right relationship with soldiers. But probably he would have been as ineffective in non-military spheres of leadership as well. For Proxenus's very virtues created a certain lack of firmness or toughness which can lead to a loss of respect. Without respect, leadership is fatally impaired. A weak leader exposes himself to exploitation by his more unscrupulous subordinates. Bad leadership of this kind looks remarkably the same whatever the field or area of human enterprise.

Xenophon, who sat at the feet of Socrates, the Western world's first great teacher of leadership, now shows us what *he* meant by leadership.

A LEADER IN ACTION

Imagine yourself on a sun-baked, stony hillside on the southern edge of Kurdistan (on the borders of what is now Iraq and Turkey) watching this scene unfold before you. It is about noon; the sky is clear blue, except for a line of white clouds almost motionless above a distant mountain range. Marching through these foothills comes the advance guard of the Ten Thousand. The hot sun glints and sparkles on their spears, helmets and breastplates. They are hurrying forward, eager to reach the safety of the mountains in order to be rid of the Persian cavalry snapping like hunting dogs at their heels. But first they have to cut their way through the Carduci, the warlike natives of the region. Across the pass you can see a strong contingent of these tribesmen already occupying the lower heights of a steep hill which commands the road. Now the Greek advance guard has spotted them, too, and it halts. After some deliberations you can see a messenger running back. A few minutes later a horseman – it is Xenophon – gallops up to the commander of the advance guard, a seasoned Spartan captain named Chirisophus. Xenophon tells him that he has not brought up a reinforcement of the light-armed troops that had been urgently requested because the rearguard – still under constant attack – could not be weakened. Then he carefully studies the lie of the land. Noticing that the Carduci have neglected to occupy the actual summit of the hill, he puts his plan to his Spartan colleague:

> 'The best thing to do, Chirisophus, is for us to advance on the summit as fast as we can. If we can occupy it, those who are commanding our road will not be able to maintain their position. If you like, you stay here with the main body. I will volunteer to go ahead. Or, if you prefer it, you march on the mountain and I will stay here.'
>
> 'I will give you the choice,' replies Chirisophus, 'of doing whichever you like.'

It would be an arduous physical task, Xenophon points out, and he tactfully says that being the younger man he would be the best one to undertake it. Having chosen some 400 skirmishers, armed with targets and light javelins, together with 100 hand-picked pikemen of the advance guard, he marches them off as fast as he can go towards the summit. But when the enemy see what the Greeks are doing, they too begin to head for the highest ground as fast as they can go.

> Then there was a lot of shouting, from the Greek army cheering on its men on the one side and from Tissaphernes' people cheering on their men on the other side. Xenophon rode along the ranks on horseback, urging them on. 'Soldiers,' he said, 'consider that it is for Greece you are fighting now, that you are fighting your way to your children and your wives, and that with a little hard work now, we shall go on the rest of our way unopposed.'
>
> Soteridas, a man from Sicyon, said: 'We are not on a level, Xenophon. You are riding on horseback, while I am wearing myself out with a shield to carry.'

As the commander, Xenophon had several options open to him. He could have ignored the man. Or he could have threatened him. Or he could conceivably have had him arrested and punished later. Xenophon took none of the courses. Writing of himself in the third person he told us what happened next:

> When Xenophon heard this, he jumped down from his horse, pushed Soteridas out of the ranks, took his shield away from him and went forward on foot as fast as he could, carrying the shield. He happened to be wearing a cavalry breastplate as well, so that it was heavy going for him. He kept on encouraging those in front to keep going and those behind to join up with them, though struggling along behind them himself. The other soldiers, however, struck Soteridas and threw stones at him and cursed him until they forced him to take back his shield and continue marching. Xenophon then remounted and, so long as the going was good, led the way on horseback. When it became imposs-

ible to ride, he left his horse behind and hurried ahead on foot. And so they got to the summit before the enemy.

Note that it was the other soldiers who shamed Soteridas into taking back his shield. Although Xenophon, burdened with a heavy cavalry breastplate, eventually fell back behind the ranks as the men rushed up the hill, yet he encouraged the men forward and urged them to keep their battle order. Eventually he remounted and led his soldiers from the front at first on horse and then again on foot.

Once the Greeks had gained the summit the Carduci turned and fled in all directions. The Persian cavalry under Tissaphernes, who had been distant onlookers of the contest, also turned their bridles and withdrew.

Then Chirisophus's men in the vanguard of the army were able to descend through the mountain pass into a fertile plain beside the Tigris. There they refreshed themselves before facing the fearsome rigours of a winter march amid the snow-covered Armenian highlands. Eventually, in the summer of the following year, the army reached the safety of the Hellespont, the narrow straits dividing Europe from Asia. They owed much to Xenophon who, not long afterwards, became the sole commander of the Ten Thousand.

Anyone reading this story will recognize that in it Xenophon acted as a leader. He led by example. That is a universal principle or theme in the story of leadership. It is especially important where people face hardship or danger: they expect their leaders to run the same risks and shoulder the same burdens as themselves, or at least show a willingness to do so.

KEY POINTS

- Socrates wrote no books, but two of his circle – Xenophon and Plato – independently give us in his name the teaching that leadership flows to the person who knows what to do in the given situation. The situational approach, as it has later been called, dates back to Socrates.
- People are most willing to obey those who know what they are doing.
- As the experience of Xenophon himself and his observations of other generals suggests, a good leader gives direction, sets an example, and shares danger or hardship on an equal footing. He or she should win respect without courting popularity.
- There is a difference between managing – administration, planning and controlling – and leadership. A good leader does those things but transcends them: he or she has the secret of arousing the willing and enthusiastic support of others to the common task at hand.
- The story of Xenophon's assault on the Carduci illustrates another cardinal principle of leadership. Leaders *encourage* people. They renew spirits, giving others fresh courage to pursue the common course of action. Xenophon's words and deeds infused the Greeks with new confidence and resolution. His brave example inspired them.

POINTS TO PONDER

Xenophon mentions more than once in this opening description the personal *qualities* required in a general. In the *Cyropaedia* he listed the qualities of an ideal ruler as: temperance, justice, sagacity, amiability, presence of mind, tactfulness, humanity, sympathy, helpfulness, courage, magnanimity, generosity and considerateness. Aristotle, Plato's greatest pupil, suggested just four qualities of leadership: justice, temperance, prudence and fortitude. Field Marshal Montgomery quoted them with approval. His colleague Lord Slim also taught four qualities but they are different: courage, willpower, initiative and knowledge. What qualities does a business leader require?

It's helpful first to distinguish *qualities* of personality and character from *knowledge* in the technical or professional sense that Socrates had in mind. Then, think in terms of levels of qualities.

First, a leader should possess or exemplify the qualities expected or required in their working groups or organizations.

Exercise 1   Look back on the last chapter and list the five core qualities of a good soldier, regardless of rank. Keep it by you, and amend it as you read the rest of the book.

Exercise 2   What do you think are the five qualities expected or required in a good nurse, teacher and engineer?

Exercise 3   In your business what qualities of personality and character do you expect everyone to have? Do you – by common consent – exemplify those qualities?

These qualities, you should note, are *necessary* but not *sufficient* – they won't make you a leader, but you cannot be one without them.

There are some more generic qualities associated with leadership, in any field, such as enthusiasm, integrity (the quality that makes people trust you), energy, toughness or being seen and accepted as a leader.

Exercise 4 Using this brief list, and adding to it as you read on, identify your own strengths and weaknesses in terms of leadership qualities.

2

LEADERSHIP SKILLS

'There is nobody who cannot vastly improve his powers of leadership by a little thought and practice.'

Lord Slim

The question of leadership transferability had a special importance in Athens in the days of Socrates. The various offices in the Athenian army and navy, including the generalships (which were roughly equivalent to the commands of large territorial infantry battalions today), were open to all citizens by election. To secure one of these commands was a first step for any ambitious young man aspiring to become a political leader in Athens. There were other offices, too, such as being choir-master of one of the city's choirs. Like the regiments, these choirs were based upon the old tribal structure of Athens. The Greeks were extremely competitive, and a choir that won the prize in competition brought much credit to its tribe and its choir-master.

Therefore Socrates and Xenophon had a contemporary reason for being interested in the question of whether or not any transferable or personal skills existed, as distinct from professional ones (which would equip a young man to lead in business or politics, in the arts, such as music, or in the Athenian army or navy). Athenians were essentially civilians. Like Socrates, when Athens went to war they had to fight in the phalanx of spearmen or pull an oar in the navy's warships. For the notion of having professional officers or soldiers was alien to the Greek states, except for Sparta – a nation of soldiers.

In the following discussion Socrates explored the issue of transferability by arguing provocatively that a successful business man will make an effective general. During the course of it, incidentally, Socrates became the first person in history to identify what today would be called leadership functions.

THE CASE OF NICOMACHIDES

Once on seeing Nicomachides returning from the elections, Socrates asked him, 'Who have been chosen generals, Nicomachides?'

'Isn't it like the Athenians?' he replied. 'They have not chosen me after all the hard work I have done since I was called up, in the command of company or regiment, though I have been so often wounded in action.' (Here he uncovered and showed his scars.) 'They have chosen Antisthenes, who has never served in a marching regiment nor distinguished himself in the cavalry and understands nothing but money-making.'

'Isn't that a recommendation,' said Socrates, 'supposing he proves capable of supplying the men's needs?'

'Why,' retorted Nicomachides, 'merchants also are capable of making money, but that doesn't make them fit to command an army!'

'But,' replied Socrates, 'Antisthenes also is eager for victory, and that is a good point in a general. Whenever he has been choir-master, you know, his choir has always won.'

'No doubt,' conceded Nicomachides, 'but there is no analogy between the handling of a choir and of an army.'

'But you see,' said Socrates, 'though Antisthenes knows nothing about music or choir training, he showed himself capable of finding the best experts in these activities. And therefore if he finds out and prefers the best men in warfare as in choir training, it is likely that he will be victorious in that too; and probably he will be more ready to spend money on winning a battle with the whole state than on winning a choral competition with his tribe.'

'Do you mean to say, Socrates, that the man who succeeds with a chorus will also succeed with an army?'

'I mean that, whatever a man controls, if he knows what he wants and can get it he will be a good controller, whether he control a chorus, an estate, a city or an army.'

'Really, Socrates,' cried Nicomachides, 'I should never have thought to hear you say that a good businessman would make a good general!'

By his familiar method of patient cross-examination, Socrates won agreement from Nicomachides that successful businessmen and generals perform much the same functions. Then Socrates proceeded to identify six of these functions or skills:

- selecting the right person for the job;
- punishing the bad and rewarding the good;
- winning the goodwill of those under them;
- attracting allies and helpers;
- keeping what they have gained;
- being strenuous and industrious in their own work.

'All these are common to both,' Nicomachides accepted, 'but fighting is not.'

'But surely both are bound to find enemies?'

'Oh yes, they are.'

'Then is it not important for both to get the better of them?'

'Undoubtedly; but you don't say how business capacity will help when it comes to fighting.'

'That is just where it will be most helpful,' Socrates concluded. 'For the good businessman, through his knowledge that nothing profits or pays like a victory in the field, and nothing is so utterly unprofitable and entails such heavy loss as a defeat, will be eager to seek and avoid what leads to defeat, prompt to engage the enemy if he sees he is strong enough to win, and, above all, will avoid an engagement when he is not ready.'

The amazement expressed by Nicomachides at Socrates' line of argument in this dialogue rings true. For the teaching of Socrates, that people will only follow leaders who have the authority of knowledge relevant to a given situation, must have been well known in Athens. Moreover, in that city, as in Britain during much of this century, businessmen were held in low social regard. Young gentlemen from good Athenian families would seek military and political careers, but they did not become merchants. Of course the scale of commerce and industry before the Industrial Revolution was relatively small and the scope for leadership was correspondingly limited. Armies and navies, by contrast, remained the largest and most important forms of common human enterprise until relatively recent times. In the mid-eighteenth century, for example, the Royal Navy was the largest industry in Western Europe.

Socrates did challenge this Athenian snobbery that has

cast such a long shadow in history. 'Don't look down on businessmen, Nicomachides,' he said towards the end of their discussion. 'For the management of private concerns differs only in point of number from that of public affairs. In other respects they are much alike, and particularly in this, that neither can be carried on without men, and the men employed in private and public transactions are the same. For those who take charge of public affairs employ just the same men when they attend to their own; and those who do understand how to employ them are successful directors of public and private concerns, and those who do not, fail in both.'

HUMAN NEEDS AND LEADERSHIP FUNCTIONS

Because of his observation that men are common to both armies and business, Xenophon focused on leadership as the ability to supply the men's needs. He made this point early in the conversation with Nicomachides, and it is repeated in other dialogues. A good leader meets the needs of his men, just as a good shepherd looks after his flock. The thought, too, that leadership is essentially about helping people to achieve a better life does strike a chord in our own age. It suggests a theme, destined for greater prominence in the future, that leadership is a form of service to one's fellow men and women.

Within the compass of human needs in working groups, we can now distinguish clearly three distinct but overlapping or interacting areas of need: to achieve the common *task*, to be maintained as a *team*, and the needs of which *individuals* as such bring with them by virtue of being human.

These three kinds of need should not be conceived as being separate entities: they overlap or interact in a rich variety of ways, sometimes with good and sometimes with ill-effects. If, for example, an organization fails completely to achieve its task, it will tend to disintegrate. Individual needs will then suffer, for our needs for money, security, recognition and personal or professional growth are to a large extent bound up with the common task. By drawing these areas of need – task, group and individual – as three overlapping circles, as below, it is much easier to visualize these interactions. For, as the Chinese proverb says, 'A picture is worth a thousand words.'

Why use the term *needs?* If the common task has sufficient value for them, people in enterprises, organizations and groups experience a need to accomplish it successfully, and they look for leaders who will help them to do so. They also need to be built up and held together as a working team. Such social cohesiveness is more than physical; it is a matter of harmony between minds and spirits. Individual needs include the basic ones for food and for shelter, for care when wounded or sick, and for security in time of danger. But we are personal as well as human, and so we seek the social acceptance and esteem which come from recognition by others of our personal contribution to the common task or the common good. The Greeks differed from other contemporary nations in their heightened sense of being individuals. It flowed from, and also fed on, competitive desire for the fame or renown that comes from some notable act or achievement. They thirsted for individual recognition.

Leadership *functions* – such as identifying direction, planning, controlling, setting and maintaining standards, giving encouragement – are necessary if these three areas of need are to be met. Here are some of those key functions set out in relation to the three overlapping areas of need:

TASK FUNCTIONS
Defining the task
Setting objectives
Making a plan
Allocating work and resources
Controlling quality and tempo of work
Checking performance against the plan
Adjusting the plan

TEAM FUNCTIONS
Setting standards
Maintaining discipline
Building team spirit
Encouraging, motivating,
giving a sense of purpose
Appointing sub-leaders
Insuring communication
within the group
Training the group

INDIVIDUAL FUNCTIONS
Attending to personal problems
Encouraging individuals
Giving status
Recognizing and using individual abilities
Training the individual

Obviously a leader needs *knowledge* in order to help a group or organization to achieve its task. But where do leadership *qualities* fit into the picture? What a leader is, in terms of personality and character, will shape or colour the style in which he or she performs those *functions* listed above. Qualities such as tenacity, firmness, fairness, enthusiasm and a sense of humour will inform the way in which the essential functions of leadership are performed.

The three circles model does have the drawback of looking rather static. Leadership in reality, of course, is much more dynamic and ever moving. It is an always changing interaction between the needs and personalities of people and their leaders within an environment.

A LEADER IN MANAGEMENT

When Xenophon was not campaigning for his friends the Spartans in the later decades of his life, he managed his estates and wrote a variety of books on the history of his times, constitutions, hunting, horsemanship and cavalry command.

He returned to the theme of leadership in his most influential book, the *Cyropaedia*. In later centuries it became the text book on leadership for many of the great leaders of Rome. As the strange-sounding title suggests, the *Cyropaedia* is a philosophical dialogue about the education of Cyrus the Great, who in fact does little more than lend his name to an ideal king ruling an ideal state.

In it, Xenophon advocated that a leader should demonstrate that in summer he can endure the heat, and in winter the cold; and he should show that in difficult times he can endure the hardships as well as, if not better than, his men. Moreover, a leader should rejoice with, if not better than, his men. Moreover, a leader should rejoice with them if any good befall them, and sympathize with them if any ills overtake them, showing himself eager to help in times of stress. 'It is in these respects that you should somehow go hand in hand with them,' wrote Xenophon. 'All this contributes to the leader being loved by his men.'

Xenophon added the interesting observation that it was actually easier for the leader to endure heat and cold, hunger and thirst, want and hardship, than his followers. 'The general's position, and the very consciousness that nothing he does escapes notice, lightens the burden for him.'

The same principle, Xenophon held, would apply in all areas of human work, simply because men and their needs are the same. In another of the books he wrote on his estate at Scillus, the *Oeconomicus* or *The Economy*, as we would call it – the world's first book of management – he put across this distinctive view with characteristic style and compelling vigour. It reflected his own experience running these estates under the shadow of Mount Olympus.

Much of the book is concerned with technical farming matters and the organization of the estates. But Xenophon urged upon his readers the importance of leadership on large farm estates. 'Nobody can be a good farmer,' he said, 'unless he makes his labourers both eager and obedient; and the captain who leads men against an enemy must contrive to secure the same results by rewarding those who act as brave men should act and punishing the disobedient. And it is no less necessary for a farmer to encourage his labourers often, than for a general to encourage his men. And slaves need the stimulus of good hopes no less, nay, even more than free men, to make them steadfast.'

This general leadership ability, as relevant to agriculture as to politics or war, was often absent, he noted, in those who held positions of authority. Xenophon instanced the Greek warships of his day, which, it must be remembered, were rowed by free men and not by slaves.

On a man-of-war, when the ship is on the high seas and the rowers must toil all day to reach port, some rowing-masters can say and do the right thing to sharpen the men's spirits and make them work with a will. Other boatswains are so unintelligent that it takes them more than twice the time to finish the same voyage. Here they land bathed in sweat, with mutual congratulations, rowing-master and seamen. There they arrive with dry skin; they hate their master and he hates them.

Xenophon's mind ranged back to the generals he had known, who also differed widely from one another in this respect.

For some make their men unwilling to work and to take risks, disinclined and unwilling to obey, except under compulsion, and actually proud of defying their commander: yes, and they cause them to have no sense of dishonour when something disgraceful occurs. Contrast the genius, the brave and skilled leader: let him take over the command of these same troops, or of others if you like. What effect has he on them? They are ashamed to do a disgraceful act, think it better to obey, and take a pride in obedience, working cheerfully, every man and all together, when it is necessary to work. Just as a love of work may spring up in the mind of a private soldier here and there, so a whole army under the influence of a good leader is inspired by love of work and ambition to distinguish itself under the commander's eye. Let this be the feeling of the rank and file for their commander, then he is the best leader – it is not a matter of being best with bow and javelin, nor riding the best horse and being foremost in danger, not being the perfect mounted warrior, but of being able to make his soldiers feel that they must follow him through fire and in any adventure. So, too, in private industries [Xenophon continued], the man in authority – bailiff or manager – who can make the workers keen, industrious and persevering – he is the man who gives a lift to the business and swells the profits.

ARE LEADERS BORN OR MADE?

For Xenophon, this kind of leadership is quite simply 'the greatest thing in every operation that makes any demand on the labour of men'. If leaders are made in the sense that they can acquire the authority of knowledge, are they born as far as the capacity to inspire is concerned? It is tempting to conclude so. The ability to give people the intellectual and moral strength to venture or persevere in the presence of danger, fear or difficulty is not the common endowment of all men and women. Xenophon, however, did believe that it could be acquired through education, though not 'at sight or at a single hearing'. He was not specific about the content or methods of such an education for leadership, but Socratic discussion must have been one strand in it.

As Xenophon implied, some degree of leadership potential has to be there in the first place. Many people possess it without being aware of the fact. Given the need or opportunity to lead, some encouragement and perhaps a leadership course or programme, most people can develop this potential. Those with a greater amount of natural potential can correspondingly become greater leaders within their spheres, providing that they are willing to work hard at becoming leaders.

Learning about leadership happens when sparks of relevance jump in between experience or practice on the one hand, and principles or theory on the other hand. One without the other tends to be sterile. It is a common fallacy that leadership is learned only through experience. Experience only teaches the teachable, and it is a school which charges large fees. Sometimes people graduate from it when they are too old to apply the lessons. Leadership is far better learned by experience *and* reflection or thought, which, in turn, informs or guides future action. Other people, as examples or models, teachers or mentors, have an important part to play in this process. Socrates, for example, most probably acted as Xenophon's own mentor.

The belief that theories or principles, imbibed from books or courses, can by themselves teach a person to lead, is equally a half-truth. All the academic study of leadership does is to teach one *about* leadership, not how to lead. It is certainly useful for people to clarify their concepts of leadership, either as a prelude or as an interlude in the practical work of leading others. But leadership is learnt primarily through doing it, and nothing can replace that necessary cycle of experiment, trial-and-error, success and failure, followed by reflection and reading. Following this path of self-development, a person may become so effective as a leader that others will say 'He or she was born to it.' Little will they know the work it took!

KEY POINTS

* Apart from the *qualities* approach – what you have to be – and the *knowledge* approach – what you have to know – there is a third *functional* approach to leadership which centres on what you have to do in order to lead.

- The debate about transferability – would a businessman make a good general – led Xenophon into foreshadowing the functional approach as we know it today. He identified these common skills:

  ❑ selecting the right individuals (judgement of people)

  ❑ rewarding and disciplining (justice)

  ❑ winning the goodwill of those under you (motivating)

  ❑ building good relations with colleagues, allies and suppliers (team building)

  ❑ setting a personal example of hard work (energy)

- The objection of Nicomachides – that businessmen know nothing about fighting – is here apparently dismissed because Xenophon is emphasizing the other side of the coin. In reality, *both* knowledge related to the field or situation *and* skill in these more general leadership functions is required of a leader. And your *qualities* will colour or give your personal stamp to the actions you take as a leader.

- Although Xenophon did perceptively see leadership as a means of meeting human needs of groups and individuals, he was not systematic about this insight. The three-circles model of needs – task, team and individual – repairs that deficiency. It enables us to relate *functions* more closely to needs.

- Again, Xenophon, by his word and example on his estates, reminds us of the gulf that lies between exercising coercive power over people and using the inner power that stems from firm leadership and personal example. He demonstrated, too, that leading from the front had the same effect upon farm labourers as it had upon soldiers in battle. Human nature doesn't change – that is one message of this book.

POINTS TO PONDER

In Athens, said Pericles, 'What counts is not membership of a particular class, but the actual ability which the man possesses'. Education for the few with this natural leadership talent, both to develop them as whole men and later to enable them to acquire the technical or professional knowledge in their chosen departments of civic life, was central to the Greek way of life. Good leadership, they know, is essential for a democratic society. And, as Plato said, 'What a country honours will be cultivated there. Do we place a similar value on leadership?'

The Greeks certainly believed that leadership could be learnt, whatever your level of natural aptitude. Both Alexander the Great and Julius Caesar read Xenophon's books. Another Greek writer, Plutarch, wrote the first book of leadership case studies for the benefit of the Romans. In the middle of the Second World War, Winston Churchill said that 'Every prospective officer should follow General Gordon's recommendation and read Plutarch's *Lives.*' After the Renaissance, largely inspired by Plato's *Republic*, schools and universities sprang up like mushrooms to equip people to be leaders not as a consequence of birth or social rank but because they had the personal qualities, appropriate knowledge and transferable skills of leadership. Do you think schools and universities are still fulfilling that original social purpose?

In classical education up to modern times the place of 'theory' in leadership development was supplied by such authors as

Xenophon, Plato, Plutarch, Caesar and Cicero, all read in their original Greek or Latin. How should we now convey the philosophy or principles of good leadership – and leadership for good – in school and university?

3

A LEADER OF LEADERS

'Not the cry but the flight of the wild duck leads the flock to fly and to follow.'

Chinese proverb

Daniel Boone, a famous American frontiersman, was once asked if he had ever been lost in the trackless forests of Kentucky. 'I can't say that I was ever lost,' he replied, 'but I was once sure bewildered for three days.' By definition, leaders are never lost, even though they are occasionally bewildered. Within their field they have a sense of direction.

In changeful situations sensing the way forwards, and giving a clear lead in that direction, is a leader's main contribution to achieving the common task. But on that journey of change leaders are also responsible for building or maintaining the team and for meeting individual needs. The biblical image of the shepherd well illustrates that three-fold responsibility. It was exemplified by one of the great leaders of antiquity – Alexander the Great – on his journey through Asia. The word *leader* itself suggests the importance of guidance on a journey forwards in time.

The Anglo-Saxon root of the words *lead, leader* and

leadership, incidentally, is *laed*, which means a path or road. It comes in turn from the verb *laeden*, to travel or to go. The Anglo-Saxons extended it to mean the journey that people make upon such paths or roads. Being seafarers they used it also for the course of a ship at sea. A leader was the person who showed the way. On land he would do so normally by walking ahead, or taking the lead as we say. At sea he would be the navigator and steersman, for in those days the same man performed both functions.

In order to keep one's feet on the ground in studying leadership it is important not to stray too far from this basic journey image of the leader as one who shows the way ahead, holds people together as a group and encourages individuals – by example and word – to keep going despite the hardships and dangers of travel. These abilities are exemplified in Alexander the Great. He is one of the few unchallengeable geniuses when it comes to leadership. He certainly had his share of human failings and imperfections, but despite these lapses, Alexander's contemporaries, especially his companions and followers, revered him as an exceptional leader. The following story helps to reveal why they did so.

IN THE GEDROSIAN DESERT

Imagine a desolate desert of barren rocks and sand and scrub, scorched by the sun. It is midsummer, hence the furnace-like heat. Across this arid plain in Asia Minor, called the Gedrosian Desert, marches Alexander's Greek army of some 30,000 foot soldiers with cavalry units in the rear. The best and most reliable historian of his conquests, Arrian – a Greek writer of the second century AD with the

Latin name Flavius Arrianus, who saw himself as a second
Xenophon – tells the story of what happened next.

> Alexander, like everyone else, was tormented by thirst, but he
> was none the less marching on foot at the head of his men. It was
> all he could do to keep going, but he did so, and the result (as
> always) was that the men were better able to endure their misery
> when they saw it as equally shared. As they toiled on, a party of
> light infantry which had gone off looking for water found some –
> just a wretched little trickle collected in a shallow gully. They
> scooped up with difficulty what they could and hurried back, with
> their priceless treasure, to Alexander; then, just before they
> reached him, they tipped the water into a helmet and gave it to
> him. Alexander, with a word of thanks for the gift, took the helmet
> and, in full view of his troops, poured the water on the ground.
> So extraordinary was the effect of this action that the water
> wasted was as good as a drink for every man in the army. I
> cannot praise this act too highly; it was a proof, if anything was,
> not only of his power of endurance, but also of his genius for
> leadership.

The test of Alexander's leadership in the Gedrosian
Desert was not yet over. After taking the army first to the
left and then to the right, the guides hired by the Greeks
from the local natives eventually admitted that they no
longer knew the way. The familiar landmarks, they
declared, had been obliterated by the drifting yellow sands.
There was nothing in that vast and featureless desert on
which they could get their bearings – no trees and no hills.
   With more than 30,000 thirsty men, their horses and
pack animals under his command, Alexander suddenly
found himself in a crisis. It was not unknown for an entire
army to disappear in deserts, every man dying of thirst

before the wind blew the sands and entombed them. Alexander gave no signs of panic. With commendable calmness he gave directions to the army.

Feeling by intuition that they should be heading more to the left he decided to reconnoitre ahead with a small party of mounted men. It was a calculated risk. When the horses began to succumb to the heat he left most of his party behind and rode on with only five men. At last they caught sight of the blue sea from a low rise in the dunes. Scraping away the shingle on the beach, they came upon fresh water. The whole army soon followed, and for seven days marched along the coast getting its water from the beach. Finally the guides once more recognized their whereabouts, and a course was set for the interior again. Thus by his sure leadership Alexander saved the army from a potentially terrible disaster.

CREATING UNITY AND TEAMWORK

Alexander had inherited from his father, Philip of Macedon, the title 'Leader of the Greeks'. His courage and leadership in battle are renowned. But here we see him more as a shepherd leading a very large human flock than as a general in action, resplendent in his shining armour. For in a sense his extended journey in the East was more like an explorer's expedition than a conqueror's campaign. Indeed Alexander was accompanied by those whom we should now call scientists. Before Alexander finally turned for home his soldiers had marched a staggering 11,500 miles. It was a journey that took them years, with many more days on the march than in battle. The above incident in the Gedrosian Desert, on the long, weary way back to

Greece from India, shows us a non-military example of Alexander's true leadership in literally giving direction to his army.

While Alexander is before our eyes it is worth remarking that he also met the other two areas of need we have identified. Less than half of his army came from Macedonia: the cities and states of mainland Greece supplied the rest. The Greeks were competitive by nature and not famous for co-operating well together. Homer captured their spirit in a phrase: 'Always to excel and to be superior to others'. Alexander succeeded in creating a spirit of unity in his army. In it, Greeks of diverse backgrounds and skills — cavalry and infantry, staff and engineers — had the unusual and rewarding experience of really working well together as a single unbeatable team.

This unity helped to produce teamwork on the battlefield between the different arms. They moved in unison like choristers singing at a competition, an analogy actually used by Herodotus in his description of one Greek army in battle. Even today choirs teach teamwork. Thus the cavalry did not look down upon the foot soldiers as their inferiors, nor did the pikemen despise the skirmishers or slingers. The Macedonian invention of staff officers, each entrusted with a special function, developed a sense of complementary skills interlocking like a jigsaw puzzle. Hephaestion, for example, was often charged with the matters of supply and transportation; Diades was the engineer; and Laomedon served as a provost marshal — a wise move because it took the potentially unpopular matter of policing the army out of Alexander's hands. Alexander even had a signals officer on his staff. Apart from a medical service he also developed a specialist unit with portable river-crossing equipment, together with catapult artillery to cover the crossing. A balanced force, lean and fit, Alexander's army proved to be invincible as long as it retained its cohesion.

CARING FOR INDIVIDUALS

Of course Alexander could not have known as individuals all the Macedonians, let alone all the Greeks in his army. But it was part of his genius as a leader that they felt he did. He met their individual needs. Arrian recorded plenty of examples of Alexander's humanity and care for his soldiers as individuals and persons. He never regarded them as mere spears or swords, but rather as companions and brothers-in-arms. After one battle Arrian writes: 'For the wounded he showed deep concern; he visited them all and examined their wounds, asking each man how and in what circumstances his wound was received, and allowing him to tell his story and exaggerate as much as he pleased.'

It was this care for individual needs, this deep sense of comradeship and humanity, which endeared Alexander to his troops. It appears again in his thoughtful concern for the young Macedonian pikemen who had hastily married on the eve of the expedition, perhaps on the grounds that they might not return from the wars. Feeling that some consideration was due to these men, Alexander dismissed them at the end of the first summer, sending them home to spend the winter with their wives. 'No act of Alexander's ever made him better beloved by his native troops.'

Whence did this gift of genius for leadership come? Did Alexander have charisma, or did he perhaps manufacture it? These are deeper questions about him which we shall explore in the next chapter.

KEY POINTS

- Our word *leader* comes from a root meaning a path, road or course of a ship at sea. It is a journey word. If your organization is not on a journey don't bother about leadership – just settle for management.

- A leader is not always literally the person in front – on the military analogy that may be scouts, pioneers or an advance guard. But a leader is expected to guide or give direction, keep the party together – staying in touch – and, thirdly, to care for individual needs on the journey.

- Journeys are sometimes hazardous, not least military ones that end in a crisis of violence. A leader shares the hardships and privations, risks and dangers, on an equal footing with others, as Alexander did in the Gedrosian Desert.

- Alexander personified the cardinal military virtues, such as physical courage, as well as the mental qualities of a brilliant commander. He also had a genius for leadership which transcends time and place.

- A team is made up, like a jigsaw puzzle, of complementary parts fitting perfectly together. Under Alexander's compelling leadership the Greek army worked as a high performance team. However desperate his circumstances, Alexander was able with its aid to defeat much bigger armies time after time. Teamwork was the key to his success.

- The Greeks, like us today, were very individualistic. Apart from caring for his men's individual needs – food and water, security, family – Alexander also ensured that the outstanding received personal recognition. He knew their names and praised them in public.

- Alexander had vision. He was not just out for himself or for Macedon. What mattered to him was spreading the humanistic values of Greece throughout the known world. What is your vision?

POINTS TO PONDER

A chairman of a large company recently awarded himself and his fellow directors a 40 per cent pay rise, and new contracts with share options and very generous terms if they were terminated.

At the same time, pleading the state of the economy, he asked the workforce to accept a 3.5 per cent pay rise and a cut in annual holidays. Profits were non-existent, he explained, and the company was in danger of being taken over. Those being compulsorily made redundant, he added, would receive only the legal minimum in redundancy payments. How do you think this chairman measures up as a business leader, compared to Alexander the Great in the Gedrosian Desert?

If the purpose of business is simply profit and the main motive in it is personal greed for money, perhaps that chairman and his fellow directors acted rationally. But these are not the actions of good leadership. What do you think? What is the true purpose of business enterprise? Does it call for leaders of Alexandrian greatness? Or is it only the battlefields of this world that evoke the best as well as the worst from human nature?

4

CHARISMA

'True charm is an aura, an invisible musk in the air; if you see it working, the spell is broken.'

Laurie Lee

As one manager said to me, 'Alexander must have had incredible charisma.' But what is *charisma*?

Webster's Dictionary defines it as a 'personal magic of leadership arousing special popular loyalty or enthusiasm for a statesman or military commander'. It has since been applied much more widely to leaders in fields other than politics or war. Indeed it is now in danger of losing all its distinctive meaning and becoming synonymous with public attractiveness: a mixture of good looks, a striking manner and self-proclamation. So often such *charisma* proves to be like a coat of unrenewable fresh paint, which shortly reveals a lasting inadequacy underneath it.

THE DIVINE GIFT

Our modern use of *charisma* stems from the work of Max Weber, a German sociologist who died in 1920. Weber was interested in how authority becomes legitimatized in various societies. He postulated three forms of authority: traditional, charismatic and bureaucratic (or rational–legalistic). According to Weber, charisma is 'a certain quality of an individual personality by virtue of which he is considered extraordinary and treated as endowed with supernatural, or exceptional forces or qualities'. Consequently, charismatic authority was inner-generated – it derived from the capacity of a particular person to arouse and maintain belief in himself or herself as the source of knowledge and authority. History showed plenty of examples of such inspired leaders challenging the traditions of their day. Their informal groups of followers, however, tended to move towards the rational–legal basis (bureaucratic) once they grew bigger and when the original leader died. Sometimes, as in the case of St Francis and the Franciscans, it happened before the founder's death, and he could find himself an alien in a large organization that was rapidly losing his spirit. There are counterparts in every field, not least in industry when the entrepreneur gives way to the manager.

JIM JONES

In 1974 a pastor called Jim Jones established a commune of the People's Temple Sect in Guyana, which he called Jonestown. The sect originated in San Francisco's black community. Complaints of oppression led to a visit by a United States congressman, who was promptly shot with his companions. Then Jones gathered his disciples together and preached a long sermon which ended with an invitation to mass suicide. Most submitted to him with blind and unquestioning obedience, while his guards coerced those backsliders unwilling to administer the cyanide to the children. In this dreadful deed, one leader was responsible for the deaths of 914 people, including over 240 children. Clearly, extraordinary personal authority can be used for misguided ends as well as good ones.

Weber's categories need not detain us any longer, for they are vague and ambiguous and therefore difficult to make operational. In fact, Weber had in turn borrowed the concept of charisma from the writings of Rudolf Sohn, a Strasbourg Church historian, who in turn took it from the Greek New Testament where *charisma* means divine gifts of extraordinary powers in people given by God.

The Greeks were specifically religious in the sense that they believed in the existence of divine beings or gods who were distinctly human in some respects. In other words, the distinguishing line between divine and human was not drawn firmly. 'Hero' was the Greek name given to men of superhuman strength, courage or greatness of soul, gifts which showed that they were favoured by the gods. Later in Greek history these men were regarded as demigods and immortals. The archetypal hero, Heracles, served as a model for both Alexander the Great and Mark Anthony. Both aspired to become heroes in those senses. Alexander once commented that only the needs for sex and sleep made him still feel human.

Now the Greeks as a whole were quite prepared to acknowledge that leadership is a gift of the gods. But, unlike the Romans, they were reluctant to take the step of hero-worship: according divine honours to a human being. The Greeks had sufficient respect for the gods, or fear of their vengeance, to avoid insulting them in this way. On the other hand, despite their sophistication, the Greeks were children of their tribal times. It was an age of animistic belief: divine spirits were seen or felt to inhabit tree, river and mountain. Why not also the heart of a man? An unscrupulous leader could exploit human credulity. Given some accomplices, he could seek to establish himself as a person of divine or semi-divine powers and worthy of the awe, reverence and unquestioning obedience reserved for the gods. In other words, he could invoke hero-worship.

Among superstitious people, for example, the power to hypnotize others might be interpreted spontaneously as evidence of a god at work. In the context of leadership, certain physical characteristics were often taken as evidence of a person's inspired nature. Brightness of eye, and a penetrating gaze which made the recipient feel as if his or her innermost heart was being scrutinized, were especially potent signs of charisma. In turn, the eyes of such a leader's followers became riveted on him. A voice which arrested attention, by both its musical rhythm and the content of the message, was another focal point. The aura of such a person, working through eyes and voice, was like the two magnetic forces; one attracted the followers closer, the other made them draw back and keep their distance as unworthy of such company. In so far as listeners succumbed to the spell, they became disciples of the teacher or leader in question. Sometimes they did so against their better judgement.

EVOCATION AND INVOCATION

There is a useful distinction to be made between *evocation* and *invocation*. Evocation happens without design, but invocation is a conscious intention. Charisma could be deliberately invoked (as opposed to being passively evoked) in several ways. A leader might associate himself, for example, with a sacred object. Alexander had a 'sacred shield' – the shield from the temple of Athene at Troy – kept by him and carried before him in battle.

SERTORIUS – FRIEND OF THE GODS

The Roman general Sertorius, campaigning in Spain, was presented with a milk-white fawn, which became his pet. 'Little by little,' wrote Plutarch, 'he began to build up the impression that there was something sacred and mysterious about the creature. He declared that she was the gift of Diana and possessed the power of revealing secrets to him, for he knew that the barbarians are naturally prone to superstition.' After it had strayed off and been found again, the fawn was reunited with its master, leaping upon the tribunal where he was hearing petitions. The stage-managed scene had the desired effect. 'The spectators were dumbfounded at first, and then, breaking into shouts of joy and loud applause, they escorted him to his house,' continued Plutarch. 'They were convinced that he was beloved of the gods and possessed supernatural power, and this assurance filled them with hope and confidence for the future.'

Before one of his early campaigns, Attila the Hun appeared before his troops with an ancient iron sword in his grasp, which he told them was the god of war their ancestors had worshipped. The sword-god had disappeared, but Attila claimed that a herdsman tracking a wounded heifer by the trail of blood, had found it standing in the desert, as if it had been hurled down from Heaven. The possession of such a supernatural weapon gave him immense influence over the barbaric Hunnish tribes.

Attila described himself as 'Descendant of the Great Nimrod'. But Alexander claimed not only descent from Heracles but also to be Heracles – or at least a god – in the flesh. It was this kind of claim that provoked a negative reaction from the Greeks. As Herodotus made plain in the earliest extant debate on the relative merits of democracy, monarchy and oligarchy, written more than a century before Alexander's campaigns, the Greeks thought the time was long since past 'for any one man amongst us to have absolute power'. Monarchy was widely regarded as being neither pleasant nor good. 'For wealth and power,' wrote Herodotus, 'lead a king to the delusion that he is something more than human.' The Greek passion for freedom made them wary of kings. A king's claim to be divine invariably preceded a demand for unconditional obedience, with a consequent loss of personal freedom and civil liberties.

When complete personal loyalty and blind obedience enter the picture, it is the end not only of equality and freedom but also of leadership. For the king or politician who achieves absolute rule is no longer a leader. In the conclusion to his book on estate management, Xenophon had made that distinction clear. He acknowledged that an exceptional leader required great natural gifts. 'Above all, he must be a genius. For I reckon this gift is not altogether human, but divine – this power to win willing obedience: it is manifestly a gift of the gods to the true votaries of wisdom. Despotic rule over unwilling subjects they give, I fancy, to those they judge worthy to live the life of Tantalus, of whom it is said that in hell he spends eternity, dreading a second death.'

ALEXANDER AS CHARISMATIC LEADER

Perhaps no man has a better right to being called a charismatic leader than Alexander, and so he makes a good case study for the phenomenon. Yet in one sense he lacked presence. For physical height was deeply associated with superiority in the ancient mind, possibly because tall men had an advantage in hand-to-hand fighting and tended to be chosen as war leaders.

When the prophet Samuel, for example, chose Saul as the first King of Israel, his only qualification seems to have been the fact that he was a head taller than the other Israelites. Now Alexander was less than middle height. When he first sat on the throne of Cyrus the Great his servants had to replace the footstool with a table. When he met some Persian emissaries they initially made their obeisances to one of his staff who was the tallest man in the royal party. The Medes, incidentally, first introduced high-heeled shoes for men to give their leaders extra height. In our own century leaders as various as Herbert Hoover, head of the American FBI, and Ceaucescu, the deposed *Cundator* or 'Leader' of Romania, used to stand on boxes behind their desks to give them the appearance of height. But Alexander did have physical features which suggested to others his genius for leadership. His portraits emphasized his large staring, luminous eyes. He could evidently speak effectively and move men's emotions with his words. His enthusiasm and energy seemed to be boundless. Add to these assets his royal birth and unbroken string of successes, and it is not difficult to see why an aura of divinity seemed to emanate from the young man. But at the core of it lay his extraordinary gifts as a leader.

As an inspirer or motivator of soldiers it is hard to think of anyone in history who has excelled Alexander. He shared in the men's dangers, as the scars of his wounds testified. Alexander would remind them on occasion that he ate the same food as they did. He was highly visible. In the siege preparations against Tyre, for example, when a massive stone pier had to be constructed in the harbour under enemy fire, Alexander was always on the spot. He gave instructions, but he also spoke many words of encouragement backed up by rewards for outstanding effort. In the assault which followed, he fought hard himself but he was ever on the watch for any acts of conspicuous courage in the face of danger amongst his men. As a general, Alexander possessed that all-important power of being able to sum up the inevitably confused situations on battlefields and then to take the appropriate action in a calm, effective way. He had a sure intuition – a feeling for the real situation long before it becomes plain to others.

The source of the troubles that almost broke his matchless army lay in its very success. How often success leads to failure! As victory succeeded victory and the epic unfolded, a group of obsequious courtiers around the young king (Alexander was only twenty-two years old when he crossed the Hellespont) fed him with a heady mixture of proper compliments and insincere flattery. They blew up the bladder of his conceit, ascribing the string of successes and conquests to Alexander's own courage and brilliance as a general, not to the combination of the army's superb qualities as a fighting team and Alexander's leadership. It is a fatal error for leaders to take credit rather than give it.

This inflated self-importance was questioned one night with dramatic and tragic consequences. Some six years had passed since the expedition had set out from Greece, and

the army was encamped at Samarkand. Alexander and some
of his officers had been drinking heavily. The flatterers were
at work plying Alexander with the notion that he was
superior to the very gods to whom he had been sacrificing
that day, and superior even to the god Heracles. Only envy
deprived him of the divine honours due, the courtiers told
him. This was too much for Cleitus, commander of the
Companion cavalry, who was as drunk as his master. In
angry tones he denounced such insults to the gods. Moreover, he continued, they grossly exaggerated the marvellous
nature of Alexander's achievements, none of which were
mere personal triumphs of his own; on the contrary, most
of them were the work of Macedonians as a whole. The
young king lost his temper and in the ensuing brawl he
speared his friend Cleitus to death.

Despite Alexander's subsequent remorse, he had not
really learnt his lesson. By this time he was the ruler of the
old Persian empire and so Persian noblemen at his court
had reason to join the flatterers and encourage Alexander's
pretensions to divinity. The Persian and Greek contexts
were quite different regarding the cultural forms of leadership. In Persia the Great King had been worshipped as a
god. The subjects of his new eastern domains deemed it
inconceivable that a great conqueror such as Alexander was
not a god in human form.

The Greeks were happy to concede to Alexander the
descent he claimed from Heracles and to acknowledge him
as a genius. Neither committed them to the doctrine that
Alexander was a living god before whom they must
prostrate themselves. They preferred a leader who was a
companion, albeit better than them in all respects; they
wanted to remain on the plain of reasoned argument, not to
descend into oriental submission to a despot. Being Greeks

they knew how to wait for the right moment and then how to make their points as tactfully as possible to Alexander.

The day for speaking the truth to Alexander about his zeal for wars came eventually on the western bank of the river Hypasis in India. Beyond it lay green jungles and plains, already alive in Alexander's fertile imagination with Indian princes and princesses, with rubies, sapphires and pearls in abundance, lords of the largest herds of the most courageous elephants on the continent . . . But the monsoon rains, incessant for days, had dampened the men's appetite for more adventure. Some swore that they would march no further, not even if Alexander himself led them. When rumours of this discontent reached him, Alexander called a meeting of his officers. But his plan to cross the river was greeted with a long silence. At last Coenus, a brave Companion, spoke up and told Alexander the truth as tactfully as he could – that the army was now longing to return home. 'No longer in poverty and obscurity, but famous and enriched by the treasure you have enabled them to win. Do not try to lead men who are unwilling to follow you; if their heart is not in it, you will never find the old spirit or courage . . . Sir, if there is one thing above all others a successful man should know, it is when to stop. Assuredly for a commander like yourself, with an army like ours, there is nothing to fear from any army; but luck, remember, is an unpredictable thing, and against what it may bring no man has any defence.'

A burst of spontaneous applause followed these plain words. With a flash of temper Alexander abruptly dismissed them. Next day he told his officers that, while not wishing to put pressure on anyone, he at least intended to continue the advance. For two days he awaited a change of heart. But officers and men remained silent; they were angry at

Alexander's outburst and determined not to let him influence them. Using the excuse of the sacrificial omens, Alexander gave in. His message that the army would turn towards home caused much rejoicing. It is said to have been Alexander's only defeat.

THE PERSIAN METHOD

Probably for political reasons, more than out of vanity, Alexander persistently put pressure on his Greek officers to prostrate themselves before him. Maintaining law and order in a vast empire when the ruler is perforce absent is much easier, the Persians had discovered, if the ruler is perceived to be a god by his subjects. The worship of such a single man served to focus loyalty and to create unity amid the diverse tribes and nations that made up the patchwork of empire.

For the most part his Greek officers refused to comply: such an act was completely against their traditions. In the event, Alexander compromised. While accepting the obeisances of his Persian subjects – lying flat on their faces before him – he promised his Greeks that the need to prostrate themselves would not in future arise. To confirm that dispensation, Alexander organized a mass wedding in the Persian fashion for eighty of his Companions. He led the way, as always, by marrying two wives himself. 'Alexander was capable of putting himself on a footing of equality and comradeship with his subordinates,' wrote Arrian, 'and everyone felt that this act of his was the best proof of his ability to do so.'

The Persians had introduced prostration as part of a novel method of the creation of an aura of divinity around their kings. Herodotus told the story of how it came about. A Mede called Deioces, who lived in the ancient time when the Medes had escaped from under the yoke of Assyria, made a local reputation as an arbiter of disputes by his fairness and integrity. Eventually the Medes chose him as their first king. Deioces ordered his subjects to build him a palace, which became the centre-piece of a new capital city, ringed on its commanding hill by seven high walls. As far as possible he then vanished from their sight, surrounding himself with a new ceremonial of royalty and strict protocol. For example, it was forbidden to laugh or spit in the royal presence. 'This solemn ceremonial was designed as a safe-guard against his contemporaries, men as good as himself in birth and personal quality, with whom he had been brought up in early years,' wrote Herodotus. 'There was a risk that if they saw him habitually, it might lead to jealousy and resentment, and plots would follow; but if nobody saw him, the legend would grow that he was a being of different order from mere men.'

One can see how the Persian method of creating a divine aura by setting a *distance* between the ruler and the people is in clear contrast to the Greek tradition of maintaining *closeness* between leader and followers. In the latter, leaders are prized who share the same hardships and dangers, and eat the same food. That principle applied even in such Greek states as Sparta which had kings. In the one culture, the head of state is virtually invisible; in the other, he is expected to be among his people. The drawback of the more democratic concept, of course, is that closeness dispels any notion of divinity. If a man is seen and known at close quarters it is unlikely that people will believe him to be divine. Therefore the Persian method was antithetical to leadership. It was designed to create rulers, not leaders. The logical climax of it was the declaration of the king's divinity.

A direct descendant of Deioces four generations later, Cyrus the Great, is said to be the monarch who introduced prostration into Persia. Incidentally, he balanced the evocation of worship directed towards himself with a remarkable toleration to other religions in his domains, such as the cult of Marduk at Babylon. Cyrus even allowed the Jewish exiles to return from Babylon and rebuild their temples in Jerusalem. Hence, in part, his reputation for wisdom in the Greek world, and why young Greeks like Xenophon revered his memory.

THE MAGIC OF NAPOLEON BONAPARTE

Napoleon is perhaps Alexander's only rival for the title of the greatest military leader of all time. He clearly possessed charisma, at least as far as the French nation of his day was concerned. Those closest to Napoleon felt his magnetic attraction most powerfully. When, for instance, in Egypt an angry General Davout came to complain about getting an insignificant appointment, Napoleon saw him and, during their conversation, converted him into a devoted follower. From then Napoleon was his god, and Davout became the most faithful marshal of them all. Painful experience revealed to the more intelligent among the marshals and generals the cynical, egocentric and Machiavellian side of Napoleon's personality. 'I have always been the victim of my attachment to him,' wrote a sadder but wiser Marshal Lannes. 'He only loves you by fits and starts, that is, when he has need of you.' And yet the memory of the extraordinary *esprit de corps* created by Napoleon's leadership lingered long. In his retirement, Marshal Marmont wrote, 'We marched surrounded by a kind of radiance whose warmth I can still feel as I did fifty years ago.'

'The 32nd Regiment would have died for me,' Napoleon once said, 'because after one engagement I wrote, "The 32nd was there, I was calm." The power of words over men is astonishing.' Following his defeat at Waterloo, Napoleon abdicated with the apparent intention of going into exile in America. He arrived at Rochefort to find ships of the Royal Navy blocking the harbour. He decided to surrender to the British and went aboard the *Bellerophon* to do so. An English passenger described him thus:

> His countenance is sallow, and as it were deeply tinged by hot climates; but the most commanding air I ever saw. His eyes grey, and the most piercing that you can imagine. His glance, you fancy, searches into your inmost thoughts. His hair is dark brown, and no appearance of grey. His features are handsome now, and when younger he must have been a very handsome man. He is extremely curious, and never passes anything remarkable in the ship without immediately demanding its use, and inquiring minutely into the manner thereof.

The Greeks were too intelligent to recognize Alexander's charisma as anything more than a gift of leadership from the gods, despite his attempts to invoke worship from them. The Persian doctrine, that a great empire could only be ruled by a king-god, was destined to triumph, however, at first among Alexander's successors and then among the Romans. Western European kings, presidents and dictators have applied the same Persian or Eastern formula in their own day with varying degrees of success.

The infusion of Persians into the army in ever-growing

numbers did impose immense strains on its unity. Only the remarkable personality and presence of Alexander, his consistent leadership, could hold this flock of Greek rams and Persian he-goats together. After Alexander's death the unity of his army disintegrated, for it had all depended too much on him.

Alexander's generals who succeeded him were lost without him. Some years later, when they met to try to find that lost unity and peace, they chose to come together before his empty throne in his old tent. In death, as in life, Alexander was the only one who could hold them together.

Perhaps as they stood again in that familiar tent, Alexander's former generals — now his quarrelling successors — recalled their last sight of their young master as he lay on his deathbed under the tent's shade. The army had reached Babylon on its meandering way home, not twenty-five miles from the battlefield of Cunaxa where Xenophon had first encountered the Persian hosts. As word had spread among the Greeks in the now polyglot army that Alexander lay dying, the veterans crowded into the centre to see him, their hearts full of grief. They were bewildered, too, at the thought of what lay in store for them without Alexander as their leader. At last, on that sad Tuesday beside the waters of Babylon, they were allowed into the royal tent, filing past Alexander on his couch in their thousands. Lying speechless as the men passed, Alexander could be seen struggling to raise his head. In his eyes, once so famous for their intensity, there seemed to be a look of recognition for each individual as he passed. He was then thirty-two years and eight months old.

KEY POINTS

- Charisma is a personal magic or charm which arouses unusual devotion from others. Leaders who have it attract a special kind of personal loyalty and enthusiasm.

- A charismatic leader may be credited with an almost supernatural inner or personal authority, in contrast to those who derive their authority from knowledge or position and rank in a hierarchy.

- As a form of personal power or influence, sometimes hypnotic in its effects, charisma can be used for evil as well as good ends (see Adolf Hitler, page 221).

- All leadership is in the gift of the followers. You can be appointed a commander or manager in a hierarchy of one kind or another, but you are not a leader until your appointment is ratified in the hearts and minds of those who work for you.

- The charismatic phenomenon is an extension of that principle, in that the followers perceive or endow some superhuman endowment in the leader. Some may unselfconsciously *evoke* that reaction by their looks or appearance or manner. They may, for example, have penetrating eyes or a musical voice. Others may deliberately try to *invoke* that reaction in order to increase their hold over others, for instance, associating themselves with the divine.

- How do you endow ordinary mortals who find themselves kings or queens with prestige and charisma? The Persian method, emulated by the Romans and many others, was to turn them into gods by making a *distance* between the rulers and their people, spreading ideas or rumours of their divinity, and ultimately requiring worship by prostration.

• For political reasons and personal ambition, fed by unscrupulous flatterers, Alexander half-adopted the Persian approach. But he remained for the Greeks no more than a divinely gifted leader, one who lived, fought, suffered, feasted and died in their midst.

POINTS TO PONDER

❏ Charisma is a kind of personal aura, visible in arresting eyes and audible in a compelling voice. But it is not the essence of leadership. That is not to deny that some leaders do have such magnetic personalities. For there are people who are able to arouse popular loyalty or enthusiasm in their fellows to an uncommon degree. But the tests of leadership are always its fruits or effects: does the *task* get done successfully; is the *team* held together, and do *individuals* feel as much satisfaction as possible? As Mike Brearley, a former captain of England's cricket team and a man with a talent for leadership, pointed out in his book *Art of Captaincy* (1987):

> Charisma does not imply steadiness, patience, concentration, or considerateness, all invaluable in a captain. Above all, placing too much emphasis on charisma might well involve ignoring the central requirement of a captain, namely, that he knows his task. Charisma is not the same thing as leadership.

❏ One of the dilemmas of modern rulers is that the demands of personal security compel them to *distance* themselves from their subjects when the democratic ethos calls for a greater *closeness* between leaders and citizens. Television offers a partial solution to the dilemma, but that medium is open to stage-management for effect. They are torn between the

Persian style of creating distance and Greek style of maintaining closeness.

❏ Security is, however, not the only issue. How much did the British royal family lose by allowing its members to give very personal interviews on television? Do biographical revelations of extramarital sex diminish the authority of our national leaders?

❏ In the New Testament, St Paul argues that the supreme and overriding gift or *charisma* from God is self-forgetful love. It is the touchstone of all other charismas, including the gift of leadership.

5

THE SERVANT—LEADER

'Let the greatest among you become as the least and the leader as one who serves.'

Jesus of Nazareth

We are not accustomed to thinking of leaders as servants. We tend to emphasize position rather than responsibility. Leaders in our society are paid more than others; they enjoy the other rewards of privileges and status. Leadership stands for power and dominance over others. That is not unlike the pattern of leadership that Jesus saw both among the Gentiles and with Israel in his day: rulers who lorded it over their subjects, intent upon subservience and hungry for public recognition.

True, Xenophon had identified the common element of service in all leadership, by insisting that the core responsibility of leaders is to meet human needs. Moreover, he had found that it worked in practice. If you came down from your height – literally in the case of a mounted commander and metaphorically in that of a landowner – and worked among people, this action would inspire willing obedience. The Roman leaders who followed Xenophon's example and teaching found that the same principle worked for them.

Both Greeks and Romans were essentially pragmatists. By the exercise of practical reason, they sought to discover what works in leadership, and to a large measure they did so.

SHARING THE HARDSHIPS AND DANGERS

The Roman general Marius was cast in the Spartan mould. As a young man, he served on the staff of a Roman army then campaigning in North Africa. Although lacking in wealth and eloquence, he had an intense confidence in himself, coupled with a great capacity for hard work. In writing about this period of Marius' life Plutarch made some comments about Roman soldiers which are both illuminating and generally applicable to all soldiers, if not to all workers:

> It was a hard war, but Marius was not afraid of any undertaking, however great, and was not too proud to accept any tasks, however small. The advice he gave and his foresight into what was needed marked him out among the officers of his own rank, and he won the affection of the soldiers by showing that he could live as hard as they did and endure as much. Indeed it seems generally to be the case that our labours are eased when someone goes out of his way to share them with us; it has the effect of making the labour not seem forced. And what a Roman soldier likes most is to see his general eating his ration of bread with the rest, or sleeping on an ordinary bed, or joining in the work of digging a trench or raising a palisade. The commanders whom they admire are not so much those who distribute honours and riches as those who take a share in their hardships and dangers; they have

more affection for those who are willing to join in their work than for those who indulge them in allowing them to be idle.

Marius, to continue the story, was responsible for a major reorganization of the Roman army in the second century BC. He had himself elected Consul seven times, the first Roman in history to do so. But he was no political leader. In the Senate, when his victories had already brought him a huge reputation, Marius used to behave quite timidly if hecklers attacked him. All the steadfastness and firmness which he showed in battle seemed to drain from him when he stood up to speak in a popular assembly, so that he could not cope with even the most ordinary compliments or criticisms. Clearly his style of military command was not transferable to the world of politics, where essentially equal citizens look to someone for a lead. Marius lived to be seventy, his harsh nature turning savage and vindictive by the possession of supreme power. He gave the Romans their first real taste of tyranny. It was the fear of another dose of such tyranny that led to Caesar's assassination.

The deepest flaw in natural leadership, you can see, is usually arrogance. The root of arrogance is an inflated pride which makes a person in a position of leadership act in an excessively determined, overbearing or domineering way. This insistence on being dominant is always based upon a real or an assumed superiority. Because of an exaggerated sense of self, and excessive pride in wealth, station, learning or achievements, the arrogant person takes upon himself more power or authority than is rightly his.

The antidotes to the disease of arrogance in relation to leadership go back as far as Lao Tzu, a Chinese thinker in the fourth century BC, and to Jesus. These Eastern antidotes may not have been very effective against the virus of pride in centuries past, but their value is beginning to be appreciated today. In the concept of leadership advanced by both Lao Tzu and Jesus there is a marked absence of aggressive egotism, a lack of vanity or presumption. Instead there is the feeling that a leader should see his or her part as something moderate or small in scale, especially in comparison to the contributions of others.

THE TEACHING OF LAO TZU

Lao Tzu was a native of Ch'u, a large state on the southern periphery of civilized China in ancient times. Almost nothing is known about him apart from what can be gleaned from the legends that surround his name. He probably served one of the ruling princes of China as a court sage and then he became a recluse in a hermitage. Even his book of sayings, entitled the *Tao Te Ching*, has been much revised by later hands. So much so, in fact, that some scholars have doubted if Lao Tzu ever existed as an individual. In order to fill the gap of knowledge about Lao, events connected with various characters in Chinese mythology were ascribed to him at an early date.

In the early days, before it received its present name, Christianity was often called 'the Way'. That is also the literal meaning of *Tao* in Chinese. The 'way' that Lao has in mind is not easy to define. It is really Nature's way: the order, course or pattern of all things created.

For the school of Chinese philosophers who thought as Master Lao, every person and thing is only what it is in relation to others. Events fall into harmony if left alone.

Someone who intuitively understands this energy in Nature, and works intelligently with the grain of natural phenomena, is a follower of the *Tao*.

'The *Tao* principle is what happens of itself,' wrote Lao Tzu. The art of living, then, is more like steering a boat than struggling with an opponent. The image of water, flowing or still in cool, clear ponds, is never far from Lao's mind. *Tzu jan*, 'Nature', is that which is of itself. It is spontaneous. Everything grows and operates independently, on its own, but in harmony with all.

The principle of *wu wei*, of not forcing things, is a natural corollary to this vision of the world. Working with the grain, rolling with the punch, swimming with the tide, trimming sails to the wind, taking the tide at its flood: these are metaphors that reflect the spirit of *wu wei*.

If the follower of the *Tao* understands the principles, structures or trends of human nature, human society and the natural order, then he can expend least energy in dealing with them. When he does exert his power at the right moment, his efforts will have a spontaneous, natural or unforced quality about them. The Taoist writer associated this *ch'i* – effortless effort – with breathing. The same principle can be seen in *judo* today: because the opponent is off-balance or has over-extended himself, the least effort will topple him.

There is an even more superior form of *wu wei*, which does not seem to aim at anything in particular. Things are not done with an effect in mind; they are expressions of inner being. 'When good things are accomplished, it does not claim (or name) them,' wrote Lao Tzu. He called it *te*, which is close in meaning to power or virtue. It is something within a person, and it is enhanced by following the *Tao*, or 'that from which nothing can deviate'.

Chuang Tzu, a later member of the Taoist school of thought, expressed it thus: 'In an age of perfect virtue, good men are not appreciated; ability is not conspicuous. Rulers are mere beacons, while the people are as free as the wild deer. They love one another without being conscious of charity. They are true without being conscious of loyalty.'

THE TAO OF LEADERSHIP

It is this quality of doing things spontaneously and in an unselfconscious way, without regard to their effects upon other people's perceptions of oneself, that links Lao Tzu with the teaching of Jesus. There is a freedom from acting for show, or indeed for outward things. It stems from this intuitive awareness of the inevitability of things as they follow their natural water courses into the sea, and the power that is naturally directed.

'The best leaders of soldiers in their chariots do not rush ahead,' wrote Lao. Socrates had appeared to say much the same thing when he suggested to a young cavalry commander that he had not sought that appointment in order to be first into battle — that honour belonged to the mounted skirmishers. But Lao is making a different point. The leader who follows the *Tao* does not need to dominate others or seize the glory first. Thus, in his behaviour, the sage (as Lao called the ruler who exemplifies these precepts) does no more than reflect the ultimate reality, the inner core of Nature itself. For 'the Tao loves and nourishes all things, but does not lord it over them.'

This refusal to dominate or lord it over others again parallels the teaching of Jesus. It is the attitude that man should adapt to all things — animals, birds and fish, mountains, lakes and sea – as well as to his fellow humans. It is because the sage has power or virtue that he does not use force. It is close to the 'meekness' which Jesus advocated.

The natural badge of such inner humility towards all things is silence. 'Silence is of the gods,' says a Chinese proverb. Again there is a paradox here, for the Greek and Roman traditions exalted the place of oratory in leadership. For Greek leaders, who had to persuade their fellow citizens by reason, it was speech that was golden, not silence. Yet listening is important, and it is difficult for a leader to listen if he or she is talking all the time.

JOHN HAMPDEN – A LISTENING LEADER

John Hampden was the first great leader of England's House of Commons. Hampden, who had first attracted public attention by his courageous refusal to pay the illegal Ship Money tax, emerged as a leader in the Long Parliament which met in November 1640. The reformist majority in the Lower House, leavened by the Puritan group led by John Hampden and John Pym, clearly enjoyed overwhelming support in the country. 'When this Parliament began,' wrote the Earl of Clarendon in his *History of the Great Rebellion*, 'the eyes of all men were fixed on Hampden as their *patriae pater* (father of his country), and the pilot that must steer their vessel through the tempests and rocks which threatened it. And I am persuaded that his power and interest at that time was greater to do good or hurt than any man's in the Kingdom, or any man of his rank has had in any time. For his reputation for honesty was universal, and his affections seemed so publicly guided that no corrupt or private ends could bias them.'

Although he was a Royalist, and therefore on the opposite side in the House, Clarendon clearly admired Hampden and observed him closely. He imputed to him a considerable degree of Machiavellian subtlety, but recognized also his gift for leadership. Hampden, he wrote, 'was not a man of many words, and rarely began the discourse, or made the first entrance on any business that was assumed; but a very weighty speaker, after he had heard a full debate and observed how the House was like to be inclined, took up the argument and shortly and clearly and craftily so stated it that he commonly conducted it to the conclusion he desired'. Hampden, he added, always showed civility and modesty, listening to others as if he mistrusted his own judgement. He summed up John Hampden as 'a very wise man, and of great parts, and possessed with the most absolute spirit of popularity, that is the most absolute faculties to govern the people, of any man I know'.

Lao envisaged a leader who practises humility, being neither self-assertive nor talkative. In St Paul's famous words, he 'seeks not his own', but spends himself without hope of any human reward. As Lao wrote:

The sage is ever free from artifice and practises the precept
 of silence.
He does things without desire for control.
He lives without thought for private ownership.
He gives without the wish for return.
Because he does not claim credit for himself he is always
 given credit.

Therefore the sage
Puts himself in the background yet is always to the fore;

Remains outside, but is always here.
Is it not just because he does not strive for any personal end
That all his personal ends are fulfilled?

'Such a ruler benefits ten thousand people and yet is content in places which men disdain,' added Lao. The analogy of water as always is not far from his mind. 'The highest good is like that of water,' wrote Lao. 'The goodness of water is that it benefits ten thousand creatures, yet itself does not wrangle, but is content with the places that all men disdain. It is this that makes water so near to the Tao.' Water, then, is the symbol of the lowly, the yielding, the unassertive and the inconspicuous; it is content to find the lowest level in order to rest. Water also, streaming down the hillsides to the valleys, receives all kinds of defilements, but it cleanses itself and is never defiled. It reminds us vividly of Jesus baptising his followers or, taking a towel and a basin of water, kneeling to wash his disciples' feet. Lao wrote:

How did the great rivers and seas get their kingship over
the hundred lesser streams?
Through the merit of being lower than they; that was how
they got their kingship.
Therefore the sage, in order to be above the people,
Must speak as though he were lower than they,
In order to guide them
He must put himself behind them.
Thus when he is above the people have no burden,
When he is ahead they feel no hurt.
Thus everything under heaven is glad to be directed by him
And does not find his guidance irksome.
The sage does not enter into competition
And thus no one competes with him.

It may well be that the thoughts of Lao Tzu would bear a different interpretation if they were placed in a historical context. Possibly in the China of the fifth century BC a ruler who appeared to do little or nothing would be the best preserver of traditional society. Lao made no suggestion, for instance, that a wise ruler should seek to educate his subjects. But thoughts of prophets and poets enjoy a life of their own; the golden grains of truth in them transcend whatever may have been their original social context. On leadership, for example, the following words of Lao Tzu have become justly famous:

> A leader is best,
> When people are hardly aware of his existence,
> Not so good when people praise his government,
> Less good when people stand in fear,
> Worst, when people are contemptuous,
> Fail to honour people, and they will fail to honour you.
> But of a good leader, who speaks little,
> When his task is accomplished, his work done!
> The people say, 'We did it ourselves.'

For Lao it is always some want within the inner life of the ruler that causes trouble among the people. If the leader lacks faith or trust, so will the people. The principle that 'There are no bad students but only bad teachers' is very much in keeping with the spirit of Taoist thought. So too is the military maxim that 'There are no bad soldiers, only bad officers.' These sayings invite leaders to look in the mirror before they find fault with others.

JESUS AND HIS DISCIPLES

The teaching of Jesus on leadership stands out more sharply against a background of some of the disciples strongly vying for his favour and perhaps ultimately for position in the new community they sensed would come about through him. Selected from a largely self-chosen band of disciples, both men and women, who accompanied Jesus as he went about the country teaching and healing, the Twelve came to see themselves as the corps of leaders for the new movement. Jesus saw that they clearly needed instruction in that role, and especially in a style of leading other disciples or followers in 'the Way' that would not be divisive. Their quarrels over precedence gave him several opportunities to teach them about the true nature of leadership.

Jesus apparently promised the disciples that when the kingdom of God came on earth they would sit on twelve thrones, as the judges or rulers of Israel. According to Matthew's Gospel, this reward for their share in his offerings was not enough for the mother of James and John, sons of Zebedee. She came up to Jesus with her sons and knelt before him in order to ask him for something. 'What do you want?' Jesus asked her. She replied: 'Command that these two sons of mine may sit, one at your right hand and one at your left.' In Luke's version of the story, it is the two disciples themselves who make this self-seeking request.

When the ten heard it, the story continues, they began to be indignant at James and John. Jesus called them to him and said to them, 'You know that the rulers of the Gentiles exercise lordship over them; and those in authority over them are called benefactors. But not so with you;

rather let the greatest among you become as the youngest, and the leader as one who serves. For which is the greater, one who sits at table, or one who serves? Is it not the one who sits at table? But I am among you as one who serves.' The emphasis upon humility in leadership is unmistakable.

According to John's Gospel, this distinctive teaching of Jesus on the need for a humble style of leadership reached a climax shortly before the end of his life on earth, in the most extraordinary scene in the whole history of leadership:

> Jesus . . . rose from supper, laid aside his garments, and girded himself with a towel. Then he poured water into a basin, and began to wash the disciples' feet, and to wipe them with the towel with which he was girded. He came to Simon Peter; and Peter said to him, 'Lord, do you wash my feet?' Jesus answered him, 'What I am doing you do not know now, but afterwards you will understand . . .' When he had washed their feet, and taken his garments, and resumed his place, he said to them, 'Do you know what I have done to you? You call me Teacher and Lord; and you are right, for so I am. If I then, your Lord and Teacher, have washed your feet, you also ought to wash one another's feet. For I have given you an example, that you also should do as I have done to you. Truly, truly, I say to you, a servant is not greater than his master, nor is he who is sent greater than he who sent him. If you know these things, blessed are you if you do them.

Both in this action and the accompanying teaching there is an element of Eastern hyperbole, but that is precisely what makes it so memorable. No leader should take it too literally. By becoming the group's slave a leader would cease to lead. Jesus would be unknown today if he had spent all his time meeting the physical needs of his disciples. What comes across to us, however, is the double message of Jesus: that a leader is one who meets needs and that his or her style should reflect that reality.

SERVANT–LEADERSHIP IN PERSPECTIVE

Neither humility nor even modesty was a virtue particularly admired by the Greeks, although arguably Socrates exemplified them both. In contrast to Xenophon, Aristotle and the Romans after him seem to have assumed that slaves were, by definition, mentally and spiritually inferior to free men. The Romans learned the error of that opinion when the slaves rose in revolt under Spartacus and inflicted several defeats on the legions. The idea of self-effacing leadership ran contrary to the Greek desire for personal glory and distinction. Xenophon, for example, wrote his history of the Persian expedition primarily to ensure that his own exploits as a leader were not overshadowed. For other commanders wrote memoirs which had considerably played down his part in comparison to their own.

The teachings of Lao Tzu and Jesus on humility in leadership should not, however, be lightly dismissed as unrealistic. Many people – not only Christians – would argue that Jesus was the greatest transformational leader in history: he came to change human nature or to restore it to God's original vision. It may be that we are becoming the kind of people who will value and respond to the kind of servant–leadership Jesus advocated. It does have strength and it does arouse admiration.

There is evidence of a pragmatic kind from Greek and Roman times that, even in such a hierarchical society as an army, troops respond warmly to leaders who come down to their level, eating the same food and sharing the same hardships. These leaders are never more powerful than when they divest themselves, so to speak, of the artificial 'garments' of office and rely solely upon the authority of their knowledge and personality.

WU CH'I

'Regard your soldiers as your children, and they will follow you into the deepest valleys; look on them as your own beloved sons, and they will stand by you even unto death.'

Tu Mu drew an engaging picture of the famous general Wu Ch'i: 'He wore the same clothes and ate the same food as the meanest of his soldiers, refused to have either a horse to ride or a mat to sleep on, carried his own surplus rations wrapped in a parcel, and shared every hardship with his men. One of his soldiers was suffering from an abscess, and Wu Ch'i himself sucked out the virus. The soldier's mother, hearing this, began wailing and lamenting. Somebody asked her, saying: 'Why do you cry? Your son is only a common soldier, and yet the commander-in-chief himself has sucked the poison from his sore.' The woman replied, 'Many years ago, Lord Wu performed a similar service for my husband, who never left him afterwards, and finally met his death at the hands of the enemy. And now that he has done the same for my son, he too will fall fighting I know not where.'

'If, however, you are indulgent, but unable to make your authority felt; kind-hearted, but unable to enforce your commands; and incapable, moreover, of quelling disorder: then your soldiers must be likened to spoilt children; they are useless for any practical purpose.'

Hsun Tzu, *The Art of War*, (c. 500 BC)

For leadership at its most sublime touches the human spirit. That indefinable spirit includes the power we have to transcend ourselves for the common good, even to the point of laying down our lives. Experience of that spirit in man does breed a sense akin to humility in a leader: it deepens respect, trust and love. Such a leader will come to look upon leadership as a privilege in itself, not as a passport to privileges which would otherwise be denied to him.

HUMILITY – A TEST OF GREATNESS

I believe the first test of a truly great man is his humility. I do not mean by humility, doubt of his own power, or hesitation in speaking his opinions; but a right understanding of the relation between what *he* can do and say, and the rest of the world's sayings and doings. All great men not only know their business, but usually know that they know it, and are not only right in their main opinions, but they usually know that they are right in them; only, they do not think much of themselves on that account. Arnolfo knows he can build a good dome at Florence; Albrecht Durer writes clearly to one who had found fault in his work, 'It could not have been done better'; Sir Isaac Newton knows that he has worked out a problem or two that would have puzzled anybody else; – only they do not expect their fellow-men therefore to fall down and worship them; they have a curious under-sense of powerlessness, feeling that the greatness is not *in* them, but *through* them; that they could not do so or be anything else than God made them. And they see something Divine and God-made in every other man they meet, and are endlessly, foolishly, incredibly merciful.

John Ruskin, *Modern Painters* (1843)

The tradition of Lao Tzu lends support to this view. The leader senses the powers at work in groups of people and individuals: he works with these powers, like a carpenter working with the grain of the wood. He is humble before his materials, just as a good craftsman or artist might be. His humility also allows him to stand back in the hour of success. For he knows that it is the power of the group, which he has guided and served, which has achieved the result. 'When his task is accomplished, his work done, the people say, "We did it ourselves."'

The difficulty, of course, is that leaders tend to be men and women with a higher than average level of self-assurance. They are often what are called strong personalities. These qualities do not mean that leaders are also necessarily self-centred or selfish: some are and some are not. But they do make it hard for many leaders to be self-effacing in the style taught by Lao Tzu and Jesus. Such strong leaders can make for weak teams (see Margaret Thatcher, page 198).

The world has been reluctant to learn that lesson. The English, for example, have always been more comfortable with the word *modest*, rather than *humble*, or *lowly* or *meek*. Modesty is a classically based concept, which means essentially staying within one's limits.

GEORGE WASHINGTON

Washington's great-grandfather, John Washington, stepped ashore in Virginia in 1657 and acquired for himself a handsome estate. George was born in 1732, third son of a second wife. He trained as a surveyor and at sixteen journeyed to the Shenandoah Valley and the region of the Blue Ridge Mountains.

He grew to be a tall man of 6 feet 2 inches, with blue-grey penetrating eyes and a commanding countenance, acquired while leading Virginian companies in the wars against the French and Indians. In 1775 he was appointed to command the American forces struggling against the British Redcoats.

Unity among the revolutionary army was essential. It was not an easy task to create it. At the outset of the war, for example, many units refused to obey orders from officers who did not come from their own colonies. Patrick Henry, Governor of Virginia, spoke as a statesman when he declared: 'The distinctions between Virginians, Pennsylvanians, New Yorkers and New Englanders are no more. I am not a Virginian, but an American!' Washington established his authority slowly, carefully and firmly in the army largely through the power of his personality. Virtually everyone who met him found him dignified and modest. Abigail Adams, for instance, who met most of the leaders of the Revolution and approved of few of them, was deeply impressed by Washington. To her husband, she wrote: 'You had prepared me to entertain a favourable opinion of him, but I thought the one half was not told me. Dignity with ease and complacency, the gentleman and soldier look agreeably blended in him. Modesty marks every line and feature in his face.'

Another friend recalled: 'There was so much native dignity in his deportment, that no man could approach him without being impressed with a sensation that he accosted a superior being: yet, there was a small mixture of timidity in his general demeanour, lest he might commit an error, and his modesty was exceeding prepossessing. It gave a mildness and kindess to his manner . . .'

Too often humility in people is not renunciation of pride but the substitution of one pride for another — being proud that they are not proud. Humility simply means to make a right estimate of oneself. It is one facet of true greatness, for really great men and women feel that greatness is not in them but through them. Golda once told a colleague that he wasn't great enough to be humble! False modesty and low self-esteem are as much the opposites of greatness as self-pride or arrogance. 'Humility is just as much the opposite of self-abasement as it is of self-exaltation,' wrote Dag Hammarskjöld in *Markings* (1964). When Lady Violet Bonham-Carter taxed Winston Churchill with his pride he replied: 'I accept that I am a worm, but I do believe that I am a glow-worm!'

THE JAPANESE CONTRIBUTION

Contact with Japanese society in various ways has served to remind us of the servant nature of true leadership and the humility which accompanies it. Bernard Leach, for example, Britain's most distinguished potter, once studied under another famous potter called Hamada in Japan. Unlike Western potters, Hamada did not sign his pots for he did not wish to put an accent on his personality. It was not a signature that mattered but the integrity of the act. 'The work, the doing, the activity for its own sake is no longer the actual goal,' wrote Bernard Leach. 'Our salvation lies in preserving humility in a world of widening and changing demand.' Leach saw Hamada much later at Mashiko. The famous potter had been offered a variety of teaching positions in Europe and America, but he preferred to live in Japan and to hire himself out as a thrower. He did this lowly work partly to gain acceptance of himself as a human being and good workman, and partly to rid himself of all pretence and self. He used to call it 'getting rid of his tail'.

If not disciples of Taoism, the Japanese still reflect something of that Eastern tradition in which Lao Tzu is the brightest star. 'One who excels in leading others,' he wrote, 'humbles himself before them.' For the Japanese practise a more self-effacing style of leadership than is customary in the West. In Japan the group is still valued more highly than the individual, and this induces a degree of what looks like humility in the leaders.

PUTTING THE TEAM FIRST

In the Japan—China War of 1895 there was a daring and successful attack by Japanese torpedo boats on the Chinese flagship in Wen-hai-wei bay.

'No Japanese officer who participated will tell you his share. I once asked one of these, whom I met, about the famous action. "Oh yes," said he, "I was there. It was a very cold night."

Subsequently I learnt from another officer that this particular one had commanded the boat that sank the *Ting-Yuen*. "But," added my informant, "he would not tell you, and you should not ask. All did well; some were lucky, some were not. Since all did well they agreed not to speak of it after, and say who did this and who did that, for all were equally worthy of praise."'

Frederick T. Jane, *The Imperial Japanese Navy* (1904)

Japanese managers tend to wear the same uniforms and eat in the same canteens as their work people. It is not unknown for Japanese managers to do such menial (or servant) tasks as sweeping the factory or cleaning out the lavatories. These are variations of a half-forgotten theme which lies deep within the world's emerging global tradition of leadership.

KEY POINTS

- Leadership as service emphasizes responsibility for the three areas of need – task, team and individual – as opposed to position, rank or privilege. A servant–leader is with or among people as well as being over them.

- The besetting temptation of leaders – the overgrown fruit of personal self-confidence – is arrogance; an overweening attitude of superiority is often accompanied by an excessive sense of being right, an overbearing manner and dominance. The antitude and opposite to arrogance is humility.

- The teaching of Lao Tzu set leadership in the context of Nature's harmonious and holistic *Tao* or Way. Don't force things – let them take their natural course. Leadership is within you. Express it without self-consciousness or self-importance, without pride or show. Have all things but do not dominate them.

- Listening and silence, paradoxically, are often the badges of such a leader. 'No one can safely appear in public unless he himself feels that he would willingly remain in retirement,' wrote the medieval Christian writer Thomas à Kempis. 'No one can safely speak who would not rather be silent. No one can with safety command who has not learned to obey.'

- Again, paradoxically, the leader who puts himself or herself into the background, so that the people say, 'We did it ourselves', will always be to the fore. 'But you made a difference,' the people may well add, when they have had time to think about it. Acceptance of proper recognition gracefully is a sign of humility, just as a false embarrassment at praise suggests its absence.

- As G. K. Chesterton said, 'It is always the secure who are humble.'

POINTS TO PONDER

❑ How does the idea of servant–leadership relate to today's hierarchical organizations and the barriers which so often exist with them? All organizations are hierarchical, for organization *is* hierarchy: it is being organized into orders or ranks each subordinate to the one above it. The principal reason for it was originally communication rather than authority: that means by which a leader could communicate effectively with a large body of people.

The real choice is between elaborate organizations with many layers or ranks and much more simple structures. For a variety of reasons, modern organizations have become flatter as unnecessary levels of management have been stripped out. We are moving towards just three broad and overlapping bands: strategic, operational and team leaders.

But this is still a hierarchy. Leadership is paradoxical in that it can and does work in a formal structure, fulfilling managerial roles and respecting order and system as the necessary means to achievement. At the same time, however, leaders can seem anarchical. They persist in seeing others as free and equal partners. Such leaders put themselves on an equal footing with others without losing the respect that stems from their inner leadership. But even the unseen and entirely justifiable differentials in salary, they believe, should better reflect this essential equality of all team members in the common enterprise.

❑ Qualities, knowledge, skills – all have been much emphasized in the context of leadership. But inner attitudes – the way you think and the way you are inside yourself – are as fully important. For, by a kind of extra-sensory perception, your people will always come to sense who you are. You cannot hide your inner self as a leader. As the Zulu proverb says: 'I cannot hear what you say, because what you are is shouting at me.' Leadership is just being you.

6

NELSON

'I never saw a man in our profession . . . who possessed the magic art of infusing the same spirit in to others which inspire their own actions . . . all agree there is but one Nelson.'

Admiral Lord St Vincent, writing to Nelson

Perhaps once or twice in its history every nation produces a person with a genius for leadership. Horatio Nelson was such a genius. His leadership style was particularly remarkable given that it was being exercised in the Royal Navy in the conditions of the late eighteenth century, but of course Nelson, like all geniuses, transcends both his times and the limited military context. As long as the British are interested in leadership they will always study Nelson.

Nelson reveals almost all the core qualities of leadership identified in this book. He had the authority of knowledge and personality, as well as of rank and position. He gave clear directions; he built teams; and he showed a real concern for the individual. As Nelson's career unfolded, it also became clear that he possessed a great leader's gift of drawing out the best from people. These are the reasons why Nelson's story is worth telling again in this context.

EARLY LIFE

Nelson's family and social background were relatively humble. His father, a country vicar in Norfolk, had eleven children. His paternal grandfather, another rector, who had been educated at Eton and Emmanuel College, Cambridge, had married the daughter of a butcher in Petty Cury in Cambridge. His mother, a relative of the Walpole family, kept up her links with the Walpoles, but she had other relatives nearer to home, notably the Suckling family. When Spain threatened the Falkland Islands and Horatio's uncle Captain Maurice Suckling was making ready for sea, he invited one of his Nelson nephews to accompany him. Horatio, the younger of the two, a well-spoken boy with a certain charm of manner, accepted with alacrity. As a midshipman, he sailed with Suckling to the West Indies. He also voyaged to the Arctic, and finally to the East Indies, where he was stricken by a fever.

On his way home to England in the *Dolphin* (the voyage took over six months) Nelson suffered a severe depression, caused first by his fever and then by his apparent lack of prospects. Under the kindly eye of the captain his health returned and his spirits revived. Nelson thought he perceived a radiant orb which beckoned him on. 'A sudden glow of patriotism was kindled within me,' he would tell his officers later, 'and presented my King and Country as my patron. My mind exulted in the idea. "Well, then," I exclaimed, "I will be a hero, and confiding in Providence, I will brave every danger."'

With Captain Suckling as his patron, Nelson rose fast in the service. He was extremely ambitious; he had a gift not only for getting noticed by those who mattered in his career but also for establishing excellent relations with most of his superiors without any hint of subservience or servility. He was captain of a thirty-two-gun frigate at the age of twenty-one, but then endured five years on the beach with half pay in England, fretting for action. Like Alexander the Great, Nelson thirsted for battle. He desperately desired a great name and all the honours that accompanied success.

Nelson's impatience becomes more intelligible when it is remembered that he had yet to take part in a major sea battle. His enforced stay on land came to an end in 1793, when he was appointed to command the *Agamemnon* of sixty-four guns, under Lord Hood. Two days later England declared war on France. His new command brought him sudden glory, the loss of his right arm at Tenerife, and, from 1798 onwards – after the Battle of the Nile in Aboukir Bay – general fame. Such universal popularity might have been unwelcome to a man of different temperament, but Nelson loved it. He basked in the limelight of England's hero-worship. Nelson's enjoyment of his success was marred only by the effects of the nasty wound above the eyebrow he received in Aboukir Bay (Lady Emma Hamilton taught him later to cover up the scar by combing his hair forwards). He had lost his right eye in Corsica, and the sight in his remaining eye was beginning to fail.

THE MAN AND THE LEGEND

Later, Nelson took care to foster his own legend. He understood and practised the art of public relations. After actions at sea he excelled at writing what he called 'a famous account of your own actions'. He arranged for these despatches to be leaked immediately to the press, directing that where he had written 'I' and 'my' the third person should be substituted, to give the impression that some other hand had written them. He loved having his portrait painted. One of his mentors, the crusty old Lord St Vincent, told some ladies that Nelson, 'foolish little fellow, has sat to every artist in London'. (Nelson was only 5 feet 2 inches in height.) Soon Nelson's image, drawn from these portraits, appeared everywhere: on souvenir jugs and mugs, patriotic handkerchiefs, and swinging inn signs. In Yarmouth, when the landlady of the Wrestlers Inn asked leave of Nelson to rename her hostelry the Nelson Arms, he smiled and replied: 'That would be absurd, seeing that I have but one!'

People seldom forgot their first meeting with Nelson. It was in Admiral Hood's ship the *Barfleur* that Prince William, son of the reigning monarch and later England's eccentric sailor king, met Nelson, then a twenty-three-year-old frigate captain. His appearance made the straitlaced Prince stare. The Prince was midshipman of the watch on deck 'when Captain Nelson, of the *Albemarle*, came in his barge alongside, who appeared the merest boy of a Captain I ever beheld: and his dress was worthy of attention. He had on a full-laced uniform: his lank untidy hair was tied in a stiff hessian tail, of extraordinary length; the old-fashioned flaps of his waistcoat added to the general quaintness of his figure, and produced an appearance which particularly attracted my notice; for I had never seen anything like it before, nor could I imagine who he was, nor what he came about. My doubts, however, removed when Lord Hood introduced me to him. There was something irresistibly pleasing in his address and conversation; and an enthusiasm, when speaking on professional subjects, that showed he was no common being.'

That youthfulness and enthusiasm never left Nelson. But

in his later years his sandy-grey hair turned almost white. His face, with its irregular features lined with suffering, looked older than his years. Nelson improved his dress. In later life he customarily wore his blue naval uniform with gold epaulettes, adorned with his four orders of chivalry, the ribbons of two of them, and the gold medals awarded to all captains of ships-of-the-line after the battles of Cape St Vincent and the Nile.

NELSON MEETS WELLINGTON

It was where he was not known that Nelson wished to impress. The classic instance occurred during his chance meeting with the future Duke of Wellington, then Sir Arthur Wellesley. This took place in September 1805, immediately before Nelson left England for the last time. Wellington was eleven years younger than Nelson, but even at the age of thirty-six he had acquired a great reputation in India. Ahead of him was a succession of victories in Europe, culminating in Waterloo.

'Lord Nelson was, in different circumstances, two quite different men,' Wellington said later. 'I only saw him once in my life, and for, perhaps, an hour. It was soon after I returned from India. I went to the Colonial Office in Downing Street, and there I was shown into the little waiting room on the right hand, where I found also waiting to see the Secretary of State, a gentleman, whom from his likeness to his pictures and the loss of an arm, I immediately recognized as Lord Nelson. He could not know who I was, but he entered at once into conversation with me, if I can call it conversation, for it was almost all on his side and all about himself, and in, really, a style so vain and so silly as to surprise and almost disgust me.

'I suppose something that I happened to say may have made

him guess that I was somebody, and he went out of the room for a moment, I have no doubt to ask the office keeper who I was, for when he came back he was altogether a different man, both in manner and matter. All that I had thought a charlatan style had vanished, and he talked of the state of the country and of the aspect and probabilities of affairs on the Continent with a good sense, and a knowledge of subjects both at home and abroad, that surprised me equally and more agreeably than the first part of our interview had done; in fact, he talked like an officer and a statesman.

'The Secretary of State kept us long waiting, and certainly, for the last half of three-quarters of an hour, I don't know that I ever had a conversation that interested me more. Now, if the Secretary of State had been punctual and admitted Lord Nelson in the first quarter of an hour, I should have had the same impression of a light and trivial character that other people have had, but luckily I saw enough to be satisfied that he was really a very superior man; but certainly a more sudden and complete metamorphosis I never saw.'

During the long war with France, when at one point Britain was threatened with invasion by Napoleon's Grand Army, the nation needed a saviour. In fact it found two – Wellington and Nelson. The two men possessed very different backgrounds and characters.

Wellington came from the aristocracy. He had a certain aloofness about him, together with a lordly indifference to what people thought or felt about him – especially his social inferiors. He practised the virtue of self-control to the point of being taciturn. Wellington won victories and he won respect, but did he also win hearts? Wellington always seemed more at home with his officers, in their red coats and gold epaulettes, than the rank and file, those scourings of society – the 'scum of the earth', as he once called them. The British Army, he added, had turned these men into fine soldiers. Popular as 'Old Nosey' was for winning victories, for the good administration and even-handed discipline he maintained in his army, Wellington remained a commander rather than a leader.

In strange company Nelson usually said very little, although occasionally he could be boastful. He disliked any form of public speaking. Among friends Nelson spoke in a simple and unaffected way, his face animated. One of his nephews said that, 'At his table he was the last heard among the company, and so far from being the hero of his own tale, I never heard him allude voluntarily to any of the great actions of his life.'

As Wellington's story illustrated, Nelson could switch from one part to another with rapidity. Vanity and modesty fought for position in him. For Nelson's soaring ambition for glory and honour was confronted by a genuine humility before God – to whom he prayed night and morning – and before his fellow men. One of his captains, Sir Alexander Ball, tells the story that after the glorious battle of the Nile, he and his fellow captains commissioned an artist to paint Nelson's portrait. The artist had difficulty in even getting started. At last he admitted that the task was beyond his powers. 'There is such a mixture of humility and ambition in Lord Nelson's countenance,' he said, 'that I dare not risk the attempt.'

ACHIEVING THE TASK

'Nothing can stop the courage of English seamen,' wrote Nelson exultantly after one fight against the French in the Mediterranean. Nelson exemplified physical courage. He gave evidence in childhood that he had little sense of fear. As we have noted, he had an abnormal thirst for action which recalls Alexander the Great. The odds against him seldom mattered. Luck and the devotion of his colleagues and subordinates saw him through – at least until Trafalgar. In the boat attack on Cadiz in 1797, he and a crew of thirteen men attacked a Spanish barge with a crew of thirty. They fought it out with swords and pistols. John Sykes, the coxswain, twice saved Nelson's life with his cutlass; a third time he dived forwards and received on his own head a slash meant for Nelson. 'We all saw it,' wrote one sailor. 'We were witnesses to the gallant deed, and we gave in revenge one cheer and one tremendous rally. Eighteen of the Spaniards were killed, and we boarded and carried her, there not being one man left on board who was not either dead or wounded. "Sykes," said Nelson as he caught the gallant fellow in his arms, "I cannot forget this." But my wounded shipmate only looked him in the face, and smiled as he said, "Thank God, Sir, you are safe."'

On 25 July 1797 Nelson attacked Santa Cruz and had his right elbow shattered. The amputation of his arm without an anaesthetic proved to be an agonizing ordeal, but according to an eyewitness Nelson bore it with 'firmness and courage'.

'Authority flows from the man who knows,' says the proverb. Having gone to sea at the age of twelve, after briefly attending three schools, Nelson had little formal education but he read voraciously while he was at sea. He applied himself, too, to mastering his profession, passing his Lieutenant's Certificate at nineteen, one year below the permitted age (it helped having his mentor, Captain Suckling, on the examining board!) 'I have been your scholar,' Nelson wrote to William Locker, captain of the *Lowestoffe* on which he served as a lieutenant, 'it is you who taught me to board a Frenchman . . . and my sole merit in my profession is being a good scholar.'

Sea battles usually consisted of two long lines of stately white-sailed wooden ships sailing in parallel and pounding each other with broadsides. Nelson showed his flair and imagination in varying this theme. He spent much of his time thinking – thinking hard – about how to best use his 'grey-geese', as he sometimes called his beloved ships. Off Cape St Vincent his self-confidence and flexibility of mind led him to ignore conventional tactics and turn his ship the *Captain* out of line and across the head of the enemy column. At the Battle of the Nile, Nelson surprised the French fleet by attacking them at anchor on the landward side where their gunports were inoperative. At Trafalgar he approached the French line at right angles with two columns of ships. 'What do you think of that?' he had asked one of his captains to whom he had explained the plan while they strolled in the gardens of his Merton house before leaving England. 'Such a question I felt required consideration, I paused,' recalled Captain Keats. 'Seeing it he said, "But I'll tell you what *I* think of it. I think it will surprise and confound the enemy! They won't know what I am about. It will bring forward a pell-mell battle, and that is what I want."'

Nelson was exceptionally good at communicating his ideas and plans to his officers. After joining the fleet off

Cadiz before Trafalgar, he gave a dinner for fifteen commanding officers in his stateroom aboard the *Victory* on 29 September, his birthday, and to as many other captains on the succeeding day. 'I believe my arrival was most welcome, not only to the Commanders of the Fleet, but to almost every individual in it,' he wrote to Lady Hamilton, 'and when I came to explain to them the *"Nelson touch"* [his idea of bringing on a confused fight] it was like an electric shock. Some shed tears, all approved – "it was new – it was singular – it was simple!" and, from Admirals downwards it was repeated – "It must work, if ever they will allow us to get at them. You are, my Lord, surrounded by friends, whom you inspire with confidence."'

BRINGER OF HARMONY

In all his command, Nelson both inspired confidence and created harmony. Whether it was with an individual ship, a squadron or a fleet, he demonstrated that he was a natural team-builder. Nelson began with an unusually high opinion of his fellow officers and seamen. He trusted them and they in turn resolved not to let him down. Months after the Nile, in a letter of congratulation to him, Lord Howe said how notable he thought it was that *every* captain had done his duty on that day. Alas, he added, in his long experience that had not always been the case. Nelson replied, 'I had the happiness to command a Band of Brothers; therefore night was to my advantage. Each knew his duty, and I was sure each would feel for a French ship.'

This gift of creating or enhancing harmony wherever he went extended to the lower deck. He had the knack of finding the golden mean as far as discipline was concerned.

The harshness of some naval commanders, who relied overmuch on fear and corporal punishment to enforce their orders, often caused dissension and even mutiny with the fleet. That unimaginative disciplinarian Prince William, when he commanded a ship under Nelson, was quite indiscriminate on occasion: he once had a visiting German journalist whipped with a cat-o'-nine tails for some remarks which were not to his liking. Nelson eschewed such brutality. On one occasion in the West Indies, he courted unpopularity with his seniors for saving from the hangman's noose a drunken deserter called Able Seaman William Clerk. Nelson had powers to suspend the court martial sentence, but not to pardon or discharge the man: he did both. Lord St Vincent, one of the old school, commented: 'He used a hatchet where I would have used a penknife.'

Once a crew was working as a team and was infected with the right spirit, Nelson gave them his whole-hearted and warm affection. 'Nobody can be ill with my ship's company,' he wrote of the *Agamemnon*, 'they are so fine a set.' He turned down the offer of a bigger ship in order to stay with them in what he regarded as 'the finest ship I ever sailed in'. During a time when Spain allied itself somewhat uncertainly to Britain, Nelson paid a friendly visit to the Spanish fleet in Cadiz. 'Very fine ships, but shockingly manned,' was his professional judgement. 'The Dons may make fine ships,' he remarked, 'but they cannot, however, make men.' By contrast, the Royal Navy, like Wellington's army, did make men out of unpromising and sometimes unwilling material. 'My seamen,' he once wrote to his wife, 'are now what British seamen ought to be . . . almost invincible: they really mind shot no more than peas.'

Nelson once told a friend that at the Battle of the Nile his daring plan rested upon the outstanding abilities of his captains and crews. Without knowing the men he had to trust, he would not have hazarded the attack: there was very little room, but he was sure each would find a hole to creep in at. 'Having caught sight of the French fleet,' Nelson added, 'I could not help popping my head every now and then out of the window (although I had a damned toothache) and once, as I was observing their position, I heard two seamen quartered at a gun near me, talking, and one said to the other, "Damn them, look at them. There they are, Jack, if we don't beat them they will beat us." I knew what stuff I had under me, so I went into the attack with a few ships only, perfectly sure the others would follow me, although it was nearly dark and they might have had every excuse for not doing it, yet they all in the course of two hours found a hole to poke in.'

MEETING INDIVIDUAL NEEDS

Nelson's early life in a country rectory in Norfolk had taught him to care for others. His financial generosity to those who had some claim on him was one expression of this. Nelson had plenty of that liberality which Sir Thomas Elyot had expected an English governor or leader to show. He was always an affectionate man, especially to children such as his youngest sister Kate or, later, to his future wife's five-year-old son. A friend of hers once surprised the 'great little man of whom everyone is afraid', at play under the dining-room table with young Josiah.

Like any good naval officer of the day, Nelson concerned himself with the sailors' material needs, on one occasion providing one crew with fifty blankets at his own expense. He insisted that the men's quarters were properly ventilated and kept as free from damp as possible. He encouraged music and dancing, and any other activity which could help to sustain morale. He obtained Bibles and other Christian literature for the sailors. But such good works do not explain his extraordinary effect upon the lower deck. That was much more to do with his personality and charm.

THINKING FIRST OF OTHERS

'You must remember well that all those from whom you expect obedience will, on their part, expect you to take thought for them,' wrote Xenophon. The best leaders have always observed that principle.

As General Sir Ralph Abercrombie was carried, fatally wounded, from the battlefield of Aboukir Bay in 1801, a folded blanket was placed beneath his head. 'What is that?' he asked. 'Only a soldier's blanket,' replied an officer. 'Only a soldier's blanket!' exclaimed the general. 'A soldier's blanket is of great consequence and you must send me the name of the soldier to whom it belongs that it may be returned to him.'

'God bless your honour,' cried his soldiers as he was borne away, and soon after he was dead.

THE SAILOR'S RESPONSE

Apart from Nelson's reputation, which preceded him like an ever-mounting bow wave, the seamen loved him for his humanity and fellow-feeling. At Aboukir Bay, when a piece of iron shot ripped across his forehead above the eye leaving the bone white and skin hanging down over his face, Nelson was carried down to the cockpit. He was convinced that he was a dead man, for the spurting blood had blinded him. He spite of being in intense pain, when the surgeon broke away from a sailor he was attending in order to dress the wound, Nelson stopped him. 'No,' he said, 'I will take my turn with my brave fellow.'

After Nelson's early days as a lieutenant, the seamen of the *Lowestoffe* presented him with an ivory model of their frigate filled with dominoes. Later it was a familiar sight in Nelson's cabin, a valued token of affection from his 'brave fellows'. In his despatch after that first major success off Cape St Vincent, Nelson added in a postscript that one sailor from his ship the *Captain* had come up to him on board the captured *San Joseph*, and shaken him warmly by the hand, saying he might not soon have such another place to do it in, and 'assuring me he was heartily glad to see me'.

As Captain of the *Boreas*, an officer on that ship recalled, he used to call the midshipmen his children. He never rebuked the more timid of them, but always wished to show them he desired nothing of them he would not instantly do himself. 'I have known him say — "Well, Sir, I am going a race to the mast-head, and I beg I may meet you there."' The officer added that Nelson never seemed to notice the timid boy's lack of alacrity in climbing the mast, but 'when he met at the top, began instantly speaking in the most cheerful manner, and saying how much a person was to be pitied who could fancy there was any danger, or even anything disagreeable in the attempt'. Who could resist a Commander-in-chief who, asked by a fond mother to deliver a last-minute note to a midshipman on his first voyage, requested her to kiss it, so that he 'might take the kiss to him too'?

Trust in his colleagues and subordinates was the key to Nelson's leadership. It is summed up in the original form of his famous flag signal at Trafalgar. He ordered this signal to be hoisted on to the *Victory* yardarm high above the amber-and-black sides of the ship as the two British columns inched towards the waiting French lines at an agonizingly slow speed of two knots. It was to read as follows: NELSON CONFIDES THAT EVERY MAN WILL DO HIS DUTY. He agreed to an officer's suggestion with commendable modesty – that NELSON should be changed to ENGLAND. As CONFIDES would have had to be spelt out letter by letter, Nelson also accepted the suggested substitution of EXPECTS. At least on one quarter-deck the response was characteristically British. 'What is Nelson signalling about?' grumbled Admiral Collingwood at the head of the other column. 'We all know what we have to do.'

THE POWER OF EXAMPLE

Paul Nicholas was scarcely sixteen when he embarked on the sixty-four-gun *Belleisle* in October 1805 as an ensign in the Royal Marines. He wrote a vivid account of his experience at Trafalgar which included his first discovery about leadership:

'At half-past ten the *Victory* telegraphed "England expects every man will do his duty." As this emphatic injunction was communicated through the decks, it was received with enthusiastic cheers, and each bosom glowed with ardour at this appeal to individual valour . . .

'The determined and resolute countenances of the weather-beaten sailors, here and there brightened by a smile of exultation, were well suited to the terrific appearance which they exhibited. Some were stripped to the waist; some had bared their necks and arms; others had tied a handkerchief round their heads; and all seemed eagerly to await the order to engage. My two brother officers and myself were stationed, with about thirty men at small arms, on the poop, on the front of which I was now standing. The shot began to pass over us and gave us an intimation of what we should in a few minutes undergo. An awful silence prevailed in the ship, only interrupted by the commanding voice of Captain Hargood: "Steady! starboard a little! steady so!" echoed by the Master directing the quartermasters at the wheel. A shriek soon followed – a cry of agony was produced by the next shot – and the loss of the head of a poor recruit was the effect of the succeeding, and as we advanced, destruction rapidly increased. A severe contusion on the breast now prostrated our Captain, but he soon resumed his station. Those only who have been in a similar situation to the one I am attempting to describe can have a correct idea of such a scene. My eyes were horrorstruck at the bloody corpses around me, and my ears rang with the shrieks of the wounded and the moans of the dying.

'At this moment, seeing that almost every one was lying down, I was half disposed to follow the example, and several times stooped for the purpose, but – and I remember the impression well – a certain monitor seemed to whisper, "Stand up and do not shrink from your duty." Turning round, my much esteemed and gallant senior [Lieutenant John Owen] fixed my attention; the serenity of his countenance and the composure with which he paced the deck, drove more than half my terrors away; and joining him I became somewhat infused with his spirit, which cheered me on to act the part it became me. My experience is an instance of how much depends on the example of those in command when exposed to the fire of the enemy, more particularly in the trying situation in which we were placed for nearly thirty minutes from not having the power to retaliate.'

After Nelson's death at Trafalgar the sense of elation which swept through the British fleet at its great victory was tempered by the great shock of losing such a leader. 'I never set eyes on him,' wrote a sailor in his letter home, 'for which I am both sorry and glad, for to be sure I should have liked to have seen him. But there, all the men in our ship who have seen him are such soft toads. They have done nothing but blast their eyes and cry since he was killed. God bless you! Chaps that fought like the Devil sit down and cry like a wench.'

NELSON'S LEGACY

Apart from his physical frailty, Nelson had other human weaknesses. Some would describe them as flaws of character. At Leghorn in 1794, for example, he is known to have shared his Captain's cabin with an untidy and slovenly woman — 'he makes himself ridiculous with that woman,' wrote a brother officer. Some critics thought that Nelson had made a fool of himself with Lady Hamilton too, but there was a depth and permanence in their relationship which balanced his outward adoration of her and silenced all but a few critics. Among them, alas, was his sovereign, King George III, for whom he had ventured so much loyalty. According to a friend of Lady Hamilton's she said that his besetting sins were 'venery and swearing', but neither fault was untypical of the sailors of his, or any other, day. Besides, in the military, political and industrial fields, leaders have what has been called an 'idiosyncrasy credit': grateful for success, their colleagues discount human failings and peccadilloes. The British nation, and certainly the Navy, had no difficulty in over-looking his affair with Emma, for he was careful to observe the conventions of propriety. In this respect his charm helped him, for he remained on excellent terms with Emma's lawful husband, Sir William Hamilton, who actually died in Nelson's arms. Such faults may have made him less of a paragon, but paradoxically they made his virtues more accessible to those who would emulate him as a leader.

Of course Nelson had luck — lots of it. So many of his successes could have turned into disasters, and branded him for ever as foolhardy. But most of the risks he took were carefully calculated. Nor could he have achieved his pinnacle of fame unless he was supported by other superb leaders, captains and commanders in the Royal Navy, who fell not far short of him in courage, professional knowledge and even leadership. Ovid's words in *Heroides* again come to mind: 'He was a leader of leaders.' Nor should his glory detract from the real heroes, those seamen who endured the long blockades at sea with him and fought their guns in the infernos of smoke and flame between decks. What distinguished Nelson was his rare combination of leadership qualities and abilities. Fused together, and with a certain but indefinable personal charm, Nelson achieved excellence as a leader.

None of the portraits quite captures Nelson's personal magnetism, nor do any of the descriptions of him convey it. It is best deduced from the extraordinary effects he had upon others. Yet the memory of his inspirational leadership is central to the legacy he left to the British Navy. 'Not the least glory of the Navy is that it understood Nelson,' wrote Joseph Conrad. 'He brought heroism into the line of duty. Verily he is a terrible ancestor.' By that last remark Conrad meant that, for officers of the Royal Navy in particular, Nelson was a very hard act to follow.

'May humanity after victory be the predominant feature in the British Fleet.'

Nelson, 21 October 1805

KEY POINTS

- Nelson possessed a genius for leadership, just as Mozart – born two years before him – had a genius for music. In his life and career as a leader most of the strands of leadership identified so far, and more besides, come together in harmony.
- A combination of patriotic fervour – a sense of duty and love of England – blended in Nelson with an extraordinary ambition for personal fame. Yet he established and maintained excellent relationships with his colleagues as well as his superiors and subordinates. He did promote his own reputation by every means at his disposal, not always wisely. He was an odd mixture of humility and ambition.
- Possessed of boundless natural courage, Nelson led from the front in battle. He mastered his profession by study and experience, acquiring thereby the authority of knowledge. He could think quickly and from first principles, giving him a confidence, clarity and flexibility of mind.
- Nelson believed in communication through channels of command and in small groups, but oddly enough there is no record of him making a speech to a ship's crew or a large gathering. He was no public speaker.

- As a builder and inspirer of teams, Nelson was without equal. He showed considerable humanity in his treatment of individuals, balancing firmness and fairness on the one hand with understanding and empathy on the other. He was as proud of his 'brave fellows' the sailors as they were proud of him.

POINTS TO PONDER

☐ One of Nelson's captains who survived Trafalgar refused to travel on the first steam-engined train journey on the grounds that it was too dangerous! The world of Nelson's navy seems far distant from the grimy factories and mills of his own day, let alone the business world of today. His Royal Navy was the largest industry in Europe of its day; the National Health Service presently holds that title. Do you think Nelson would have been equally effective today in the National Health Service? How would you translate his example into practice today in industry or commerce?

☐ Why are there no leaders of genius in industry and commerce? Is it to do with the nature of the common task – the apparent lack of a sublime cause or purpose that evokes the best from human nature? Or is it more due to cultural factors that have deflected natural leaders away from careers in management? That situation is changing, but is it changing fast enough?

☐ Despite the legacy of Nelson as a hero and role model, the Royal Navy takes pains to train its officers in leadership. Against that benchmark, what is your organization doing to train or develop its leaders for tomorrow?

7

MAKING THE RIGHT DECISIONS

'Reason and calm judgement, the qualities especially belonging to a leader.'

Tacitus

In order to guide a group, organization or nation in the right direction a leader needs the ability to think and decide. It could be called the intellectual dimension of leadership. Practical reason, intuition and imagination are all included under that heading. But it is not only a matter of the leader having some or all of these attributes. He or she has to be able to guide a problem-solving or decision-making body, such as a board of directors, whose members may have different mental abilities as well as different personalities. The case study of Clement Attlee below shows how important it is to select the right team members and to lead decision-making meetings in an effective, business-like way. Climate matters, too, when it comes to thinking together for results. A good leader will remain cool, calm and collected, and encourage others to do so. If things go wrong, he or she accepts full personal accountability.

THINKING TO SOME PURPOSE

The core activity is undoubtedly *thinking*. The Canadian entrepreneur Roy Thomson, who built up a vast publishing empire and owned *The Times*, insisted upon its importance. In his autobiography *After I Was Sixty* (1975) he wrote:

> Thinking is work. In the early stages of a man's career it is very hard work. When a difficult decision or problem arises, how easy it is, after looking at it superficially, to give up thinking about it. It is easy to put it from one's mind. It is easy to decide that it is insoluble, or that something will turn up to help us. Sloppy and inconclusive thinking becomes a habit. The more one does it the more one is unfitted to think a problem through to a proper conclusion.
>
> If I have any advice to pass on, as a successful man, it is this: if one wants to be successful, one must think; one must think until it hurts. One must worry a problem in one's mind until it seems there cannot be another aspect of it that hasn't been considered. Believe me, that is hard work and, from my close observation, I can say that there are few people indeed who are prepared to perform this arduous and tiring work.

The fact that Roy Thomson left school at fourteen warns us against equating the ability to think or reason with having attended a university. Reason in this context means the sum of a person's intellectual powers. Practical reason is a phrase that suggests intellectual powers disposed to action as opposed to speculation or abstraction.

The Greeks called this practical common sense, or practical wisdom when it is found to an uncommon degree, *phronesis*. The traditional English translation of it (by way of the Latin word for foresight) is *prudence*. But modern-usage prudence has acquired nuances of thoughtful restraint; it is almost a synonym for caution. The Greek concept is much more positive. Aristotle instances Pericles, the Athenian statesman and leader, and others like him as demonstrating the nature of *phronesis*, 'because they can envisage what is good for themselves and for people in general'. He added that this quality belonged to those who understand the management of estates, the forerunners of modern industry, as well as political states.

MAKING TIME TO THINK

The power to give sustained thought to the way ahead is part of a strategic leader's competence. He or she is subject to a heavy schedule and many distractions. It is a part of the competence to take time to think through issues.

Soon after assuming office, President Ronald Reagan complained he had little time to think. He added that one gets used to it! President Sadat, on the other hand, took plenty of time to think, to meditate and formulate his daring strategy with Israel and its follow-up. He refused to be tied up in details. Shimon Peres, Israel's opposition leader (later Prime Minister) wrote in *The Times* after Sadat's assassination:

> He (Sadat) told me that he kept moving 'from one cabin to another cabin', not only because he was in need of relaxation, but because he was in search of loneliness. It was this loneliness which freed him in many ways from daily routine and permitted him to remain alone to meditate. This inclination he had to be alone — to think without being interrupted, to be in command of his time, to prefer

> a tree to a desk, a flower to a file – made him
> into a model leader as it is so often described in many
> books and is so rarely found in real life; to have more time
> for contemplation and use less time for fussing.'

In a famous funeral oration delivered at the burial of the fallen in battle, Pericles celebrated the values and spirit which made Athens so powerful in its time and so influential throughout later ages. During the speech, Pericles praised the ability of the Athenians to base their decision on *phronesis* or practical wisdom:

> We Athenians, in our own persons, take our decisions on policy
> or submit them to proper discussions for we do not think that there
> is an incompatibility between words and deeds; the worst thing
> is to rush into action before the consequences have been properly
> debated. And this is another point where we differ from other
> people. We are capable at the same time of taking risks and of
> estimating them beforehand. Others are brave out of ignorance
> and, when they stop to think, they begin to fear.

As Athens was a democracy, Pericles assumed that all citizens would share in the work of solving the problem of what to do in a given situation: defining the aim or goal, identifying possible courses of action, selecting from them the feasible alternatives, debating the pros and cons of each in terms of foreseeable consequences, and, finally, making the best decision possible in the light of the information available.

Sometimes the Greek tendency to talk and debate could get out of hand. During the war between Athens and Sparta, for example, Thucydides recorded that the Athenian

general Demosthenes showed inspiring leadership in opposing a landing by superior Spartan forces. But first he had to
quell the natural Athenian tendency to analyse the situation
in detail. Having drawn up his hoplites in order to stop the
enemy from landing, he spoke to them as follows:

> Soldiers, all of us together are in this, and I do not want any of
> you in our present awkward position to try to show off his
> intelligence by making a precise calculation of the dangers which
> surround us; instead we must simply make straight at the enemy,
> and not pause to discuss the matter, confident in our hearts that
> these dangers, too, can be surmounted. For when we are forced
> into a position like this one, calculations are beside the point:
> what we have to do is to stake everything on a quick decision.
> And in fact I consider that the odds are on our side, so long as
> we are determined to hold our ground and do not throw away
> our very real advantages through being frightened by the enemy's
> numbers.

Where time is short for decision-making, as for instance
in a crisis situation where life and death are involved, a
leader will normally be expected to exercise his or her own
practical common sense and make a decision. Military
leaders in particular need this ability to take a decision on
their own, as do people in commercial fields. The Spartan
general Clearchus, as you may recall (see page 16), took
upon himself that responsibility, although he had the
benefit of listening first to a debate by his intelligent
colleagues on their predicament, and what might be done.

From the angle of leadership, the involvement of people
in decision-making in this way has one enormous advantage.
For the more that people share in decisions which affect their
lives, the more they are motivated to carry them out. As

leadership and motivation are so closely related, that factor must always loom large in any leader's mind. Especially when there are few if any other means of motivating people, or when the leader lacks the authority of position (as in voluntary organizations), engaging people in the decision of what to do or where to go is vitally important.

POWER OF PERSUASION

A trait always noticeable in a successful leader is his ability to persuade others. There are times, of course, when every leader must make a decision and see that it is carried out regardless of what others might think. But whenever men can be persuaded rather than ordered — when they can be made to feel that they have participated in developing the plan — they approach their task with understanding and enthusiasm.

Churchill was a persuader. Indeed, his skill in the use of words and logic was so great that on several occasions when he and I disagreed on some important matter — even when I was convinced of my own view and when the responsibility was clearly mine — I had a very hard time withstanding his arguments. More than once he forced me to re-examine my own premises, to convince myself again that I was right — or accept his solution. Yet if the decision went against him, he accepted it with good grace, and did everything in his power to support it with proper action. Leadership by persuasion and the wholehearted acceptance of a contrary decision are both fundamentals of democracy.

General Dwight Eisenhower

As the ancient Greek proverb says, 'Two heads are better than one.' The quality of the decision will often be higher if more than one person has been involved in the prior process of practical reasoning. Our common experience of decisions in everyday life supports that conclusion.

Only an arrogant person will assume that he or she has all the information and all the wisdom necessary to make a decision. In order to guarantee that the best possible decision is taken, a wise leader will encourage as full a debate as possible among the members of the team and listen to it carefully. As Shakespeare wrote: 'Rightly to be great, is not to stir without great argument.'

But others involved in the argument do not necessarily have the same responsibility for action as the leader. It is the leader who is usually charged with ensuring that a decision is taken and that it is then implemented. Time, time that waits for no man, can now become a critical factor. 'Nine-tenths of wisdom,' said Theodore Roosevelt, 'is being wise in time.' Consensus or mutual consent among all upon what should be done, is always highly desirable, for no leader who wishes to be effective wants a minority of dissenters who will drag their heels because they are uncommitted to the course of action adopted. But that unanimity is not always attainable. Cromwell voiced the exasperation of many a leader when he declared in the House of Commons one day, 'I am as for consent as any man, but where shall it be found?'

FROM IDEAS TO RESPONSIBLE AND DECISIVE ACTION

A leader, then, accepts the responsibility for seeing that decisions are taken and that the correct action ensues. In both respects, he or she must be a progress-chaser. 'I am certainly not one of those who need to be prodded,' Churchill said, with a characteristic twinkle in his eye. 'In fact, if anything, I am the prod!'

The invention and production of what came to be known as Mulberry Harbours illustrated well Churchill's foresight and prodding insistence on action at work. Without harbour facilities the Allied invasion of Normandy in 1944 could not have taken place. As the enemy held all the French harbours, the Allies would have to invent a new harbour facility and take it with them. In 1941, three years before the event, Churchill wrote a memo to Admiral Mountbatten, then in charge of combined operations:

> We must devise pierheads for the major unloading of thousands of tons. The piers must float up and down with the tide. The anchor problem must be solved. Don't argue the matter, the difficulties will argue for themselves.

A good leader will also accept complete personal responsibility if the decision he has made leads to failure. He will not 'pass the buck' to his colleagues or subordinates. After the failure of his first attack on Quebec, General Wolfe wrote:

> The blame I take entirely upon my shoulders and I expect to suffer for it. Accidents cannot be helped. As much of the plan as was defective falls justly on me.

Eisenhower also shouldered the responsibility of failure. The weather conditions in the first few days of June 1944 caused his air commander to argue for further postponement of the invasion of Europe. After consultation with his generals and specialist advisers, Eisenhower himself took the momentous decision to take the risk and go ahead on 6 June 1944. Before the invasion fleet set out he wrote this press release, to be used if necessary:

> Our landings have failed and I have withdrawn the troops. My decision to attack at this time and place was based upon the best information available. The troops, the air and the Navy did all that bravery and devotion to duty could do. If any blame or fault is attached to the attempt it is mine alone.

Hitler exemplified the opposite side of the coin – irresponsibility. He persistently blamed the failure of his military plans upon the incompetence of his subordinates or their lack of will-power, while taking for himself the credit of the early successes. When the roof fell in, Hitler castigated the German people for letting him down. He could neither see nor face his ultimate responsibility as leader.

A LEADER'S HUMILITY

'A sense of humility is a quality I have observed in every leader whom I have deeply admired. I have seen Winston Churchill with humble tears of gratitude on his cheeks as he thanked people for their help to Britain and the Allied cause.

'My own conviction is that every leader should have enough humility to accept, publicly, the responsibility for the mistakes of the subordinates he has himself selected and, likewise, to give them credit, publicly, for their triumphs. I am aware that some popular theories of leadership hold that the top man must always keep his "image" bright and shining. I believe, however, that in

> the long run fairness and honesty, and a generous attitude
> towards subordinates and associates, pay off.'
>
> General Dwight Eisenhower

The emphasis upon decisiveness in leadership is important because of the danger that those in posts of leadership
will never stop taking evidence, and accumulating and
weighing facts. As the future is, by definition, not entirely
predictable, it is impossible to have all the facts and
information before you make a decision. In this respect,
decision-making differs from the kind of problem-solving
where all the information is there but has to be sorted out
into a solution, like a jigsaw puzzle. In life, bits of the
jigsaw are often missing. A leader must often decide – or
press a group to decide – whether to trade more time and
money for more information, or to act upon the best
information available. That is a choice which in itself calls

EXECUTIVE ACTION

Lincoln Steffens, author of *The Shame of the Cities*, belonged to
a group of young reformers – one of the first pressure groups in
modern times – who through novels and popular writing laid bare
the abuses which had crept into American political, social and
economic life early this century. Railroads, finance, food adulter-
ation, traffic in women and children, and fraudulent claims for
drugs were among their targets. In 1906 Theodore Roosevelt
compared them to the muckraker in *Pilgrim's Progress*, more
interested in the filth at his feet than the celestial crown – hence
their nickname 'The Muckrakers'. But their writings led to construc-
tive, progressive legislation. In his autobiography Steffens quotes

a conversation with Woodrow Wilson, while the late President was in France, in which President Wilson said:

'An executive is a man of action. An intellectual – such as you and I [he smiled] – is inexecutive. In an executive job we are dangerous, unless we are aware of our limitations and take measures to stop our everlasting disposition to think, to listen, to – not act. I made up my mind long ago, when I got into my first executive job, to open my mind for a while, hear everybody who came to me with advice, information – what you will – and then, some day, the day when my mind felt like deciding, to shut it up and act. My decision might be right; it might be wrong. No matter, I would take a chance and do – something.'

for judgement. The desire to look at all sides of the question and to collect more information is a tendency among those professionally given to study and reflection. That is why they seldom make good leaders. In his book *The Art of Leadership* (1929), Ordway Tead summarized this key importance of decisiveness. 'Ultimately the leader has to get results,' he wrote.

There must be action and accomplishment. The group objective must be measurably realized. This is vital. To cut across indecision with decision, to galvanize indifference into enthusiastic performance, to translate doubt of possibilities into the swing of going actuality – to effect these translations is the leader's peculiar prerogative and duty. 'He did the job' is the tribute from which leadership cannot escape. How he did it, what motives he summoned and what residuum of achieved satisfaction he has left with his followers – these too are intrinsic aspects of his success. But leadership is at a premium because so many people are loath to make irrevocable decisions, are tepid in their enthusiasms, timid in their faith in themselves and others, afraid of the burden of responsibility and undecided about their direction.

CASE STUDY: CHAIRING THE CABINET

Clement Attlee served as Prime Minister of Great Britain from 1945 to 1951. 'In the Driver's Seat', an article which appeared in the *Observer* on 18 October 1964, contains his thoughts on leading a team which was itself composed of leaders (some of them, such as Aneurin Bevan, Herbert Morrison and Ernest Bevin, with a tendency to be prima donnas). It is written in Attlee's characteristically succinct, even terse, style of talking. He began with some reflections on judgement:

> Judgement is necessary because the Cabinet is the instrument by which decisions are reached with a view to action, and decisions stem from judgement. A Cabinet is not a place for eloquence — one reason why good politicians are not always good Cabinet Ministers. It is judgement which is needed to make important decisions on imperfect knowledge in a limited time. Men either have it, or they haven't. They can develop it, if they have it, but cannot acquire it if they haven't . . . Some men will be ready to express a view about everything. They should be discouraged. If necessary, I would shut them up. Once is enough. Ernie Bevin held forth on a variety of subjects, but Ernie had an extraordinary variety of practical knowledge.
>
> It is a curious thing that nearly every Cabinet throws up at least one man, whether he is a departmental Minister or not, of whom a newcomer might ask, 'What is he doing here?' He is there because he is wise. You will hear a junior Cabinet Minister being

told by the Prime Minister, perhaps, 'If you are going to do that, you would be well advised to have a talk with X.'

The ability to talk attractively in Cabinet is not essential. Being able to put a case clearly and succinctly and simply is what counts. The Cabinet is certainly not the place for rhetoric. Though an excellent head of department and a conciliator of genius, Nye Bevan used to talk a bit too much occasionally. Usually he was extremely good, often wise, and sometimes extremely wise. '75 per cent of political wisdom is a sense of priorities,' I remember him saying once – an admirable remark, and good advice for Cabinet Ministers.

The occasions when he talked too much were when he got excited because he felt that our policies were falling short of the pure milk of the word. This goes for most such interruptions, and a Prime Minister should try to avoid these time-consuming expressions of guilt – or electoral fear – by trying to reassure from time to time the pure in heart who feel the Government is backsliding . . .

The Prime Minister shouldn't speak too much himself in Cabinet. He should start the show or ask somebody else to do so, and then intervene only to bring out the more modest chaps who, despite their seniority, might say nothing if not asked. And the Prime Minister must sum up. Experienced Labour leaders should be pretty good at this; they have spent years attending debates at meetings of the Parliamentary Party and the National Executive, and have to sum those up. That takes some doing – good training for the Cabinet.

Particularly when a non-Cabinet Minister is asked to attend, especially if it is his first time, the Prime Minister may have to be cruel. The visitor may want to show how good he is, and go on too long. A good thing is to take no chance and ask him to send the Cabinet a paper in advance. The Prime Minister can then say, 'A very clear statement, Minister of . . . Do you need to add anything?' in a firm tone of voice obviously expecting the answer, no. If somebody else looks like making a speech, it is sound to nip in with 'Has anybody any objection?' If somebody starts to ramble, a quick, 'Are you objecting? You're not? Right. Next business,' and the Cabinet can move on.

It is essential for the Cabinet to move on, leaving in its wake a trail of clear, crisp, uncompromising decisions. That is what government is about. And the challenge is how to get it done quickly.

INTUITION AND IMAGINATION

The practical wisdom of a leader consists of more than the mental skill of analysing people or things. As we have seen, paralysis by analysis is a common failing in leaders who have not learned to be decisive. Analytical or logical thinking is a valuable asset in a leader at any level, and an education which develops that ability is to be prized. A leader who does not have a mind schooled in some discipline which has taught him to think clearly and systematically would be wise to include among his counsellors those who are so trained. One of Hitler's many mistakes as a leader was to despise the German General Staff, disciplined experts in logical thinking within the confines of war.

Hitler certainly possessed intuition. This attribute is often present in the intellectual powers of a leader above a certain level. 'Intuition comes very close to clairvoyance,' writes Alexis Carrel in his *Reflections Upon Life*. 'It appears to be the extrasensory perception of reality. All great men are gifted with intuition. They know without reasoning or analysis what they need to know.'

Leaders are often deterred from recognizing and using

their own intuitive powers because they feel that, somehow, intuition is not intellectually respectable. It is certainly, they believe, not scientific enough. The cult of the rational manager has an iron grip on such minds. But this is nonsense. Some of the most celebrated scientists have been intuitive in their work. Some words by Einstein prove that point:

> There is no logical way to the discovery of these elemental laws. There is only the way of intuition, which is helped by a feeling for the order lying behind the appearance.

Intuition, then, is the power or faculty of immediately apprehending that something is the case. Apparently, it is done without intervention of any reasoning process. There seems to be no deductive or inductive step-by-step reasoning, no conscious analysis of the situation, no employment of the imagination – just a quick and ready insight – 'I just know.' It is important, however, that intuition is soundly based upon experience and a history of sound reasoning.

TRUSTING YOUR INTUITION

Mrs Golda Meir, former Israeli Prime Minister, once said she caused the initial debacle in the 1973 Yom Kippur war and ruined her political career, because she ignored her own intuition.

In her autobiography, Mrs Meir revealed that when, on Friday, 5 October 1973, news was received that the Russian advisers were leaving Syria in a hurry, she had an intuition of what was to come. 'I tried not to become obsessive,' she wrote. 'Besides, intuition is a very tricky thing. Sometimes it must be acted upon at once, but sometimes it is merely a symptom of anxiety.'

She was reassured by Moshe Dayan, then Minister of Defence, the Chief of Staff and also by the Chief of Intelligence. They did not think war was imminent. Nor did General Bar Lev, a former Chief of Staff.

She added: 'Today I know what I should have done. I should have overcome my hesitations that Friday morning. I should have listened to the warnings of my own heart and ordered a call-up. For me, that fact cannot and never will be erased and there can be no consolation in anything that anyone else has to say.'

A person who consistently deploys an instinctive power of discernment in a certain field is said to have flair. He or she can 'smell' a good prospect or in what direction the truth might lie, rather than reasoning towards a goal in a step-by-step manner. Indeed flair comes from the French verb *flairer* meaning to smell. J. Paul Getty gave this example:

When I first started drilling in the Oklahoma oil fields the consensus of expert judgement held that there could be no oil in the so-called Red Beds region. But like so many oilmen, I chose to temper all 'analytical' thinking with a healthy dose of non-logical subjectivity. To me, the area looked as if it might hide oil. Largely on the basis of a hunch, I decided to see for myself. I began drilling in the Red Beds, and struck oil and brought in a vast new producing field. I rather suspect that by relying upon such nontextbook thought-processes and taking attendant risks, the biggest fortunes have been made – in oil and other endeavours.

Business flair is a consistent theme in the lives of great industrial leaders. They can intuitively spot an opportunity for making money. They can smell a potential profit where others can see nothing but present losses. It is an instinct apart from the dictates of reason or logic which guide more plodding minds. When it is not followed, such businessmen frequently find out their mistake later, just as Golda Meir did. For, as the Arab proverb says, 'Dawn does not come twice to awaken a man.'

THE COMPUTER OF PRACTICAL REASON

I must now ask myself: what was it that gave me this self-confidence, this determination and adventurous spirit in business . . . at sixty-seven.

It was at least partly due to my discovery over a fairly long period, but more than ever during these latter years in Edinburgh and London, that experience was a very important element in the management side of business and it was, of course, the one thing that I had plenty of. I could go further and say that for management to be good it generally must be experienced. To be good at anything at all requires a lot of practice, and to be really good at taking decisions you have to have plenty of practice at taking decisions. The more one is exposed to the necessity of making decisions, the better one's decision-making becomes.

At various times during my business life I have had to take some important decisions, and, particularly in the early days, I often got these wrong. But I found later that the early mistakes and, for that matter, the early correct decisions stood me in good stead. Most of the problems that I was confronted with in London were in one way or another related to those earlier ones. It was often a matter of just adding some zeros to figures and the sums were the same. In a great many instances I knew the answer immediately.

I cannot explain this scientifically, but I was entirely convinced that, through the years, in my brain as a computer, I had stored details of the problems themselves, the decisions reached and the results obtained; everything was neatly filed away there for future use. Then, later, when a new problem arose, I would think it over and, if the answer was not immediately apparent, I would let it go for a while, and it was as if it went the rounds of the brain cells looking for guidance that could be retrieved, for by next morning, when I examined the problem again, more often than not the solution came up right away. That judgement seemed to be come to almost unconsciously, and my conviction is that during the time I was not consciously considering the problem, my subconscious had been turning it over and relating it to my memory; it had been held up to the light of the experiences I had had in past years, and the way through the difficulties became obvious . . . It is only the rare and most complex problems that require the hard toil of protracted mental effort.

Roy Thomson, *After I Was Sixty* (1975)

As a general rule, the sooner an intuition comes to a leader, the more time he or she should take to verify it as far as that is possible. By contrast, intuition that is born out of a longer period of thought, study and experience, is more likely to be true. Consequently intuition later in life can perhaps be trusted more than earlier on, because of experience and practice in reasoning.

In this context, imagination and intuition are closely related. A leader needs imagination in many situations – where the next move is not blueprinted. It is true that as a leader you do not have total freedom. You do not have the relative freedom of someone writing a television script or the composer of a poem. You are more like a person crossing an unmapped plateau with others. You have to think things out for yourself and then suspiciously try out possible ways of getting where you want to be – and the solutions to these problems are not in books, nor can they be recalled from your memory bank. For you have never been here before. You have to originate or innovate, and you cannot innovate by following established precedents or by applying common recipes. John Sainsbury, a former chairman of the highly successful chain of grocery supermarkets which bears his name, stated:

> The characteristic in a good manager which I appreciate almost above all else is that of imagination. The good manager has to be imaginative in order to be a successful innovator. Success in that respect brings not only a valuable contribution to any enterprise, but also the considerable personal satisfaction of creative achievement. It is imagination which is needed to anticipate events and to respond to change. It is only those with a lively imagination who can really develop sensitive understanding of others, be they customers, colleagues or shop floor workers. To be able to do this is a vital ingredient of success in commerce or industry.

Imagination should not be promoted to top place in the hierarchy of thinking abilities. It should be a team player, not the captain. The specific role of imagination is to lead us into innovating, inventing, creating, exploring, risk-taking and adventuring. It is the vanguard or the advanced scouting party of thinking.

LAWRENCE OF ARABIA

'They taught me that no man could be their leader except he ate the rank's food, wore their clothes, lived level with them, and yet appeared better in himself.' So wrote T. E. Lawrence about the

Bedouin. He fought alongside them during the First World War, while acting as a political adviser to the Arab Revolt. General Allenby, his superior, described him as 'a brilliant tactician with a genius for leadership'. W. F. Stirling, who served as a staff officer with the Arab Army, came close to Lawrence's secret as a leader. Yet Lawrence occupied a low place in the military hierarchy. Whence his influence? Writing in *T. E. Lawrence by His Friends* (1937), Stirling said:

> Lawrence not only saw the task more clearly than others and how it could be achieved, but also possessed a remarkable intuitive sense of what was happening in the minds of the group. Above all he led by example. He took the limelight from those of us professional soldiers who were fortunate enough to serve with him, but never once have I heard even a whisper of jealousy. We sensed that we were serving with a man immeasurably our superior.
>
> As I see it, his outstanding characteristic was his clarity of vision and his power of shedding all unessential from his thoughts, added to his uncanny knowledge of what the other man was thinking and doing . . .
>
> How did he gain his power? Chiefly, I think, we must look for the answer in Lawrence's uncanny ability to sense the feelings of any group of men in whose company he found himself; his power to probe behind their minds and to uncover the well-springs of their actions.

Lawrence's traumatic experience of war – the exposure to combat, indignities at the hands of a Turkish captor, and the necessity for a Machiavellian duplicity in British diplomacy – induced in him stress, nervous breakdown and a sense of shattered personal integrity from which he never fully recovered. Sometimes the price of leadership is a burden of personal suffering.

The leader who knowingly ventures off or beyond the beaten track, the path of well-trodden expectations, is showing some degree of imagination. His or her ventures may turn out to be fruitless, random or crazy. For leaders who dream dreams may be pathfinders, but they may also lead themselves and others into the bankruptcy courts. Of those who depart from well-established ways only a few are explorers. '*Imaginative*', '*inventive*' and '*adventurous*' are terms of praise but, equally, '*fanciful*', '*reckless*' and '*crazy*' describe those who are failed imaginative thinkers. We should therefore be on guard against any tendency to glorify the notion of imagination as an end in itself. People sometimes forget that a lively imagination can also be a silly one. Scope for originality is also freedom to be a crackpot. Both the genius and the crank are imaginative thinkers – some are both at the same time.

Yet imagination covers some crucial qualities in the leader. There are plenty of situations in leadership that call for powers of originating, inventing, improvising, discovering, innovating, exploring, experimenting and of knowingly leaving the beaten track. 'As a rule,' wrote Kenneth Grahame, author of *The Wind in the Willows*, 'grown-up people are fairly correct on matters of fact; it is the higher gift of imagination that they so sadly lack.'

CALMNESS UNDER PRESSURE

Tacitus, in the words quoted at the head of this chapter, included calmness in the qualities that belong especially to a leader. The process of deciding the cut-off point between thought and action can be fraught with anxiety in various shapes and sizes. One is the anxiety of holding the decision until as much information as possible has been gathered. The other is the anxiety of making the decision when there really isn't enough information — which, on critical decisions, is usually the case. All of this is complicated by pressures building up from those who 'want an answer'. Again, trust is at the root of it. Has the leader a really good information base (both hard data and sensitivity to feelings and needs of people) and a reputation for consistently good decisions that people respect? Can the leader defuse the anxiety of other people who want more certainty than exists in the situation?

Communication plays an important part in dispelling anxiety. But the inner calmness of the leader also has influence. Anxious people look at the faces of their leaders. An absence of visible tension or excitement when such reactions might well be expected in the circumstances has a calming effect on them. It is not that a leader lacks such emotions. Courage is not being devoid of fear; it is the will or ability to control fear and to draw from it energy and resolution. It is vital to maintain self-control if one hopes to be able to control others.

A coolness which resists excitability and a composure which gives that dignified demeanour and conduct in the midst of confusion is valuable to other people as well as to generals. Field Marshal Lord Alanbrooke, Britain's Chief of General Staff during the Second World War, recorded in his diary how people in the War Office — officers, civilians and typists — used to watch his face in the dark days of 1941 and 1942 as he walked through the corridors of the building to his room. They were scrutinizing it for signs of how the war was going. It was a struggle at times, admitted this humane and sensitive man, to prevent his face from sending out signals of alarm and despondency.

Cool, calm and collected: these words are often bracketed together. They suggest that a leader's mental resources are completely intact in the face of difficulty. 'Calm' stresses a quiet approach to a problem, devoid of hysterical actions or utterances, while 'collected' emphasizes the application of practical reason to the solution of the problem. To be free from agitation of any sort in the face of danger or provocation, to be able to concentrate the mind, eliminating distractions, especially in moments of crisis: these are indeed qualities essential in any leader of stature. As Voltaire said of John Churchill, first Duke of Marlborough, he possessed 'that calm courage in the midst of tumult, that serenity of soul in danger, which the English call a cool head'.

COOLNESS IN ACTION

General Robert E. Lee was perhaps the finest military leader in the American Civil War. At the outset both sides sought him as their Commander-in-Chief, but Lee's loyalty to his native state of Virginia drew him into the camp of the Confederacy. By skilful generalship and good leadership he waged a remarkably successful war against the North. But at the three-day battle of Gettysburg any hope of victory for the South virtually disappeared. The decisive point in the battle came when an attack led by one of Lee's subordinates, General Pickett, failed. An eyewitness was present when news of this disaster reached Lee:

'His face did not show the slightest disappointment, care or annoyance, and he addressed every soldier he met with a few words of encouragement – "All will come right in the end, we'll talk it over afterwards." And to a Brigade Commander speaking angrily of the heavy losses of his men: "Never mind, General, all this has been my fault. It is I who have lost this fight, and you must help me out of it the best way you can."'

Anthony Eden, British Prime Minister during the Suez Crisis of 1956, showed in its duration how he lacked these particular qualities of leadership. He flapped his wings ineffectively. Eden's natural irritability erupted in fits of temper. Nor could he delegate properly. His Cabinet colleagues were constantly interrupted by him as he telephoned them in a state of excitement or worry. Rather than letting ministers get on with what needed to be done, Eden kept nagging and fussing. He showed an acute lack of self-confidence. He was very nervous and could not make up his mind. In the Suez Crisis he commanded every platoon. Clearly Eden was no leader. By contrast, Harold Macmillan's 'unflappability' was a byword. In the Cabinet Room he had framed the reminder: 'Quiet, calm deliberation disentangles every knot.' That is a good practical guideline for a leader to act upon.

THE VALUE OF HUMOUR

One of Churchill's endearing characteristics was his sense of humour. His biographer, Martin Gilbert, who spent a quarter of a century on his monumental work, came to know him in a unique way. 'What of Winston Churchill himself?' he wrote, reflecting upon his experience. 'I doubt if anyone could have enjoyed delving into his life for twenty-five years if he had been an ogre. How right his daughter Mary was when she wrote to him, in 1951: "It is hardly in the nature of things that your descendants should inherit your genius – but I earnestly hope that they may share in some way the qualities of your heart."'

Gilbert added that as the years of research and writing advanced, Churchill's sense of fun was a constant companion. 'In almost every file there was something to make me laugh. Puzzled in 1941 by the silence of General Wolfe Murray at a war conference, Churchill at once renamed him General "Sheep" Murray. In 1940, wanting to speak to his principal private secretary, Eric Seal, he asked a secretary: "Fetch Seal from his ice floe."'

Apart from making conversation much lighter, humour also has a functional value: it helps to defuse tension. Anxiety can be like electricity: if it strikes the pole of humour it can be conducted safely into the ground. Because of the situational pressures inclining people to laugh in order to relieve their tension, the joke made by a leader – or anyone else in the team – doesn't have to be a particularly good one.

Remaining cool, calm and collected is essential for a leader. If, like an acrobat balancing on the high wire of risk and difficulty, a leader can smile as well – and cause others to smile – it can have a magic effect on morale. For people tend to take a cue from their leaders.

HANNIBAL AT CANNAE

Varro insisted on observing the practice whereby each consul took command of the army on alternate days. He then pitched his camp opposite Hannibal's on the banks of the river Aufidus near the town named Cannae, and at daybreak hoisted the signal for battle, a scarlet tunic hung out over the general's tent. At first even the Carthaginians were dismayed, not only by the

Roman commander's apparent boldness, but also by the strength of his army, which was more than double their own. Hannibal ordered his troops to prepare for action, while he himself with a few companions rode to the crest of a gently rising slope, from which he could look down on the enemy as they formed their order of battle.

When one of his companions, an officer of high rank, remarked that the numbers of the enemy seemed amazingly large, Hannibal looked grave for a moment, and said, 'There is another thing you have not noticed, Gisco, which is even more amazing.' When Gisco asked what this was, he replied, 'The fact that in all this enormous host opposite there isn't a single man called Gisco.' The joke caught the whole party off guard and they all began to laugh: then as they rode down from the high ground they repeated it to everyone they met, so that their high spirits quickly spread among the troops and the officers of Hannibal's staff were completely overcome with laughter.

The Carthaginians took heart when they saw this, for they thought that their general must have a great contempt for the Romans if he could laugh and joke like this in the face of danger.

Plutarch.

KEY POINTS

- Leadership is about giving direction, but it has to be the right direction. That calls for a practical intellectual ability, both natural and educated, which issues in clear thinking and correct decisions. The Greeks called it *phronesis*, which we might translate as practical judgement or transcendent common sense.

- Such thinking, as Roy Thomson says, is arduous and tiring work, but it is the chief key to success as a leader. 'If one wants to be successful, one must think,' he wrote, 'one must think until it hurts.'

- Thought and reflection on your own must be interwoven with hearing the issues discussed by your group. Feasible courses of action have to be identified, and their pros and cons debated hard. Out of such discussion arises intelligent and committed action. It produces the optimum course or way forward, not necessarily the perfect one.

- Thought precedes decision; decision leads to action. Depending on the circumstances, and especially upon the degree of crisis, as a leader you need to know when to cut off the debate and to initiate the action phase.

- Intuition is sensing situations as they really are when the evidence is incomplete. It can be distorted by anxiety or fear, and it should always be tested by reason or experiment before being accepted. 'In the country of the blind, the one-eyed man is king.' But even a leader with partial vision may sometimes rely upon the blind man's guide dog – intuition.

- Imagination is also necessary, for new circumstances call for new ideas. Again, a leader does not have to be particularly imaginative personally, but should be able to stimulate and respond to imaginative thinking in the organization.

- The ability to make things happen is essential. It helps immeasurably if a leader creates a climate of energetic purpose, in which people do what has to be done in a calm and collected way. Humour defuses tension in times of crisis and adds an element of enjoyment. Where possible, good leaders make work more fun than fun.

POINTS TO PONDER

☐ In order to understand a concept such as *leadership* you have to understand also its immediate neighbours, such as *decision-making* and *communication* (the subject of the next chapter). The foundations of effective decision-making are clear thinking, intuition and imagination. Such are the complexities of change today that we need what T. E. Lawrence called 'brainy leadership'. Do you agree that the intellectual cost of living has gone up for all leaders these days?

☐ 'The fine art of executive decisions,' wrote Chester Barnard, 'consists in not making decisions that cannot be made effective, and in not making decisions that others should make.' Do you agree?

☐ 'Nothing is more difficult, and therefore more precious, than to be able to decide,' wrote Napoleon. A leader's task is to help a group or organisation to overcome the difficulty of decision. Decision should be a step in the right direction, even if the end of the journey is not always clear.

☐ It is often said that leaders need vision and certainly great leaders show it. Vision means literally to see ahead. It is far-sightedness. Vision can also be the art or power of forming a mental image of something not actually present to the senses or never before wholly perceived or experienced in reality. It can be an imaginative and exciting concept of how things might be tomorrow. Leaders deal in visions; their stock in trade is hope. Some visions turn out to be illusions, but others are the stuff of progress. Learn to know the difference! As a leader, then, you need imagination as well as foresight if you are going to bring the gift of vision.

8

THE ART OF INSPIRING WHILE INFORMING

'Not geniuses, but average men require profound stimulation, incentive towards creative effort, and the nurture of great hopes.'

John Collier

Communication is a dimension or facet of almost all that a leader does. A leader communicates in order to achieve the common task, to build the team and to meet individual needs. Leaders and the others involved must communicate with each other. It is practically impossible for a leader, short of doing everything himself or herself, to make things happen without communicating. And effective leadership implies making the right things happen at the right time.

The simple truth that things do not happen without communication highlights the importance of *how* a leader communicates. To lead at all requires communication; to lead well requires that a leader communicate effectively. In this chapter we shall look at some examples of leaders who did communicate supremely well.

THE EFFECTIVE COMMUNICATOR

In the context of leadership, to communicate means to share with or impart to others one's thoughts and information in order to obtain a desired response. 'You make an audience say "How well he speaks!" said Demosthenes, the greatest orator in Athenian history, to a political rival. 'I make them say, "Let us march against Philip of Macedon!"'

The primary responsibility for good communication lies with the leader. In *The Art of War*, written in China by Hsun Tzu in about 500 BC and therefore the world's oldest book on the subject, the Chinese sage emphasized the importance of clarity in giving orders. 'If the words of command are not clear and distinct, if orders are not thoroughly understood, the general is to blame.'

It is not too difficult to define effective communicators. First, they know what the aim is. What are the effects or actions that should result from this communication? Second, they understand the feelings and information already present in the minds of their hearers or readers. Third, they put over what they have to say clearly, simply and vividly, using the most appropriate method of communication – personal conversation, telephone, presentation, report or letter.

In the context of human enterprise, leaders must both impart and receive a great deal of information daily. They need to be skilled both in putting across information with the necessary clarity and conciseness, and in listening to what others have to report.

People need information from their leader or leaders on where the enterprise is going. How is the common task to be achieved? What is the plan? What information is there about the opposing forces, such as competitors, who lie in wait along the way to prevent us from achieving our goal?

However, if information flows out from the centre to the periphery in organizations, so information constantly comes back from the periphery to the centre. The task of interpreting and digesting this data is partly an intellectual one, but it is also partly a matter of communication. Does the leader actually listen to those who know what is happening operationally?

'I hear what you say,' is listening on a low level. A good listener is not necessarily the one who makes the most feedback-type physical response, such as head-nodding or grunts of comprehension. A leader who is a good listener asks questions to clarify the information and to test its validity. Above all, such a leader is genuinely open to the possibility of a change of view or adding to his or her store of information as a result of the act of listening.

HERMOCRATES

This Syracusan statesman and general was much admired by Thucydides, who saw in him a Sicilian Pericles. He commanded a Syracusan squadron of ships sent to assist Sparta in one of its wars. Xenophon, in his continuation of Thucydides' history, wrote that, when Hermocrates left the fleet, he 'was particularly badly missed by those who had been in close contact with him and who now felt the loss of his guiding authority, his readiness to help and his ability to mix with his men.

'Every morning and every evening he had been in the habit of inviting to his own tent a select body of those whose acquaintance he had made, both captains and steersmen and marines, and he would discuss with them whatever he was planning to say or to do. He would explain his reasons and then ask them sometimes to express their opinions at once, sometimes to go away and think it over first. Hermocrates, as a result of this, had a very high reputation in the general assembly. He was regarded there as the best speaker and the most reliable planner.'

THE ART OF INSPIRING OTHERS

Having a worthwhile vision which one wishes to impart is one important dimension in the art of inspiring others. What is vision? The word suggests, as we have noted, the power of seeing, and by implication the ability to see further ahead and to see a wider field than others. It is, essentially, foresight together with an unusual discernment of the right way forward.

More often than not, a leader will take elements of his or her vision from others, but they still have to be internalized and synthesized. In religious contexts, a vision may be credited to supernatural sources. It may be seen in a dream, trance or ecstasy; it can be a supernatural appearance conveying a revelation. Few industrial or commercial leaders would claim divine authority for their ideas, but creative imagination does enter into the everyday visions which guide our steps forward. A visionary – one whose ideas or projects are impractical – will not last long in a leadership position. But a visionless leader – lacking in vision or inspiration – is almost a contradiction in terms.

In order to inspire others a leader first needs to be inspired. A cynic might suggest that it is the prospect of personal fame or glory, or relish in exercising power over others, which invariably motivates leaders. Neither common sense nor history entirely supports this view, although there are undoubtedly elements of truth in it. Usually it is some higher purpose or exalted cause which inspires the leader. But there is more to inspiration than communicating a vision, however exalted. An effective leader seems to impart emotion, feeling and energy as well.

It is this ability to inspire energy, to enthuse others, that history records so clearly in the lives of great leaders. Some military and political leaders in history, such as Alexander the Great, Napoleon and Hitler, saw themselves as the powerhouses of their armies and nations, constantly energizing them to great effort. That self-perception has two main disadvantages. First, a severe physical and mental toll has to be paid by the leader. Second, it breeds dependence. A better approach would be to see the power or energy as already there within the people. The leader has to locate the hidden reserves of energy, to release them and to channel them into purposeful action. His or her words and example are more like triggers than dynamos.

JULIUS CAESAR – THE GREAT MOTIVATOR

Before invading Britain, Caesar had campaigned in Gaul for eight years. There, according to Plutarch, 'He proved himself to be as good a soldier and a commander as any of those who have been most admired for their leadership and shown themselves to be the greatest generals. His ability to secure the affection of his men and to get the best out of them was remarkable.'

The Roman Army worked reasonably well operationally without inspiring leadership. It was a military machine held together by the ropes of discipline. Compliance with orders was achieved by the exercise of power; whether or not the men were willing was a matter of secondary importance to some commanders and of no importance to others. But the Roman soldier had the same human nature and desire to excel as his Greek counterpart. Greatness was always latent in the legions, awaiting the call to life from a leader of genius. Caesar was such a leader. Under Caesar's eye the Roman legions became 'an unconquered and unconquerable army'.

Caesar's very presence seemed to transform ordinary professional legionaries into men of extraordinary valour. 'Soldiers who in other campaigns had not shown themselves to be any better than average,' wrote Plutarch, 'became irresistible and invincible and ready to confront any danger, once it was a question of fighting for Caesar's honour and glory.' Plutarch cited the following example:

When Caesar's army in Gaul faced the German tribes whose incursions threatened the province, Caesar saw that many of his officers – particularly those young men of good families who had come out from Rome under the impression that a military campaign would mean comfortable living and easy money – were nervous at the prospect of fighting the formidable and frightening Germans. So Caesar summoned them and told them to go back to Rome; they must not run any undue risks, he suggested, in their present cowardly and soft state of mind. Caesar himself proposed to take just the Tenth Legion with him and to march against the Germans. He did not expect to find the enemy stronger than the fiercest of Gallic tribes had been, he declared, and he would not be thought a worse general than Marius. As a result of this speech it is recorded that the Tenth Legion sent a deputation to thank him for his compliment, and the men of other legions were furious with their own commanders. The whole army was now willing and eager for action and they followed Caesar once more to victory.

Therefore a leader has to be concerned with emotion and motive. Those two words come from the same Latin verb 'to move'. The extent to which he has to try to stir up emotion and motive force does depend upon the situations and the followers. Where people are essentially self-motivating and fully committed, attempts to make them more so can actually be counter-productive. Armies in defeat or industrial organizations in trouble are instances where the leader must give special attention to morale, which means essentially the attitude of people to their common task. Where there is low morale, people are 'switched off' in terms of the energy devoted towards the task that has to be done. Their attitude is one of indifference or defeatism. In such situations the leader must impart a positive attitude, stir up the energies of the group and redirect them into a path that is likely to lead to results.

A leader, then, is usually communicating on several levels at the same time. While he or she is imparting information (or listening to it) he or she is also communicating ideas and values, feelings and emotional energy. He or she is looking for a response on this level: a change in morale which will lead to the more energetic pursuit of an attainable success.

THE RELEVANCE OF THE SECOND WORLD WAR

Both the case studies that follow are from the military field, and in particular from British armies in the Second World War. But leadership is neither a British nor a military phenomenon. Why, then, choose two examples of the art of inspiring while informing from the military field?

There are three reasons. First, armies throw light on how leadership can be given in big organizations. The chief barriers to leadership and good communication are size and geographical distance. How do you lead and inspire an organization made up of many thousands of men and women spread in units over a country or even several continents? That problem, common to strategic leaders of large public or private corporations, appears first in history in the context of armies. The word 'strategic', incidentally, comes from two Greek words for an 'army' or a large body and a 'leader': the *strategikos* was the leader of the army.

Second, the Second World War brought about changes which led eventually to better leadership in industry, because thousands of officers and men in the citizen armies of Britain experienced there for the first time good leadership and communication. Just as the war proved to be the seedbed of technological change – radar, computers and jet engines – so it stimulated a change of attitude towards leadership. Slim and Montgomery in particular were models of leadership perceived to be appropriate in a democratic army. Their philosophy and methods had a growing influence on British industry after the war, not least because many of the officers and men who served under them subsequently became managerial leaders and 'captains of industry'.

Third, in every field of study there are classic examples which will always endure. They transcend their context. No military commander, not even among those of genius, nor any other leader in a non-military field, has left such a clear and vivid explanation of how he thought through the problem of leadership as Slim has done in *Defeat into Victory* (1956). It is still one of the best examples of a leader thinking out aloud that history can provide. The same is true in a more limited sense of Montgomery's speech to his staff in 1942, delivered shortly after he took command of the Eighth Army. Down the ages generals have always been expected to talk to their senior officers, if not to their troops, on the eve of battle. They explain their plans. If they are leaders, they will arouse emotions to a fever pitch, which is not hard to do when uncertainty, anxiety and fear are already in the air. Hatred of the enemy, justness of the cause, proffered fruits or rewards of victory, hopes of enduring fame and glory: these are some of the staple emotions or motives which must be appealed to. By their nature, such inspirational speeches are seldom recorded. By hindsight, when writing their memoirs, leaders sometimes compose the speech that they should have made! Historians are also guilty of such fictions, possibly basing their efforts on scraps of information gleaned from eye-witness accounts. Shakespeare's famous speech in *King Henry V*, 'Once more unto the breach, dear friends . . .' uttered before the English assault on Harfleur, is a good example of how a poet of genius can improve vastly on nature. Montgomery's speech, however, was taken down in shorthand, and so we know that we are getting the genuine article.

CASE STUDY: THE FORGOTTEN ARMY

In 1943 General William Slim had taken command of the Fourteenth Army. The all-conquering Japanese had driven it out of Burma, and it now sat in India, licking its wounds. Slim identified his main problem: to restore the Fourteenth Army's morale. But how was it to be done? In *Defeat into Victory* he recollected how he thought through the problem:

> So when I took command, I sat quietly down to work out this business of morale. I came to certain conclusions, based not on any theory that I had studied, but on some experience and a good deal of hard thinking. It was on these conclusions that I set out consciously to raise the fighting spirit of my army.
>
> Morale is a state of mind. It is that intangible force which will move a whole group of men to give their last ounce to achieve something, without counting the cost to themselves; that makes them feel they are part of something greater than themselves. If they are to feel that, their morale must, if it is to endure – and the essence of morale is that it should endure – have certain foundations. These foundations are spiritual, intellectual, and material, and that is the order of their importance. Spiritual first, because only spiritual foundations can stand real strain. Next intellectual, because men are swayed by reason as well as feeling. Material last – important, but last – because the highest kinds of morale are often met when material conditions are lowest.
>
> I remember sitting in my office and tabulating these foundations of morale something like this:
>
> **Spiritual**
> - There must be a great and noble object.
> - Its achievement must be vital.

- The method of achievement must be active, aggressive.
- The man must feel that what he is and what he does matters directly towards the attainment of the object.

At any rate, our spiritual foundation was a firm one. I use the word spiritual, not in its strictly religious meaning, but as belief in a cause . . .

Intellectual
- He must be convinced that the object can be obtained; that it is not out of reach.
- He must see, too, that the organization to which he belongs and which is striving to attain the object is an efficient one.
- He must have confidence in his leaders and know that whatever dangers and hardships he is called upon to suffer, his life will not lightly be flung away.

Material
- The man must feel that he will get a fair deal from his commanders and from the army generally.
- He must, as far as humanly possible, be given the best weapons and equipment for the task.
- His living and working conditions must be made as good as they can be.

It was one thing thus neatly to marshal my principles but quite another to develop them, apply them, and get them recognized by the whole army.

We had this; and we had the advantage over our enemies that ours was based on real, not false, spiritual values. If ever an army fought in a just cause we did. We coveted no man's country; we wished to impose no form of government on any nation. We fought for the clean, the decent, the free things of life, for the right to live our lives in our own way as others could live theirs, to worship God in what faith we chose, to be free in body and mind, and for our children to be free. We fought only because the powers of evil had attacked these things. No matter what the religion or race of any man in the Fourteenth Army, he must feel this, feel that he had indeed a worthy cause, and that if he did not defend it life would not be worth living for him or for his children. Nor was it enough to have a worthy cause. It must be positive, aggressive, not a mere passive, defensive, anti-something feeling. So our object became not to defend India, to stop the Japanese advance, or even to occupy Burma, but to destroy the Japanese Army, to smash it as an evil thing.

The fighting soldier facing the enemy can see that what he does, whether he is brave or craven, matters to his comrades and directly influences the result of the battle. It is harder for the man working on the road far behind, the clerk checking stores in a dump, the headquarter's telephone operator monotonously plugging through his calls, the sweeper carrying out his menial tasks, the quartermaster's orderly issuing bootlaces in a reinforcement camp – it is hard for these and a thousand others to see that they too matter. Yet every one of the half-million in the army – and it was many more later – had to be made to see where his task fitted into the whole, to realize what depended on it, and to feel pride and satisfaction in doing it well.

Now these things, while the very basis of morale, because they were purely matters of feeling and emotion, were the most difficult to put over, especially to the British portion of the army. The problem was how to instil or revive their beliefs in the men of many races who made up the Fourteenth Army. I felt there was only one way to do it, by a direct approach to the individual men themselves. There was nothing new in this; my corps and divisional commanders and others right down the scale were already doing it. It was the way we had held the troops together in the worst days of the 1942 retreat; we remained an army then only because the men saw and knew their commanders. All I did now was to encourage my commanders to increase these activities, unite them in a common approach to the problem, in the points that they would stress, and in the action they would take to see that principles became action, not merely words.

Yet they began, as most things do, as words. We, my commanders and I, talked to units, to collections of officers, to headquarters, to little groups of men, to individual soldiers casually met as we moved around . . .

NO BAD SOLDIERS – ONLY BAD OFFICERS

The real test of leadership is not if your men will follow you in success but if they will stick by you in defeat and hardship. They won't do that unless they believe you to be honest and to have care for them.

I once had under me a battalion that had not done well in a fight. I went to see why. I found the men in the jungle, tired and hungry, dirty, jumpy, some of them wounded, sitting miserably about doing nothing. I looked for the commanding officer, for any officer; none could be seen. Then as I rounded a bush, I realized why that battalion had failed. Collected under a tree were the officers, having a meal while the men went hungry. Those officers had forgotten the tradition of the Service that they look after their men's wants before their own. I was compelled to remind them.

I hope they never again forgot the integrity and unselfishness that always permeate good leadership. I have never known men fail to respond to them.

Slim, speaking to British managers (1957)

Slim then described the reactions of different nationalities to these addresses.

I learnt too, that one did not need to be an orator to be effective. Two things were necessary: first to know what you were talking about, and, second and most important, to believe it yourself. I found that if one kept the bulk of one's talk to the material things that men were interested in, food, pay, leave, beer, mails, and the progress of operations, it was safe to end on a higher note – the spiritual foundations – and I always did.

To convince the men in the less spectacular or less obviously important jobs that they were very much part of the army, my commanders and I made it our business to visit these units, to show an interest in them, and to tell them how we and the rest of the army depended upon them. There are in the army, and for that matter any big organization, very large numbers of people whose existence is only remembered when something for which they are responsible goes wrong. Who thinks of the telephone operator until he fails to get his connection, of the cipher officer until he makes a mistake in his decoding, of the orderlies who carry papers about a big headquarters until they take them to the wrong people, of the cook until he makes a particularly foul mess of the interminable bully? Yet they are important. It was harder to get this over to the Indian subordinates. They were often drawn from the lower castes, quite illiterate and used to being looked down upon by their higher-caste fellow-townsmen or villagers. With them I found I had great success by using the simile of a clock, 'A clock is like an army,' I used to tell them. 'There's a main spring, that's the Army Commander, who makes it all go; then there are other springs, driving the wheels round, those are his generals. The wheels are the officers and men. Some are big wheels, very important, they are the chief staff officers and the colonel sahibs. Other wheels are the little ones, that do not look

at all important. They are like you. Yet stop one of those little
wheels and see what happens to the rest of the clock! They are
important!'

We played on this human desire of every man to feel himself
and his work important, until one of the most striking things about
our army was the way the administrative, labour and non-
combatant units acquired a morale which rivalled that of the
fighting formations. They felt they shared directly in the triumphs
of the Fourteenth Army and that its success and its honour were in
their hands as much as anybody's. Another way in which we
made every man feel he was part of the show was by keeping
him, whatever his rank, as far as was practicable in the picture
concerning what was going on around him. This, of course, was
easy with staff officers and similar people by means of conferences held daily or weekly when each branch or department
could explain what it had been doing and what it hoped to do.
At these conferences they not only discussed things as a team,
but what was equally important, actually saw themselves as a
team. For the men, talks by their officers and visits to the
information centres which were established in every unit took the
place of those conferences.

It was in these ways we laid the spiritual foundations, but that
was not enough; they would have crumbled without the others, the
intellectual and the material. Here we had first to convince the
doubters that our object, the destruction of the Japanese army in
battle, was practicable. We had to a great extent frightened
ourselves by our stories of the superman. Defeated soldiers in their
own defence have to protest that their adversary was out of the
ordinary, that he had all the advantages of preparation, equipment, and terrain, and that they themselves suffered from every
corresponding handicap. The harder they have run away, the
more they must exaggerate the unfair superiority of the enemy. Thus
many of those who had scrambled out of Burma without waiting to

get to grips with the invader, or who had been in the rear areas in 1943, had the most hair-raising stories of Japanese super-efficiency. Those of us who had really fought him, believed that man for man our soldiers could beat him at his own jungle game, and that, in intelligence and skill, we could excel and outwit him.

We were helped, too, by a very cheering piece of news that now reached us, and of which, as a morale raiser, I made great use. In August and September 1942, Australian troops had, at Milne Bay in New Guinea, inflicted on the Japanese their first undoubted defeat on land . . .

Slim also ordered aggressive patrolling in the forward areas, and larger scale actions designed to build up unit and formation self-confidence.

We had laid the first of our intellectual foundations of morale; everyone knew we could defeat the Japanese; our object was attainable.

The next foundations, that the men should feel that they had belonged to an efficient organization, that the Fourteenth Army was well run and would get somewhere, followed partly from these minor successes . . . Rations did improve, though still far below what they should be; mail began to arrive more regularly; there were even signs of a welfare service . . .

Other steps towards higher morale included the improvement of rest and training facilities, the reinforcement of disciplinary standards such as saluting, and the institution of a newspaper. When Admiral Mountbatten arrived to take command of the newly formed South-East Asia Command, his presence and personal talks to the troops proved to be a 'final tonic' to morale. Meanwhile supplies of material gradually improved, but due to the priority of the war in Europe they remained small compared to the needs of the Fourteenth Army, a reason which Slim was careful to explain to the soldiers.

These things were frankly put to the men by their commanders at all levels and, whatever their race, they responded. In my experience it is not so much asking men to fight or work with inadequate or obsolete equipment that lowers morale but the belief that those responsible are accepting such a state of affairs. If men realise that everyone above them and behind them is flat out to get the things required for them, they will do wonders, as my men did, with the meagre resources they have instead of sitting down moaning for better.

I do not say that the men of the Fourteenth Army welcomed difficulties, but they grew to take a fierce pride in overcoming them by determination and ingenuity. From start to finish they had only two items of equipment that were never in short supply: their brains and their courage. They lived up to the unofficial motto I gave them, 'God helps those who help themselves.' Anybody could do an easy job, we told them. It would take real men to overcome the shortages and difficulties we should be up against – the tough chap for the tough job! We had no *corps d'élite* which got preferential treatment; the only units who got that were the ones in front. Often, of course, they went short owing to the difficulties of transportation, but, if we had the stuff and could by hook or crook get it to them they had it in preference to those farther back. One of the most convincing evidences of morale was how those behind – staffs and units – accepted this, and deprived themselves to ensure it. I indulged in a little bit of theatricality in this myself. When any of the forward formations had to go on half rations, as throughout the campaign they often did, I used to put my head-quarters on half rations too. It had little practical effect, but as a gesture it was rather valuable, and it did remind the young staff officers with healthy appetites that it was urgent to get the forward formations back to full rations as soon as possible . . .

The individual, we took pains to ensure, too, was judged on his merits without undue prejudice in favour of race, caste, or class . . . In an army of hundreds of thousands, many injustices to individuals were bound to occur but, thanks mainly to officers commanding units, most of the Fourteenth Army would, I believe, say that on the whole they had, as individuals, a reasonably fair deal. At any rate we did our best to give it to them.

In these and in many other ways we translated my rough notes on the foundations of morale, spiritual, intellectual, and material, into a fighting spirit for our men and a confidence in themselves and their leaders that was to impress our friends and surprise our enemies.

From this passage it is clear that 'Uncle Bill', as he became affectionately known to his troops, had the power of communicating energy while imparting information. Slim's instinctive honesty of mind and deed, natural authority and humanity came across to all who met him and won his affection. Everyone found him thoughtful, dignified, courteous and considerate. Ronald Lewin, his biographer, judged him to be a genuinely humble person, in the sense of being devoid of vanity, self-complacency or *folie de grandeur*. Not that Slim lacked personal drive or worldly wisdom, but his humility disinfected his natural ambition – 'the soldier's virtue', as Shakespeare called it. His desire to get on neither tarnished his reputation nor made him pitch his hopes too high. Instead, throughout his career Slim showed an inability to set the same high valuation upon himself as others did. Self-assurance in him was balanced by a proper measure of self-questioning. 'Life seems to glide past some people without leaving an impression; others absorb and digest,' wrote Lewin. 'Slim was a pondering man, chewing the cud of experience, and it is striking how often during his time of high command he would draw on what he had deduced from episodes, often apparently trivial, which had occurred many years ago. He was always a pupil-learner in the classroom of the world.' Slim was also a teacher – one of the few exceptional leaders to be also an outstanding teacher of the British tradition of leadership.

CASE STUDY: MONTGOMERY

On 13 August 1942 Montgomery arrived to take command of the Eighth Army, two months before the battle of Alamein. 'The atmosphere was dismal and dreary,' he wrote in his diary. That evening he addressed the entire staff of Eighth Army Headquarters, between fifty and sixty officers. As he was their fourth Army Commander within a year, he faced a sceptical audience. The seasoned commanders and staff officers plainly doubted that this new general from Britain was the man to reverse their recent defeats and failures. Montgomery knew that he had to win their minds and hearts that evening if the morale of that broken army was to be restored to full pitch.

Montgomery stood on the steps of his predecessor's caravan and bade the gathering sit on the sand. He spoke without notes, looking straight at his audience. Here is what he said:

> I want first of all to introduce myself to you. You do not know me.
> I do not know you. But we have got to work together; therefore
> we must understand each other and we must have confidence in

one another. I have only been here a few hours. But from what I have seen and heard since I arrived I am prepared to say, here and now, that I have confidence in you. We will then work together as a team; and together we will gain the confidence of this great army and go forward to final victory in Africa.

I believe that one of the first duties of a commander is to create what I call 'atmosphere'; and in that atmosphere, his staff, subordinate commanders and troops will live and work and fight.

I do not like the general atmosphere I find here. It is an atmosphere of doubt, of looking back to select the next place to which to withdraw, of loss of confidence in our ability to defeat Rommel, of desperate defence measures by reserves in preparing positions in Cairo and the Delta. All that must cease. Let us have a new atmosphere . . . We will stand and fight here. If we can't stay here alive, then let us stay here dead.

I want to impress on everyone that the bad times are over. Fresh divisions from the UK are now arriving in Egypt, together with ample reinforcements for our present divisions. We have 300 to 400 new Sherman tanks coming and these are actually being unloaded at Suez now. Our mandate from the Prime Minister is to destroy the Axis forces in North Africa; I have seen it written on half a sheet of notepaper. And it will be done. If anyone here thinks it can't be done, let him go at once; I don't want any doubters in this party. It can be done, and it will be done; beyond any possibility of doubt . . .

What I have done is to get over to you the atmosphere in which we will now work and fight; you must see that that atmosphere permeates right down through the Eighth Army to the most junior private soldier. All the soldiers must know what is wanted; when they see it coming to pass there will be a surge of confidence throughout the army.

I ask you to give me your confidence and to have faith that what I have said will come to pass.

There is much work to be done. The orders I have given about no further withdrawal will mean a complete change in the layout of our dispositions; also that we must begin to prepare for our great offensive . . .

The great point to remember, [Montgomery concluded at that famous initial briefing] is that we are going to finish with this chap Rommel once and for all. It will be quite easy. There is no doubt about it. He is definitely a nuisance. Therefore we will hit him a crack and finish with him.

As Montgomery stepped down the officers rose and stood to attention. 'One could have heard a pin drop if such a thing were possible in the sand of the desert,' recollected Montgomery. 'But it certainly had a profound effect, and a spirit of hope, anyway of clarity, was born that evening.' His Chief-of-Staff, General de Guingand, agreed: 'It was one of his greatest efforts,' he wrote. 'The effect of the address was electric – it was terrific! And we all went to bed that night with new hope in our hearts, and a great confidence in the future of the Army. I wish someone had taken it down in shorthand, for it would have become a classic of its kind.' Fortunately, it was taken down in shorthand and filed away for many years before appearing in print for the first time in 1981.

A SENSE OF PARTNERSHIP

'I made the soldiers partners with me in the battle. I always told them what I was going to do, and what I wanted them to do. I think the soldiers felt that they mattered, that they belonged.'

Field Marshal Montgomery

Whatever Montgomery's personal faults, and however much military historians may argue about the wisdom of some of his decisions, few deny the extraordinary loyalty and trust he won from the troops he commanded. His positive approach is striking: it is a model for all leaders. Montgomery's secret was simple but painstaking. He was meticulous in explaining in detail, in advance of a battle or training exercise, precisely what his plans were and why he had arrived at them. He took immense care to explain himself personally to large numbers of those in his units, and was adamant that this sharing should be conveyed to every single soldier in his command. Montgomery could not of course know every soldier, but in a real way every soldier knew him, and they gave him their trust in a fashion unsurpassed by any other army this century.

THE EFFECTS OF TELECOMMUNICATION

Like the great leaders of earlier times, Slim and Montgomery wrote their own speeches. Today political leaders in particular hire speech-writers, professionals who help them to communicate more effectively. It must be difficult, however, to appear sincere when one is using borrowed words in order to inspire others. Indeed, it may be a contradiction in terms to suppose that such speeches could ever be inspiring. Matters are made worse by the advent of radio and television. Although in some ways these media have been boons to leaders or nations or large organizations, they have also renewed an old temptation for leaders: to believe that they can create and sustain an 'image' of leadership, rather than having to develop within themselves the real qualities and abilities of a leader.

KEY POINTS

- Two-way communication is inseparable from leadership. It involves the basic skills of speaking and listening, reading and writing. A good communicator is well prepared, clear, simple and concise.

- Listening leaders are still comparatively rare. To listen well you must listen not only by giving thoughtful attention but by opening your third inner ear to the meanings and feelings that lie like music behind the words. Listen with your eyes, too, for so much communication is still non-verbal.

- Communicating at the leadership level is not just about imparting information or ideas; it is a stirring up of energy and enthusiasm for the work in hand. It is not a matter of the leader imparting his or her own energy, but releasing the greatness that is there already.

- 'Anyone can hold the helm when the seas are calm.' The test of your powers of communication come when the seas are rough with change, and people feel disorientated and out of touch. Can you communicate hope when all about you are doubting the promise of the future?

- Both the studies – Slim and Montgomery – served as strategic leaders of very large multinational organizations. Both had a passion for good communication. Although neither could be described as naturally charismatic, they mastered the art of inspiring while informing. They kept to the basics of the three circles, and added the descant of inspiration.

- The effect or result of good communication in organizations – downwards, upwards and sideways – is that everyone feels that they are partners in the common enterprise.

POINTS TO PONDER

☐ Good leaders are not impersonal transmitters of information. They also communicate their inner thoughts, emotions and spirit. In particular, they impart energy. They have the ability to inspire while they inform. As Lord Rosebery said of William Pitt the Elder: 'It is not merely the thing that is said, but the man who says it that counts, the character which breathes through the sentences.'

☐ Trust and good communication go hand in hand. Where there is trust even seemingly bad news can be communicated. The more you communicate the plain truth or the realities of the situation, the more people will trust you. 'The bird carries the wings, but the wings carry the bird.' Techniques have a place, but truth is the great communicator.

☐ Large organizations such as armies or industrial corporations, by virtue of their size and geographical spread, create major communication problems for leaders. Although systems and methods of communication, including telecommunications, have a part to play, a wise leader will seize or make opportunities to impart his or her own energetic vision – in their own words – to key groups in the organization. He or she makes the 'little wheels' feel important, not just the next level down. For a leader who is invisible and inaudible to all but a select few is seldom effective and certainly not great. What is going to be your policy when you become an operational or strategic leader?

9

LEADERSHIP IN A CHANGING WORLD

'The business of life is to go forwards.'
Samuel Johnson

Since the early part of the nineteenth century a climatic shift has taken place in human awareness. Across a broad front of human activity – philosophy, religion, politics, art and science – people felt the dawning consciousness that change was the order of the day. This first feeling of the reality and inevitability of change cheered some and depressed others. For it heralded the end of a more leisurely, more static and more privileged age.

Change and leadership are closely linked. Change tends to throw up the need for leaders; leaders seek to create change. The first of these two processes is much stronger than the second. For it is actually quite difficult for a leader to bring about change within an institution or organization which, from inside and outside, is untouched by the need for change.

This greater awareness of change brought with it a new sense of need for leaders across a broad range of political, religious, educational, social and industrial fields. For, contrary to the Marxist theory of how change happens in history, it became evident that good leaders, and leaders for good, formed a key factor in progress.

Technology had much to do with the new climate of change as the nineteenth century unfolded. The Industrial Revolution was in full swing, progress was a word much on every thinking person's lips. Originally it had been used to describe royal journeys around the country, tours marked by pomp and pageantry. Now it was applied to any journey in the sense of forward or onward movement.

Change for the better is progress. The gradual betterment of life became a central integrating purpose, a vision to inspire leaders in every field of human endeavour. Tennyson sounded the clarion call:

> Not in vain the distance beacons. Forward, forward, let us
> range,
> Let the great world spin for ever down the ringing grooves
> of change.
> Thro' the shadow of the globe we sweep into the younger
> day:
> Better fifty years of Europe than a cycle of Cathay.

For significant changes to happen, then, there usually have to be general factors or trends working together in a direction, and a movement, organization or small group pioneering the way with an effective leader or leaders at their head. If one or more elements in the combination was missing, then change either did not happen or it came about very slowly. Increasingly, leadership was seen to be a key ingredient in the process of change.

CAPTAINS OF INDUSTRY

'The Leaders of Industry,' Carlyle wrote in 1843, 'are virtually Captains of the World.' Their contemporaries saw the new industrialists as leaders in the vanguard of progress. Their products seemed self-evidently good. 'Railways exhibit the grandest organization of capital and labour that the world has yet seen,' according to Samuel Smiles in his *Lives of the Stephensons* (1868). The immense advantages of the railways to mankind profoundly impressed him. 'As tending to multiply and spread abroad the conveniences of life, opening up new fields of industry, bringing nations nearer to each other, and thus promoting the great ends of civilization, the founding of the railway system by George Stephenson and his son must be regarded as one of the most important events, if not the very greatest, in the first half of this nineteenth century.' Smiles did not live to see the First World War, in which vast armies were mobilized and moved to the various fronts largely by railway. Without Europe's railways war on such a scale could not have happened. For the successors of such men, Samuel Smiles wrote a number of books, notably *Self Help* (1860), in which he taught them the virtues of industry, perservance and self-culture. But he had nothing to say about the management of people. Nor, for the most part, had the new breed of engineers been educated in public school or university to be gentlemen leaders.

In British industry in the nineteenth century it was commonly the engineers who provided the leadership of technological change. They did so mainly by virtue of having the authority of professional knowledge. Yet there were natural leaders among the new 'Captains of the

World'. Isambard Kingdom Brunel, Victorian England's most celebrated engineer, was such a leader. His father, Marc Brunel, was a French engineer who had served in the French navy until 1792, when he went to New York. Coming to England, he was knighted for his engineering works, such as a tunnel under the Thames from Wapping to Rotherhithe. His son assisted him in the Thames tunnel project. In his own career Isambard laid some thousand miles of railway in Britain, including the Great Western Railway between Bristol and London, then the longest in the world. He also designed and built docks, suspension bridges in iron, and steamships of great size.

In the five years it took to build the Great Western, Brunel gave his attention to every detail of the line, bridges and stations, solving countless problems as the thousands of navvies inched the track forwards in all weathers. When progress fell behind the timetable, Brunel increased the work-force to 4000 men. Like a true leader, he inspired willing work by occasionally rolling up his sleeves and working alongside them. When the two gangs of navvies tunnelling through Box Hill near Bath met in the middle (it took more than two years to bore the 3212-yard tunnel), Brunel was so delighted with the accuracy of their work that he took a valuable ring from his finger and gave it to the foreman.

Brunel had in good measure one essential leadership quality – a capacity for exceptionally hard work. Such was his energy and prodigious industry that he became known as 'The Little Giant'. Writing instructions alone took four or five hours a day when he was working on the Great Western – 'I fear I sometimes pump myself dry and remain for an hour or two utterly stupid.' For four months at one stretch he worked rarely less than twenty hours a day.

Brunel's other main attribute as a leader was his vision. One key ingredient in vision is imagination. Brunel combined imagination with considerable technical knowledge, especially in mathematics which he studied at the Ecole Militaire in Paris. As a young man he said of himself, 'I am always building castles in the air, what a time I waste.' For example, he developed a vision of a high speed transport route from London to New York: the railway between London and Bristol formed the first part, and the great ships he designed, the second. The *Great Britain*, the first screw-driven steamship in the world, now lies fully restored as his monument in Bristol docks.

But the general impression one gains from studying Brunel and the other great engineers of the day is that they were very task-oriented. They were not people-oriented as well, in the sense that, for example, Nelson had been. Technical knowledge equipped them to lead in a limited sense, but they lacked most, if not all, of the more general leadership abilities. The great industrial entrepreneurs who set themselves the task of matching capital and labour to opportunity, tended to regard work people as a commodity to be bought and sold. It was plentiful and cheap. Supported by their managers and under-managers (mostly recruited from the ranks of engineers and accountants), the industrial entrepreneurs pressed on with their profitable campaigns in the cause of progress, mindless of the casualties among their workforces.

Like machines, people were seen essentially as means to ends, and not primarily as ends to themselves. In cotton mills women and children supplied the cheapest labour, working for twelve or more hours a day in an inferno of noise and heat. In coal mines women were harnessed to trucks and hauled them by chains like pit-ponies. Children of five and upwards were used to pull trucks through spaces too small for men or women. Thousands of boys worked in the Potteries for up to fifteen hours a day, dragging moulds to the furnaces.

Not all employers were so callous. The Welshman Robert Owen, who became partner and manager of the textile mills in Lanark in 1800 at the age of twenty-eight, would not employ young children and instead provided an infant school for them. He also opened schools for the older ones. He demonstrated that an employer could improve working and housing conditions, wages and general welfare, and still make a profit. He introduced a co-partnership system and a co-operative store, in contrast to those mill owners who compelled workers to take part of their wages in the form of over-priced goods from the company shop on the premises. He also encouraged thrift and cleanliness.

Factory reforms, and the opposition of Trade Unions, provided some check on their freedom of action, but for the most part entrepreneurs and their under-managers remained task-centred. With an eye ever upon the ledger books, they regarded their labourers as a set of numbers, a cost to be set against profit, an expendable human resource. 'It is the Age of Machinery, in every outward and inward sense of the word,' wrote Thomas Carlyle in *Signs of the Times*. By that he meant that the temptation grew to see industrial workers not only as minders of machines, but as actual cogs in a machine, things or 'hands' rather than as people.

If the Luddites smashed machines because they posed an economic threat to their livelihood, others feared and hated them as the new enslavers of man. In 'Prayer before Birth', the twentieth-century poet Louis MacNeice voiced these lingering fears as he prayed against:

> . . . those who would freeze my
> humanity, would dragoon me into a lethal automaton,
> would make me a cog in a machine, a thing with
> one face, a thing, and against all those
> who would dissipate my entirety . . .
> Let them not make me a stone and let them not spill me
> Otherwise kill me.

Attitudes changed slowly. Some industrialists, like the Quaker families such as the Rowntrees, Cadburys and Frys, did show a social conscience and humanitarian concern for those who worked for them. Others belatedly followed Owen's path of enlightened self-interest. They took the view that people, like machines, need to be looked after, cared for and maintained if they are to give efficient, reliable and long-lasting service. Paternalistic though this approach may now seem to us, at least it has led employers to do the right things for the wrong reasons.

But, as the twentieth century dawned, even those following this limited policy were still no more than a growing minority. The majority of industrialists still saw themselves as owners and masters, bosses and managers, but not as leaders. The great business tycoons on both sides of the Atlantic – such as Rockefeller, Carnegie and Ford in America or Mond, Leverhulme and Austin in Britain – were not memorable for their powers of leadership.

But times were changing, and the experience of two World Wars led to a revolution in social expectations, bringing with it a demand for better leadership at all levels of management.

CASE STUDY: GINO WATKINS

The years of the 1920s and 1930s saw a relative change in the climate of social relations – less hierarchy, more informality, and a greater sense of democracy. Polar exploration both mirrored the changes and to some extent blazed the trail for a style of leadership which would suit modern circumstances. One attractive exponent of it was Gino Watkins, who led expeditions to Edge Island (near Spitzbergen), Labrador and Greenland. Watkins died in 1933, drowned in a lake in Greenland while out hunting in a kayak.

The following extracts from J. M. Scott's biography of Gino Watkins concern his travels in Greenland during 1930; it is a classic description of a leader in action. The average age of the fourteen members of the party – twenty-five years – was eighteen months older than Watkins himself, and so he had the challenge of leading men who for the most part were senior to him in years.

> As quietly as if it had been a Scottish shooting party Gino had organized the greatest British expedition to the Arctic for half a century, and he was carrying it through in the same unofficial, heroic spirit . . . When he sailed for Edge Island he had no first-hand knowledge to impart. In Labrador it had been the same. Everyone he came in contact with was gratified by his respectful interest in all they said and, without fully realizing it, they did what he wanted them to do and taught him all the useful knowledge they possessed.
>
> Besides, he gave himself no privileges at all. His bed was no more comfortable than ours; probably it was less so, judging by the dog harness and rifles which were piled on top of it. His

clothes were no better and his private possessions far less numerous . . .

All that was comparatively easy. Almost anybody with a sense of humour could have done as much if his sole object was to be accepted as a member of the party. But to one who was responsible for making people do unpleasant tasks it was a self-imposed handicap which could only be overcome by a very high type of personality. There could be no bluffing in such leadership; it would either prove magnetic by its inspiring originality or lead to chaos by its non-existence.

At first there was some argument as to Gino's wisdom in following the course which he had chosen. People like the Bedouin are used to such methods: they expect a leader to be one of themselves and recognize a strong character most easily in contrast to circumstances which they themselves experience . . .

The work of the first season proved remarkably successful. Luck played a part, as in the absence of heavy ice at Kangerdlugsuak, but luck is a valuable addition to a leader's reputation. In detail the journeys had not developed exactly as expected; but the acting leaders, unrestricted by precise directions yet understanding very clearly the general objective, had used their initiative to achieve a useful end. In the course of our work we had done things that we had never done before – we had driven dogs and navigated small boats through ice – and we had found these things remarkably easy.

Knowing that so much had depended upon ourselves, our self-confidence increased and with it our confidence in Gino; for his plans were only alarming when we doubted our ability to fulfil our part in them. Having discovered the surprising fact that we were as good men as Gino thought we were, we accepted him as a splendid leader. He was exacting, he was ruthlessly indifferent to small discomforts like cold or unvaried fresh meat diets at the Base, he was disconcerting in his words and actions, but he would never be at a loss and would never blame . . .

If he told inexperienced men to do what they thought best, and if they made some fatal blunder, the responsibility would be his just as surely as if he had expressly ordered that disastrous action. The world would see it thus and so would he. It was a risky policy, but for his purpose the risk was unavoidable.

Briefly, his method of leadership was to train each man to be a leader; his ideal exploring party consisted of nothing else. These were young men and he was looking ahead towards other, more perplexing, quests.

MANAGEMENT THROUGH LEADERSHIP

The growth of the Trade Union movement, which came into being to protect the individual and to promote his or her needs over and against the needs of the task and the organization, was symptomatic of the lack of leadership in industry. Clearly entrepreneurs and directors, the new captains of industry, had no access to the tradition of leadership as set out in these pages. If they had done so, they probably could not have translated it into language that applied in their own novel situation. No wonder that industry had to reinvent the wheel of leadership.

After the Second World War ended, Clement Attlee was Britain's new Prime Minister. Like Lord Slim, he had once served as an officer in the Gallipoli campaign during the First World War. Attlee tabled for Cabinet consideration a paper by Slim suggesting that 'management through leadership' was the way forward for British industry and commerce. Perhaps Slim could introduce democratic leadership in the factories? As a first step, in 1947, Attlee appointed him as Vice Chairman of British Railways, so that he could prepare himself for becoming Chairman in due course. Yet not six months after Slim started work, Attlee asked him to leave British Railways in order to be Governor-General of Australia.

SLIM ON LEADERSHIP

Slim was a most effective communicator on the subject of leadership, which he believed in so deeply. Firms such as ICI frequently called on him to speak to their managers. Later he reached an even wider audience on the radio. Slim took immense care in writing these speeches and broadcasts. The natural teacher in him, together with a simple and natural style of speaking and writing, made what he had to say on leadership both profound and memorable. The following extract comes from one of his best speeches, given to a large audience in Adelaide in 1957. The Governor-General had this to say about leadership:

> To begin with, we do not in the Army talk of 'management' but of 'leadership'. This is significant. There is a difference between leaders and management. The leader and the men who follow him represent one of the oldest, most natural and most effective of all human relationships. The manager and those he manages are a later product, with neither so romantic nor so inspiring a history. Leadership is of the spirit, compounded of personality and vision; its practice is an art. Management is of the mind, more a matter of accurate calculation of statistics, of methods, time tables, and routine; its practice is a science. Managers are necessary; leaders are essential. A good system will produce efficient managers but

more than that is needed. We must find managers who are not only skilled organisers but inspired and inspiring leaders, destined eventually to fill the highest ranks of control and direction. Such men will gather round them close knit teams of subordinates like themselves and of technical experts, whose efficiency, enthusiasm and loyalty will be unbeatable. Increasingly this is recognised and the search for leadership is on . . .

I have talked so far about those destined for the higher appointments but the Army in which the only leaders are the generals will win no victories. All down the line there must be leaders. We have the equivalent of the supervisors and foremen of industry; they are our Warrant and Non-Commissioned Officers. You will note we call them officers. They are very definitely a part of the management, feel themselves that they are and are recognized by others as such. The position of the equivalent ranks in industry, suspended as they often are between management and workers, must be terribly difficult. The American system, where they are made to feel much more a part of management, has advantages.

The greater the size of an army, or an organization, the more difficult it becomes for the leaders to make their ideas and intentions clear and vivid to all their thousands of subordinates. All sorts of ways of doing this have been attempted. There has even grown up in industry a special class of officer whose job roughly is to keep touch between management and workers. I think there is some danger they may interpose rather than connect. Leadership is a very personal thing and like some germs it is weakened by passing through other bodies.

There are many things that can be done to keep touch, but to be effective they must all be based on two things:

- The head man of the army, the firm, the division, the department, the regiment, the workshop must be known as an actual person to all under him.

- The soldier or the employee must be made to feel he is part of the show and what he is and what he does matters to it.

The best way to get known to your men is to let them see you and hear you by going among them and talking to them. The head man should be able to walk on to any parade-ground in his command or into any factory in his firm and be recognized — even if it's only 'Here comes the old so-and-so.' It's surprising how soldiers and workmen can use an uncomplimentary expression as an endearment. The boss should talk to individuals as he moves about and occasionally — only occasionally as it should be something of an event — assemble all his staff and workers, mixed together for preference, and tell them something of what he is trying to do. To talk to men doesn't require great eloquence, only two things are needed — to know what you are talking about and to believe in yourself. The last is important.

To make anyone feel part of a show you have to take them into your confidence. Soldiers have long grown out of the 'theirs-not-to-reason-why' stage. Any intelligent man wants to know why and for what reason he's doing things. Personally I believe a good system passing on to every man information of what is going on outside his immediate view is worth more than such things as joint consultation which really only reach a few. Security I know may enter into this as it does in military matters but a little risk with security is more than repaid by the feeling chaps get that their leaders have confidence in them, that they are let into the know and that they belong.

From washing machines to electronic brains we live increasingly by technology. Technicians are vital to our industry. But we don't make a man a general in the field because he is an expert in explosives; the most brilliant surgeon is not necessarily the best man to run a hospital; nor the best-selling author to run a publishing business. The technically trained man is not the answer to the management problem. There has in some quarters been a tendency to make managers out of technical men. Some of them may make good managers because they have in them the qualities of leadership, but the better the technician, the better to use him in his own field.

We anxiously calculate stocks of raw materials, seek new minerals, study technical advances overseas and push them on at home; we devise new processes, we equip our factories with new machinery. In all these matters we take great thought for the morrow. Yet too often we just hope that tomorrow's leaders will, by some miracle, bob up when needed.

The only way in which the growing need for leadership in management can be met is to find the potential leader and then start his training and give him his chance to lead.

Here in Australia, believe me, there is no lack of potential leaders – the climate, the freedom, the tradition of this country breed them: leadership material is lying around in every factory, office and university in Australia. Unless we spot it and give it a chance, a lot of it is doomed to rust. That would be a tragedy but a greater would be that our expanding industry should lack leadership.

The raw material of leadership is there and the Australian worker, properly led, from what I have seen of him, is as good as any and more intelligent than most. But the words 'properly led' are vital. Australian industry deserves and will need leaders not just efficient managers.

In industry you will never have to ask men to do the stark things demanded of soldiers, but the men you employ are the same men. Instead of rifles they handle tools; instead of guns they serve machines. They have changed their khaki and jungle-green for workshop overalls and civvie suits. But they are the same men and they will respond to leadership of the right kind just as they have always done.

Infuse your management with leadership; then they will show

their mettle in the workshop as they have on the battlefield. Like me, they would rather be led than managed. Wouldn't you?

THE MANAGER-LEADER

'I'm just a hired hack – a professional manager, I'm proud of that – I'm not a proprietor, not dominant. I lead by example and persuasion and a hell of a lot of hard work. Not on the basis of power or authority. My skills are to help a large number to release their energies and focus themselves. It is switching on a lot of people and helping them achieve a common aim. People only do things they are convinced about. One has to create conditions in which people want to give of their best.

'The board of directors should be, in Nelson's phrase, a "band of brothers". We should be so aware of one another's views that any one of us could act for the lot of us.'

Sir John Harvey-Jones

In industry today, throughout the world, the nature of management has shifted perceptibly and irreversibly in the direction of leadership. All industrial and business enterprises are launched upon a journey, if only a journey of survival. Managing is now about taking change by the hand before it takes one by the throat. Managing change needs to be done effectively at two broad but overlapping levels. The strategic work has become the prime leadership responsibility of the chief executive officer or managing director, together with the board of directors. Operational responsibility for making it happen ought to be shared by executive directors, managers of all levels, and all other members in the organization.

KEY POINTS

- Continuity and change are the warp and weft of life. In the nineteenth century people became far more conscious of change. They became committed, too, to changing things for the better.

- Change and leadership are closely linked. Change heightens the need for leaders; leaders tend to be initiators and managers of change. Hence the proliferation of leadership in fields far removed from the political and military spheres, the traditional grounds for the exercise of leadership.

- But as education becomes more universal, and expectations rise, men and women look for something more than the traditional, authoritarian owner-bosses of industry and their lieutenants, the managers.

- The Second World War indirectly accelerated the general shift towards greater democracy and better leadership in the workplace. Outstanding generals, notably Slim and Montgomery, believed and taught that leadership could prove to be equally effective in peacetime, on the grounds that human nature does not vary.

- Only the crises of the recent decades have begun to bring home the importance of leadership to industry. We are now in the dawn of a new era of management through leadership.

- Across the broad front of human endeavour leaders contribute direction and executive action to the work of progress.

POINTS TO PONDER

❑ Why has industry, commerce and the public service been so slow to learn the value of good leadership at all levels from the military field? Why has it placed so little emphasis on selecting and training its managers as leaders?

Several possible reasons come to mind. A major one is that industry saw leadership as good human relations – the management of people. Not until change became permanent did it begin to see that leaders lead change as well as people. If your task circle includes a lot of change, you need leadership to give direction, hold the team together and care for individual needs. Communication and making the right decisions stop being desirable and become essential. Business survival, as well as business growth, depends on leadership within management.

❑ Early in the next century you will begin to see an even greater need for excellent leaders in every field of human enterprise. How do you think business schools and management courses should be changing now in order to develop such leaders?

10

WOMEN AS LEADERS

'Even when the path is normally open – when there is nothing to prevent a woman from being a doctor, a lawyer, a civil servant – there are many phantoms and obstacles, I believe, looming in her way.'

Virginia Woolf

In 1960 Sirimavo Bandaranaike of Sri Lanka became the world's first woman prime minister. Since then, Indira Gandhi, Golda Meir, Isabelita Perón, Margaret Thatcher, Benazir Bhutto and Cora Aquino are among the women who have risen to the chief position in their respective countries. Their appointments symbolize a wider trend: the emergence of many more women as leaders in fields normally associated with men. The seeds of this development lie deep within history, although it has taken a century of progress – its pace accentuated by two world wars – to bring women to the fore.

There are, however, problems and obstacles in the paths of women who wish to realize their leadership potential. Most of them are man-made. This chapter outlines the changes in values and in society which have opened the door of leadership more widely to women today. That progress has only come about because a number of women – some of whom are described below – were willing to take or make opportunities and so lead the way. Not that the story is yet over. For there are still barriers to the advancement of women as leaders that need to be dismantled, especially in industry and commerce.

THE WESTERN TRADITION

The river of Western tradition of leadership was fed from classical, tribal and biblical springs. What did each of these sources contribute to our understanding of women as leaders?

Socrates said that where women know more than men – for instance, in spinning wool – then they rightly become the leaders. For Socrates grounded authority in having the knowledge appropriate to the situation in which those concerned found themselves. In such circumstances as producing wool, he says, 'Women govern the men because they know how to do it and men do not.' In other words, the principle that 'authority flows from the one who knows' applied impartially to women as well as men. But when Socrates turned on to his other tack – arguing that leadership consists of general abilities and qualities, functional activities meeting human need which can be transferred from one working situation to another – he is silent on women. There is no suggestion, for example, that a woman who managed men in making wool could learn to take command of a Greek war trireme.

The tribal strand in our tradition does have examples of women in positions of political and military leadership (the two could hardly be separated in ancient times). For many tribes and tribal kingdoms followed the law that if a dead king lacked sons, his eldest daughter succeeded to the throne.

Some of these queens demonstrated outstanding capabilities as leaders. The Greek historian Herodotus was clearly proud of Artemisia, a former queen of his native city of Halicarnassus in Asia Minor. She commanded her own ships under Xerxes at the battle of Salamis. The Athenians, he tells us, especially resented the fact that a woman had appeared in arms against them, and offered a reward of 10,000 drachmae for anyone who captured her alive. Women were not generally esteemed. After a later defeat by the Athenians, this time on land, the son of Darius turned upon his Persian general. 'He abused him roundly, and, to crown all, told him his leadership was worse than a woman's,' wrote Herodotus. To call a man 'worse than a woman' was apparently the worst insult one could offer a Persian in those days. The enraged general was barely restrained from killing the prince with his scimitar.

THE WARRIOR QUEEN

The Iceni, a Celtic tribe in East Anglia, settled for peaceful co-existence with the Roman invaders of Britain. When King Prasutagus died in AD 60 he nominated the Emperor Nero as co-heir with his widow Boudicca and daughters. But the Romans plundered both his kingdom and his household, scourging his widow and raping his daughters.

The Iceni rose in outrage and stormed Camulodunum, where retired legionaries lived on their plots of land. Led by the vengeful Boudicca, with her daughters beside her, they massacred the small community and its garrison, marched on Londinium and completely destroyed it, and then wrought more destruction in Verulamium (St Albans). Some 70,000 people are said to have died in these three towns. Suetonius Paulinus, the Roman governor of Britain, hastened back from Wales to deal with this threat.

'Win the battle or perish!' So, according to the Roman historian Tacitus, Boudicca exhorted her troops. 'That is what I, a woman, intend to do. Let the men live in slavery if they wish!' The trained legionaries, supported by a large cavalry force, crushed Boudicca's army in battle, and boasted later of slaughtering 80,000 combatants and spectators. The Twentieth Legion received the proud title of 'the Victorious' for its work that day. Boudicca committed suicide by taking poison.

Down the ages, history records examples of other Boudiccas. Joan of Arc is well known as an inspired military leader, but we tend to forget such figures as: Theroigne de Méricourt, an opera singer who led the storming of the Bastille in 1789; Mariya Bochkareva, a Russian revolutionary in 1917; and Salyam Bint Malham, a leading warrior for the prophet Mohammad, who fought with swords and daggers strapped around her pregnant belly.

Christianity brought seeds of change in the perception of the value of women relative to men. St Paul's principle that in Christ all are equal — Jews and Gentiles, male and female, slave and free — was recorded in the Bible, which Christians considered to be the inspired word of God. Those seeds germinated slowly in the soils of Western culture, not least because of the Bible's ambivalence in parts about women. But in time they helped to produce such secular offshoots as the modern feminist movement.

Within Christianity women clearly exercised leadership

in the churches that Paul visited or established during his travels from city to city. Later, the institution of monasticism gave women another opportunity, for the abbess or prioress of a large nunnery became the head of a large organization or community dedicated to worship, learning and service.

The tribal and Christian strands come together in the person of Queen Elizabeth I, who was not only head of the state but also head of the Church of England. A woman of intellectual ability, sharpened by a Renaissance education, she used her intelligence and diplomacy with consummate skill to avoid conflict in both spheres. In 1588, when the Spanish Armada threatened England with invasion, she displayed courage and resolution. Though the Armada was defeated, for a time it was thought that the Spanish army in the Netherlands would still attempt an invasion. In this situation, and despite the fears of some for her safety, Elizabeth resolved to visit her army in Tilbury. As she passed through the army the men fell on their knees. 'Lord bless you all,' she cried. The following day, mounted on a stately horse with a baton in her hand, she witnessed a mimic battle and afterwards reviewed the army. Nothing could surpass the felicity of the speech that she made to them:

> My loving people, we have been persuaded by some that are careful of our safety, to take heed how we commit ourselves to armed multitudes, for fear of treachery. But I assure you, I do not desire to live in distrust of my faithful and loving people.
>
> Let tyrants fear. I have always so behaved myself that, under God, I have placed my chiefest strength and safeguard in the loyal hearts and good will of my subjects; and therefore I am come amongst you, as you see, at this time, not for my recreation

and disport, but being resolved, in the midst and heat of the battle, to live or die amongst you all, to lay down for my God, and for my kingdom, and for my people, my honour and my blood, even in the dust.

I know I have the body of a weak and feeble woman, but I have the heart and stomach of a king, and of a king of England too, and think foul scorn that Parma or Spain, or any prince of Europe should dare to invade the borders of my realm; to which, rather than any dishonour shall grow by me, I myself will take up arms, I myself will be your general, judge, and rewarder of every one of your virtues in this field. I know already, for your forwardness, you have deserved rewards and crowns; and we do assure you, in the word of a prince, they shall be duly paid you.

SIR FRANCIS DRAKE

Among those who responded to Elizabeth's leadership in the Armada crisis was Sir Francis Drake, one of England's greatest sailors and sea wolves.

The need to create teamwork is perennial. Drake showed himself a true leader by creating unity out of disharmony. During his epic voyage in which he circumnavigated the globe, he faced persistent troubles among his crews. A long period of cold, miserable, stormy weather accentuated one source of discord. In order to train officers for future operations against Spain's colonies, Drake had brought with him a large number of young gentlemen. They scorned to work with their hands, much to the sailors' displeasure. Behind the general low morale lay a deeper cause: Drake had not told the crews why the enterprise had been mounted in the first place. He had not won their hearts. Sensing the need, Drake decided to take action. Having mustered the three ships' companies on shore, Drake told them plainly that their mutinies and discords must cease.

'For by the life of God it does even take my wits from me to think on it. Here is such controversy between the sailors and the gentlemen and such stomaching between the gentlemen and the sailors, that it does even make me mad to hear it. But, my masters, I must have it left. For I must have the gentleman to haul and draw with the mariner and the mariner with the gentleman. What! let us show ourselves all to be of a company and let us not give occasion to the enemy to rejoice at our decay and overthrow.'

Drake then offered the *Marigold* to any who would sail home rather than work as a team. He added, however, that he would sink that vessel if it chanced into his way. Not a man raised his voice for going home. Drake then startled his captains and officers by discharging them. One or two of the worst offenders he now reprimanded by name; they humbled themselves on their knees before him. Having justified his recent controversial proceedings (in circumstances of doubtful legality he had had one gentlemen beheaded), and having communicated to them fully the reasons behind the voyage, Drake appealed to their patriotism. Finally, he restored the officers to their positions and once more impressed upon them all that they served the Queen, not himself. Thus he secured the willing obedience of all. Not long afterwards Drake changed his flag ship's name to *Golden Hind*; it was an act that symbolized the new beginning.

Some English writers also rejected Machiavelli, who died in 1527, not only because he advocated what they saw as tyranny but also because he taught what they called *subtlety*. A leader deceiving his followers or colleagues by artful methods seemed to them a contradiction in terms. But this aspect of Machiavelli's teaching in the use of craft or cunning in political life did win some converts in England. Queen Elizabeth was certainly a Machiavellian in that respect. Her restless and calculating mind was always at work, plotting a course forwards through a tangled maze of possibilities and dangers. She observed more closely and played upon their emotions as if they were the keys of her harpsichord. She alternated royal severity with a feminine touch. On one occasion, when Elizabeth had said some 'hard words' to Archbishop Matthew Parker in council the day before, it fell to his duty to meet her on Lambeth Bridge. 'She gave me very good looks,' wrote the bemused Archbishop, 'and spoke secretly in my ear, that she must needs countenance mine authority before the people, to the credit of my service.' On reflection Parker felt himself to be in a well-nigh impossible situation, as he complained to Lord Cecil: 'Her Majesty told me that I had supreme government ecclesiastical, but what is it to govern cumbered with such subtlety?'

Integrity, in the sense of plain speaking and above-the-board dealing, was the ideal set before English leaders by their school teachers and the writers of the day. As Shakespeare wrote in *Hamlet*,

> This above all: to thine own self be true,
> And it must follow, as the night to day,
> Thou canst not then be false to any man.

Although Elizabeth did manage men on occasion, in the sense of manipulating them, she never lacked integrity, that lion hallmark of the sterling leader. Therefore she enjoyed the trust and confidence of her people to the end of her days.

Queen Elizabeth never married. She promoted her image as the Virgin Queen, ruling her community of England like a wise abbess. She was expected to marry, although the choice of a suitable husband – whether an Englishman or a foreign prince, posed her with a major political problem. In the event she resolved it by remaining unmarried. In addition, Elizabeth may well have disliked the assumption of male dominance in wedlock. As Shakespeare's spirited girls and women reveal, that assumption was not unchallenged. Girls educated in the way advocated by Renaissance scholars such as the daughters of Sir Thomas More or Elizabeth herself, could not submit themselves in blind obedience to a husband selected by their parents.

LEADERSHIP IN MARRIAGE

The potentially revolutionary nature of Christian thought on the relative values placed on men and women began to emerge – and is still emerging – as Renaissance and Reformation changed the moral climate of Western Europe. John Milton steeped himself in both traditions. He was an uncompromising idealist, both in his work as a writer and in his personal life. In his early years, Milton not only dedicated himself to poetry but exemplified in his life the themes of his pen, such as chastity. 'He who would not be frustrate of his hope to write well hereafter in laudable things,' he wrote in 1642, 'ought himself to be a true poem; that is, a composition and pattern of the best and honourablest things.' The following year, when he was thirty-five, he married Mary Powell, the seventeen-year-old daughter of a Royalist in Oxfordshire, whom he had known as a girl. Within a month of their wedding Mary left him and returned home. Milton struggled in vain to reconcile his experience with the existing teaching on divorce. Therefore he wrote a book on divorce in which he argued for a new doctrine and discipline.

In Milton's new concept of marriage a woman's rights were the same as a man's. Authority rested in the husband, except where he acknowledged that his wife was more prudent and intelligent than himself, when 'a superior and more natural law comes in, that the wiser should govern the less wise, whether male or female'. But marriage was above all a spiritual affair, 'a divine institution joining man and woman in a love fitly dispos'd to the helps and comforts of domestic life'. Milton put the social end of marriage first, prizing above the procreation of children 'the apt and cheerful conversation of man with woman to refresh him against the evil of a solitary life'. That 'rational burning' for a companion had its remedy in marriage. It followed that a sexual relationship without what Shakespeare had called 'the marriage of true minds' was virtually worthless. The only course, then, was to divorce and remarry. Influential though this view of divorce has been in our times, Milton could not prevail against the overwhelming conservative opposition from all quarters to his proposed change in the Christian law. For he did not take it for granted that the man is invariably the leader in marriage. Man and wife were equal before God and equal partners in relation to the world. Leadership went to the partner who had the most natural ability to exercise it.

The English Civil War gave women new opportunities as leaders. The defence of Wardour Castle by Lady Arundel, of Corfe Castle by Lady Bankes, and of Lathom House by the Countess of Derby, showed women acting as equals to men. Within their marriage partnerships some women took the part of leader. The Royalist press accused Lady Anne, General Sir William Waller's second wife, of this usurpation of the traditional male role. The Royalist newspaper published in Oxford, *Mercurius Aulicus*, accused her of preaching in public. In the midst of the Civil War, Anne wrote to the editor denying the charge, 'for as yet (she protests) she never preached, but says she knows not what we may drive her to'. According to the newspaper she had only interpreted some difficult passages of Scripture, 'which her Ladyship called undoing hard chapters; according to which phrase her husband's army is quite expounded'. The Royalist newspaper recalled that when the couple attended religious meetings in Winchester Cathedral, Anne took the leading part. If William 'offered to speak about doctrines or uses, her Ladyship would rebuke him, saying "Peace, Master Waller, you know your weakness in these things."'

In the period of English Civil War such women as Lady Anne Waller took part in political demonstrations, grabbed attention with their religious visions and attempted to make their (generally silent) voices heard in a variety of novel ways. Within marriage, the assumption that the husband would inevitably be the leader was also called into question. Milton had picked up the Socratic tradition, which taught that authority should go to those best fitted to exercise it.

A NON-LEADER IN MARRIAGE

In 1983 a press report appeared about a divorce case. The judge granted the wife a divorce on the grounds that, in twenty-nine years of marriage, her husband –

- Only gave her two presents – a potato-peeler and a hair-drier.
- Never took her or their six children on holiday.
- Would not give her housekeeping money but sent her out to work to earn it.
- Never spoke to her unless it was to complain.
- Never asked her opinion on anything because he thought her views were worthless.

When the wife got back from work and tried to talk to her husband, all she got was a grunt. There was never any holidays because her husband thought the house was 'in the fresh air' and that was all they needed. To pay the household bills, she had to take on three part-time jobs.

Her husband was unrepentant. He explained: 'I believe the family is like a ship. You have got to have a Captain and I saw myself as the Captain. You pay the bills and you run the ship. The family can't be run as a co-operative. She told me her views and if I did not agree I did it my way. I felt as I was paying the bills I was entitled to call the tune and I had vastly more experience.

'If she came back, her attitude would have to change. I feel I am the wronged person. I provided her with a home and looked after her and the children. I fed them, clothed them, housed them and educated them, and at the end of it – well, if you have a family like mine who needs enemies.

'I would still have her back. They say better the devil you know than the one you don't. I never expected much from marriage or life in general. I can't say I have been disappointed.'

When the husband was asked in court if he would give more affection to his wife if she returned, he replied: 'It would have to be earned.'

GREAT SOCIAL REFORMERS

Prejudice dies hard. Not until the nineteenth century – the age of progress – did women begin to emerge in larger numbers as leaders, often in the face of disapproval. Women with a strong vocation to serve others led the way. Florence Nightingale, for example, transformed the poorly regarded task of nursing the sick into a new profession for women. At the age of twenty-four she began a ten-year study of nursing practices in England and Europe, becoming convinced that there was a need for women with a sense of vocation to take up the work. Her first job was the little-sought one of matron in a mental hospital.

In 1854, when Florence Nightingale heard about the terrible conditions of the wounded British soldiers in the Crimean War, she offered to lead a party of women nurses to work in the Military Hospital at Scutari. There she found conditions were appalling. The wounded, lying in disease-ridden squalor, died of fever rather than their wounds. Contrary to myth, Florence Nightingale was not known as 'The Lady with the Lamp' by the soldiers she nursed in the Crimean War. She was really 'The Lady with the Hammer', because of an incident when, defying a commanding officer's orders, she broke up a storeroom to obtain supplies. Her image as a saintly figure is also wrong. She was relentless in using influential friends, such as Sidney Herbert, Minister of War, in order to achieve her ends. A demanding and even fierce person, Florence Nightingale was a highly efficient administrator and a great manager of change. She introduced one important technique of modern reform: the use of statistics.

In 1856 the death rate at Scutari fell from 42 per cent to

2.2 per cent. It is no accident that we know the precise figure. For Florence Nightingale, as she said, 'loved to bite on a hard fact'; she added that she found statistics 'more enlightening than a novel'. In her role as a change-agent in society – reforming army medical services, hospitals and nursing education – she discovered the power of statistics and used it to the full. In 1858 she was elected a member of the newly formed Statistical Society. The main subject of the Statistical Congress two years later was her Uniform Hospital Statistics. That year, a friend wrote to her: 'I have a New Year's Gift for you. It is in the shape of Tables.' Her appetite for such facts and figures was enormous. 'I am exceedingly anxious to see your charming gift,' Florence Nightingale replied, 'especially those returns showing the Deaths, Admissions, Diseases.'

Poverty, Poor Law, Public Health, Factory Legislation, Education, Prisons: there were plenty of opportunities for social reformers who could marshal evidence in the form of compelling statistics. Florence Nightingale and Josephine Butler are the best known of the women who exercised leadership among them. Josephine Butler agitated for the admission of women to higher education, helped to secure the Married Women's Property Act, and worked for the improvement in the lot of 'fallen' women. By acquiring the authority of knowledge, expressed in tables, figures and descriptive passages (Marx culled his picture of the miseries of the English working classes from the Parliamentary Blue Books), women found that they, too, could bring about progress in society. But they still lacked the right to vote.

In October 1906, a respectable mother of five grown-up children stood in the dock at Bow Street Magistrates' Court, arrested for taking part in a demonstration by the 'Suffragettes'. Emmeline Pankhurst's upbringing was unusual for a young lady of her time. She took part in political discussions with her father and went to Paris to be educated, returning home to Manchester a graceful and elegant young lady, 'wearing her clothes and carrying herself like a Parisienne'. Two years later, at twenty-one years, she married Dr Richard Pankhurst, a barrister and radical politician. In 1903 she, her three daughters, and a few other women formed the Women's Social and Political Union. Their slogan was simple but powerful: 'Votes for Women'.

Nationwide, women took up the call. But Parliament refused to discuss their demands. Suffragettes who demonstrated for their cause were often imprisoned. When their demands to be treated as political prisoners, rather than common law-breakers, were refused, they went on hunger strike and there were even more violent demonstrations. Some women threw stones through the windows of 10 Downing Street, some chained themselves to railings, others lowered themselves down ropes into political meetings which refused to admit them. At the outbreak of the First World War, Mrs Pankhurst called on her followers to support the Government. During the war women worked in factories, on the land, on railways, in hospitals and as ambulance drivers in France. Instead of demanding equality, women demonstrated it. As so often before, war proved to be the matrix for social change.

When the war ended Emmeline Pankhurst continued her work. In 1918 women over thirty won the vote. On the very day in June 1928 that Mrs Pankhurst died, the final Bill giving women the same voting rights as men went through Parliament.

As the twentieth century unfolded, the two World Wars gave further stimulus to women to take up careers. After the Second World War many women began to emerge as leaders in their chosen fields. Dame Ciceley Saunders, for example, gave pioneering leadership to the hospice movement. The hospice of St Luke, which she founded in London, set a new standard in the care of the dying. Apart from showing the way, Ciceley Saunders has given inspiration and encouragement to those who have followed in her footsteps and established similar hospices in Britain and in other countries throughout the world.

WOMEN AS LEADER–MANAGERS

'The emergence of more women at senior positions in management will, I believe, be of immense help to industry and commerce,' wrote John Harvey-Jones in *Making it Happen* (1988).

I am bound to say that young ladies in ICI tend to react somewhat badly when I try and point out that I believe that men and women bring different approaches to thinking, and have different strengths and weaknesses. They feel that such remarks are patronising, whereas I actually intend the reverse. Perhaps the people of the East understand the relative difference between female and male approaches to things better that we. I fervently believe that, as in my family, we usually make better decisions when both sexes are involved, so the same applies in industry. Women seem to me to have better intuitive capabilities and a deeper, inbuilt, sense of fundamental responsibility. They are prepared to stick with details longer than men, and to ensure that things are actually done right. They also have a different perception of other people's reactions and, by and large, are more sensitive to them. The best decisions, and the best results, will come where men and women work together as a team, respecting their differences of view, and contributing equally from their own experience and approach to the formation of the policies which they will then try to carry out.

There is no evidence, however, that male and female qualities as such exist. There are women, for example, who lack both intuition and a sense of responsibility. Courage and aggressiveness, on the other hand, are by no means uniquely male characteristics. All attempts to generalize about the leadership qualities or abilities that women possess, as opposed to men, upon closer examination seem to collapse like a house of cards. There seems little point in labelling certain attitudes or characteristics – such as compassion, warmth, gentleness, and humility – as being 'feminine', and other qualities as being 'masculine'. For all these qualities are to be found in both sexes in different measures or combinations.

ANITA RODDICK

'Be daring, be first, be different.' Anita Roddick's philosophy of business struck a responsive chord with her customers from the start. The Body Shop, her creation, first opened its doors in 1976. Ten years later her company had grown to ninety shops in Britain and 196 more in thirty countries, bringing in profits of over £5 million. More than half of her British franchisees are women. Anita Roddick encouraged young women to follow in her steps and to set up their own retail businesses. 'Promote yourself, shout about your business,' she has told them. 'And if necessary, be brilliantly devious.'

Following the example of the first Body Shop, all Anita Roddick's shops have adopted a community care project, involving hospitals, old people's homes, or handicapped children's centres. 'It is not enough to vote a chunk of money to charity,' she has said. 'What is important is to involve people in giving, in sharing, in helping.'

The Body Shop enterprise is still run like a big family. Anita Roddick and her husband Gordon – in charge of the financial side – still know most staff by name. They give Christmas parties for them and gather managers together for summer weekend meetings in their garden. 'She's a very caring person,' a franchisee of four London shops has said, 'and that feeling of caring sifts right through the company.'

Anita Roddick has set herself the target of visiting every shop at least once a year, asking questions and offering support. She has an open telephone line for anyone to contact her. 'I have nightmares of memos in triplicate,' she said.

According to her husband, Anita Roddick is 'a volcano of creativity'; her enthusiasm and concern for others is evident in the story of the Body Shop. According to her, 'We must put back into society what we have taken out. And if we don't love our staff, our neighbours, the environment, we'll all be doomed. I want to make it attractive to be good.'

Women make valuable members of the management team, it will be granted, but do they make good leaders of that team? In Britain few women get to the top in large organizations. Their best route to senior leadership positions is to found and grow their own businesses, like Anita Roddick or the late Laura Ashley. In America, thanks in part to positive discrimination, there are more female chief executive officers and directors in major companies.

CASE STUDY: MARGARET THATCHER

Margaret Thatcher is one of the best-known leaders in the world today. Indeed she has done much to put back the concept of leadership on the political map. She emerged as leader of the Conservative Party in the mid-1970s in response to a situation which had developed within Social Capitalism in Britain. Social Capitalism, as the system that has evolved in the Western world is best called, reflects four core values, each with moral undertones: money or wealth, society, the individual and nature (or the environment). Conflicts between these values, intermeshed with class skirmishing and party political struggles, had simmered down into tensions, as all the main parties became converted to Social Capitalism. But the system had failed to achieve balance in Britain. The task of getting the economy in better order by containing inflation and raising productivity defeated the Labour Government under Harold Wilson, not least because it failed to control the powerful Trade Unions. As Prime Minister, Wilson excelled at holding his team together by tactical and sometimes devious means, but he appeared to have lacked a strategy or even a sense of direction. His successor, James Callaghan, was a graduate of that school. An excellent chairman of Cabinet and an avuncular, genial man, Callaghan could make little headway. The situation, which he had both inherited and helped to create, degenerated into the famous 'winter of discontent' in 1978. It swept Margaret Thatcher into power.

Having been defeated in two elections in 1974, the Conservative Party introduced the practice of allowing Conservative Members of Parliament to elect their leader. For many now wanted to see a change of leader. The party

JAMES CALLAGHAN ON LEADERSHIP

'I suppose it is possible to learn from textbooks and teachers how to practise the techniques of leadership, though I can't claim I've ever done so or indeed that I've ever reflected much on the techniques. No doubt I learned unconsciously when I was a young man from observing the way in which the political giants of my youth handled the problems of the thirties and forties, and certainly in adult life I've been continuing the process of unconscious learning by my addiction to political biography, which, speaking personally, I always find utterly absorbing. Nonetheless, I've never felt required to make a systematic study of the art of political leadership, although to be perfectly open, I might have been a much better leader if I had done so.

'I can claim only one extenuation: when Harlan Cleveland invited me to come to the Humphrey Institute to speak on leadership, I read my first and only book on the subject. It was an excellent study by James MacGregor Burns. To my amazement I found that in my imputed ignorance I had luckily, or instinctively, been doing much of what he said I ought to do.

'Many of my colleagues in the British Labour movement would say that their experience was similar, especially if they have emerged from the shop floor or have come to industrial or political leadership through the Trade Union movement or have sprung into Parliament as a result of being active in local constituencies.

'We were unselfconscious when we launched out on our first fluttering leadership flights. We learned how to fly by doing it. I don't know whether a bird can learn to fly in any other way. But to most birds, as to most leaders, I think doing it comes naturally.'

> From 'The Political Leader', a talk given at the
> Hubert H. Humphrey Institute of Public Affairs,
> University of Minnesota, 1982

had originally presented its then leader, Edward Heath, as a plain, straightforward man of integrity, contrasting him with the devious Wilson. As a grammar school boy from a middle-class family who had won a scholarship to Oxford, Heath could also be promoted as a representative of the new meritocracy. His appointment symbolized the end of the old Conservative Party's reliance on the privileged classes for its leader. But in office, Heath revealed to his closest colleagues a lack of talent for personal relations or communication. As a chief whip – the adjutant of the Party in the Commons – he had excelled; as commanding officer, however, he somehow fell short as a leader. He saw the need for leadership, but he failed to provide it in an effective way.

A smaller group of Conservative members, headed by Sir Keith Joseph, wanted also a change in strategy. They saw the need to make Social Capitalism more task-oriented. They were not, of course, advocating a return to primitive capitalism – that would have been impossible. But they intended to turn the helm sharply to starboard and rely far more upon traditional capitalist philosophy and monetarist techniques in order to get the ship back on course. Margaret Thatcher was not only a passionate convert to these views, she also had the courage to stand for election as leader against the formidable Heath in the first ballot.

Courage, the quality perceived in Margaret Thatcher by her sponsors in the leadership election, became her hallmark in the years that followed. Guts, nerve, pluck, resolution, backbone, all these words suggest her bold and determined attitude. Her courage is allied to her firmness, which arises from a strong belief in the moral rightness of her political position and the courses of action she advocates. She has the courage of her convictions, whatever her opponents may think about them.

Senior colleagues say that they have found Margaret Thatcher a feminine person, not above giving way to tears on occasion. She can use femininity to competitive advantage. It is said that she sometimes mistakes common politeness to her as a woman for signs of deference to her as a politician. Her concern and compassion for her staff and an extended family of friends and even acquaintances are evidence of the maternal side to her nature. In Denis Thatcher she found the right husband; by good luck children, in the shape of twins, arrived at one time, which shortened the time needed to rear them. She has been able to combine leadership in public office with family life successfully.

In groups or in public, Margaret Thatcher's colleagues have reported that she tended to be far more strident, aggressive and dominant than she was when talking to them as individuals in private. This may be a manifestation of that personal drive and need to win that she has had to develop in order to achieve her ambition. She is said to be a better listener in private than she appears to be in public.

Margaret Thatcher's emphasis has fallen on personal drive, self-reliance and self-help. She did not express any such strong beliefs in teamwork, nor did she show any talent for team-building. That lack, and its consequences, have been a flaw in her leadership. As a schoolgirl and at university she had no experience of leading teams in extra-curricular activities, preferring to develop her individual skills as a debater. Nor did her work as a chemist in industry or as a tax lawyer equip her for team leadership. William Whitelaw, who became her Deputy Prime Minister, saw this empty space and decided to work with her, complementing her driving sense of direction with his skills as a maintainer of at least an outward appearance of unity

MARGARET THATCHER ON LEADERSHIP

On a visit to Bonn in 1983 Margaret Thatcher recalled that her father had been Mayor of Grantham, and said that in a democracy one needed leadership throughout society. 'Democracy is about the distribution of responsibility,' she added.

In conversation with Max Hastings that year, reported in the *Standard* (2 June), Margaret Thatcher responded to the suggestion that it might now be time to acknowledge a greater responsibility to the unemployed. She nodded. 'We know that it is desperately depressing for a youngster not to have anything to do. But I remember when I visited Toxteth – the housing there is not bad, some of it is quite good. Yet there were weeds growing right up to some of the buildings. I said: "Surely it's possible to get a group of youngsters together and say – 'Come on and do something about this.'" But I was told: "If you do that you'll have a terrible mess the following day."

'That seems to me a very depressing attitude. What we need is more leadership at every level. You know that if you have an army, it's no good just having a general – you need leadership all the way through the system. If we have a philosophy, it is to create this leadership at every level, to say to people – 'it doesn't matter who you are or where you are or what you are, you have something to contribute to society. At the moment you find very good leadership in some places, and a total absence of it in others.'

Max Hastings commented on the interview: 'I was struck again, as many of us have been struck listening to the Prime Minister on the platform, by how little she refers to her colleagues in government, how much the thrust of her argument is unabashedly personal.'

within the Cabinet and within the parliamentary party. Whitelaw received a peerage for his services on the bridge and within the engine room of party unity.

Some of Margaret Thatcher's Cabinet colleagues, versed in the ways of clubbable English gentlemen, found her ignorant of the unwritten rules which they had acquired in their public schools, regiments and country houses. They complained that Margaret Thatcher did not know how to treat them properly. Behind the social snobbery there was an element of truth. Even quite senior ministers were seldom, if ever, invited to meet her on their own for a chat over a drink. She expected her senior colleagues to be able to look after themselves. If they ran into political trouble, they received little sympathy from her. She could be brutal in her application of the military maxim 'Never reinforce failure'. Even at Cabinet level, however, men and women do need to feel part of a team: they need to feel that their individual contributions are valued by their leader and by their colleagues.

WHITELAW ON THATCHER

As Deputy Prime Minister, William Whitelaw's influence was pervasive. It was always exercised in a calming manner – and a faithful one. He knew exactly how to get business through: when to bluster, when to cajole, when to bring out the big stick, when to produce the whisky bottle. He was good at getting people to work together and resourceful in finding solutions. His patrician and paternalist style and his open-mindedness belong to quieter political times. He did not share the Prime Minister's ideological enthusiasms, but he never tried to undermine them.

Margaret Thatcher will never become a popular politician.

Whitelaw, the former leader of the House of Lords said in an interview in *Woman's Own* (April 1988): 'She ought to be more popular, because she's a much kinder, more sympathetic person than anyone knows.' He added that Margaret Thatcher appeared 'hard and ruthless' on television because she was 'crisp and determined'. He called for 'a little compassion' in the society created in the Thatcher years.

Whitelaw hinted that Margaret Thatcher was sometimes too strident. 'A certain hesitancy is not a bad thing, because people prefer it, rather than being told all the time what to do. Hesitancy is not in the Prime Minister's vocabulary. But then she gets away with it because she has been so enormously successful.' He said that, 'She has a very different sense of humour from me, but it is not quite true to say that she has no sense of humour at all.'

Whitelaw predicted that the Conservative party would get into a muddle when Margaret Thatcher left office as Prime Minister, because she has been so dominant for so long. Finally, when asked how Thatcher had changed over the years, Whitelaw replied she had gained enormously in confidence and stature.

Strong conviction, even passion, is a great asset in a leader of either sex. It generates enthusiasm, energy and single-mindedness. People like to know where they stand with a leader. But it brings the dangers of breeding inflexibility, arrogance and ruthlessness. Too much emphasis on the strong leader can be at the expense of the team. There is always a danger, too, that restraining voices are exiled and the full Cabinet becomes a rubber stamp. Such developments may expedite the daily business, but they do not augur well for the quality of decisions in the longer term.

'The only way to safeguard yourself against flatterers,'

wrote Machiavelli, 'is by letting people understand that you are not offended by the truth; but if everyone can speak the truth to you then you lose respect.' Strong leaders in particular do need colleagues of stature, who are not afraid to speak the truth in the right place and at the right time.

'Will Margaret Thatcher take her place, with Churchill, as one of the great British political leaders of the century?' That was the question I posed in *Great Leaders* (1989), when Mrs Thatcher was still in office as Prime Minister. I continued:

> To do so, she must satisfy one criterion: she must have inspired or evoked the greatness of the British nation in order to accomplish a great necessity. Though the climate within Social Capitalism in Britain had begun to change before she took office, she presided over that change with a leader's sense of urgency. Some find that she is not inspiring as a leader. Others, however, are deeply stirred by her passionate conviction, clear and simple speech and strong sense of direction. Of her achievement, as a leader, there can be no doubt. It remains to be seen how Margaret Thatcher will face up to the last challenge of leadership: how to manage departure in a way that consolidates achievement.

Writing now, after her sudden and unwilling departure from office in 1990, it is clear that Margaret Thatcher only partly achieved that last objective of leadership. Her story as a leader ended in tears.

KEY POINTS

* People tend to follow those who know the way. As Socrates pointed out in Athens some 2500 years ago, in

industries where women are knowledgeable – for example, weaving – both men and women will accept them as leaders.

- The historical accident of law of primogeniture meant that even in centuries and in cultures where the female sex was undervalued in contrast to the male and kept out of public life, women could still be leaders of tribes, city-states or nations. Many of these women actually showed outstanding natural qualities and acquired skills as leaders.

- Not until recent times has the door for leadership been slowly opened – or forced open – for women in almost all the areas of human work. But there are still 'phantoms and obstacles' in the path of any woman who wishes to become the leader of a large organization.

- At work, women leaders rightly expect to be judged by the same inexorable criteria as their male colleagues: do they enable their group or organizations to achieve its task, while building teamwork and releasing the best that is in each individual? Those requirements can be met effectively by leaders of very different temperaments and personalities. There are most probably no specifically male or female qualities of leadership.

- Women who have no paid employment can still give leadership as wives and mothers, as neighbours and citizens. A principal strand in our hope for the future must be in the awakening of women to the needs and responsibilities of leadership.

- To enable more women to attain positions of strategic leadership responsibility in industry, commerce and the public services, should be one of the aims of society.

POINTS TO PONDER

❑ Many women do not see Margaret Thatcher as an exemplar or role model for women as leaders. Why do you think that this is the case?

❑ Men and women's brains differ as well as their bodies, it has been said. Do you agree? If so, how does it affect their style of leadership?

❑ Like men, women have to face the issue of whether or not they can pay the price of leadership and still grow as whole people. We all want to have our cake and eat it. Many women want to be happily married and have a family, and – at the same time – pursue a successful career. Having young children means that you are always on emotional first call, however much you delegate to home helpers. Can the demands of family be reconciled with the hard work, long hours and extra responsibility entailed in managerial leadership today?

11

STYLES OF LEADERSHIP

'These are hard times in which a genius would wish to live. Great necessities call forth great leaders.'

Abigail Adams, writing to Thomas Jefferson, 1790

It is fascinating to observe how leaders adopt very different styles, depending upon their personalities, their peoples and their times. These factors are illustrated by the four case studies in this chapter. The first two examples – Abraham Lincoln and Charles de Gaulle – are numbered among the great political leaders of their respective nations. Adolf Hitler is perhaps best described as a great misleader. His ruthless Machiavellian approach and lack of moral principle set him apart from the other three leaders. Yet there are lessons to be learnt from him – 'knowledge of good bought dear by knowing ill', as Byron wrote. Mahatma Gandhi's style was in total contrast to Hitler's corrupt and despotic rule, although he was also a man of charisma. His life reminds us of those truths buried in the teachings of Socrates, Lao Tzu and Jesus about the nature of great leadership.

ON GREATNESS

Greatness is a word that signifies a matter of degree. It can be applied separately or collectively to position and rank, knowledge or character – the three main strands of authority in leadership. In democracies there is a subdivision between great position and great rank, in so far as the highest born, or those first in the social order, do not necessarily rule the country. The people choose their supreme governor or governing body. They tend to elect those whom Edmund Burke called 'the natural aristocrats': men and women who exemplify the nation's virtues and who are perceived to have qualities of leadership. President Ronald Reagan's popularity in America stemmed in part from the nation's perception that he personified the qualities of a good American.

It follows that a great leader tends to hold supreme office in a nation, but may not have come from a great family (as Winston Churchill did) or even any family of rank. He or she will be seen as possessing the combined authority of knowledge and personality. But that is not enough. In order to become great in the historical sense, there must have been a really significant achievement. For greatness in history implies an accomplishment that has been critically evaluated or tested over the course of time in light of its contribution to the sum of human well-being. For this reason it is impossible to call any leader great until their accomplishment is secure.

Upon whom should the accolade of greatness amongst leaders fall? Recently a selection of people from different nations were asked that question. In reply they usually nominated the leader who had won their national freedom or independence, or preserved their countries from invasion.

For Americans, George Washington and Abraham Lincoln were such leaders, while the British would name great defenders of their freedom, such as King Alfred, Queen Elizabeth I or Sir Winston Churchill. The Dutch mentioned Prince William of Orange, of whom the historian John Motley wrote: 'As long as he lived, he was the guiding star of a whole brave nation, and when he died the little children cried in the streets.'

Greeks referred even further back in time to Alexander the Great, although Eleutherios Venizelos, a Cretan who became Premier of Greece in 1911, received some votes as a leader of stature. (The Greeks, incidentally, do not apply the word 'leader' to industrialists. Aristotle Onassis, for example, was not called a leader.) Newly emerged nations named those who led them to independence, such as Jomo Kenyatta in Kenya or Kwame Nkrumah of Ghana. In South America the name of Simon Bolivar, 'the Liberator' from Spanish colonial rule, is still pre-eminent.

Had they been asked, the North Vietnamese would have doubtless nominated a former cook at London's Carlton Hotel – Ho Chi Minh. Behind this leader's self-effacing, elusive manner was an iron will which enabled him to lead a long and bloody war against two powerful modern nations – France and the United States. Like many revolutionaries, Ho Chi Minh had suffered physically on the path to national leadership, often enduring arrest and imprisonment. In Yunnan, he was 'loaded with chains, covered in sores, put among the worst bandits, associated with the condemned, like one dead'. Ho Chi Minh, like Moses, did not live to see the final victory, but he died confident that it was an absolute certainty. Such leaders inspire a nation's lasting gratitude. They are often also seen as father-figures, person-ifications of the incipient nation's ideals and aspirations.

Abraham Lincoln, the subject of the first case study in this chapter, was such a figure in American history. Apart from his historic achievement of maintaining the unity of the United States, Lincoln's style of leadership – simple, direct and compassionate – has served as a model to those who came after him and aspired to lead their fellow Americans in the great democratic nation.

ABRAHAM LINCOLN

Lincoln's chief gift as a leader was his clarity of vision. Before his inauguration as President in May 1861, the outgoing Democratic government had already decided that it had no power to prevent any state from seceding from the Union. Lincoln judged that slavery was an issue which time and common sense would solve. But once the Union was gone it would most probably never return. North America could become like Europe, a continent torn by disunity, jealousy, economic rivalry and wars. He made his aim crystal-clear in a famous letter to Horace Greeley, editor of the *New York Tribune*:

> My paramount object in this struggle is to save the Union, and it is not either to save or destroy slavery. If I could save the Union without freeing any slave, I would do it; and if I could do it by freeing all the slaves, I would do it; and if I could save it by freeing some, and leaving others alone, I would do that.

Thus Lincoln gave the Northern states a clear aim. His strong and dignified countenance, deeply lined and touched by melancholy, imparted a calm assurance, and a proper sense of the tragedy of this war between brothers. 'Through all the doubt and darkness, the danger and long tempest of the war,' wrote William Makepeace Thackeray, 'I think it was only the American leader's indominatable soul that remained entirely steady.'

Despite his burdens as President and Commander-in-Chief during the war between the states, Lincoln found time for individuals. There is perhaps no better expression of his tender humanity than the letter he wrote to one victim of the Civil War, named Mrs Bixby:

Dear Madam,

I have been shown in the files of the War Department a statement of the Adjutant-General of Massachusetts that you are the mother of five sons who have died gloriously on the field of battle.

I feel how weak and fruitless must be any words of mine which should attempt to beguile you from the grief of a loss so overwhelming; but I cannot refrain from tendering to you the consolation that may be found in the thanks of the Republic they died to save.

I pray that our heavenly Father may assuage the anguish of your bereavement, and leave you only the cherished memory of the loved and lost, and the solemn pride that must be yours to have laid so costly a sacrifice on the altar of freedom.

Yours very sincerely and respectfully,

Abraham Lincoln

That appeal to Christian faith by Lincoln was entirely sincere. Lincoln drew deeply upon the Christian tradition in the style of leadership he chose to exercise. His simple trust in God, and humility before Him as the disposer of all things, gave him a firmness and generosity of spirit. In his second Inaugural Address, on 4 March 1865, Lincoln sounded these notes in his trumpet call to the nation:

> With malice towards none; with charity for all; with firmness in the right, as God gives us to see the right, let us strive to finish the work we are in; to bind up the nation's wounds; to care for him who shall have borne the battle, and for his widow and orphan – to do all which may achieve and cherish a just and lasting peace among ourselves and with all nations.

The great accomplishment of America under Lincoln's leadership was the preservation of the Union. 'If we do not make common cause to save the good old ship of the Union on this voyage, nobody will have a chance to pilot her on another voyage.' So Lincoln had told the inhabitants of Cleveland, Ohio, at the outset of the war between the states.

An assassin's bullet killed Lincoln as the war came to its close. Alas, great leaders have so often become lightning conductors for all the hatred, malice and envy that lurks in frustrated human souls. Lincoln left America a great legacy as far as leadership is concerned. He gave it an enduring example of what it means to be a great leader in a great Republic. Perhaps Lincoln's best epitaph is in his own words, which reflect the fields and farms of his boyhood days: 'Die when I may,' he said, 'I want it said of me by those who knew me best, that I always plucked a thistle and planted a flower where I thought a flower would grow.'

CHARLES DE GAULLE

'We navigated by the same stars,' said Winston Churchill of Charles de Gaulle. Both statesmen were guided by a sense of their nations' historic destinies. De Gaulle was imbued with a sense of France's glorious past. Grandeur, glory, greatness – the French word *grandeur*, when de Gaulle spoke or wrote it, was sometimes translated as each of these – belonged to the essence of France. He dedicated his life to leading France back to the heights. That upwards climb would give the nation its necessary common purpose. He once said, 'France is never her true self except when she is engaged in a great enterprise.' He saw himself as personifying the enduring qualities of the French people, and his leadership role as one of stirring the spirit of France.

As an officer in the French army in the First World War, de Gaulle was severely wounded and captured by the Germans. In his *The Army of the Future* (1934) he attacked French dependence on the 'impregnable' Maginot Line, and in 1940 refused to accept Marshal Pétain's truce with the Germans, becoming leader of the Free French in England. He could never have accepted the subjection of France. 'All my life I have thought of France in a certain way,' de Gaulle wrote in the opening sentence of his wartime memoirs. He saw France as a country fated to experience either dazzling success or exemplary misfortune. 'If, in spite of this, mediocrity shows in her acts and deeds, it strikes me as an absurd anomaly, to be imputed to the faults of Frenchmen, not the genius of the land.' France was not really herself 'unless in the front rank'. Only a grand national purpose to achieve excellence among the nations, putting France in the vanguard of progress, could overcome the natural disunity of the French people. 'In short, to my mind, France cannot be France without greatness.'

In order to realize this vision France needed a great leader. 'When leaders fail,' de Gaulle told an American, Admiral Harold Stark in 1942, 'new leaders emerge upwards out of the spirit of eternal France, from Charlemagne and Joan of Arc to Napoleon, Poincaré and Clemenceau.' He then added, 'Perhaps this time I am one of those thrust into leadership by the failure of others.' Not that he doubted his place in that succession. His army marched under the flag of the Cross of Lorraine, under which Joan of Arc had rallied the French people against the English in the Hundred Years' War.

In 1944 de Gaulle entered Paris in triumph. He was head of the provisional government before resigning in protest against the defeats of the new constitution of the Fourth Republic in 1946. Twelve years later, when bankruptcy and civil war loomed, he was called to form a government. As Premier he put forward a constitution subordinating the legislature to the presidency, and in 1959 took office as President. Economic recovery and the eventual solution of France's colonial problems followed, but in pursuit of national interest and *grandeur* he opposed 'Anglo-Saxon' influence in Europe. In 1969 he resigned after his government was defeated in a referendum on constitutional reform, and he died the following year.

Not only did de Gaulle practise a distinctive style of leadership, but he also wrote about it. A man of character also needs *grandeur* to be an effective leader, he believed. 'He must aim high, show that he has vision, act on the grand scale, and so establish his authority over the generality of men who splash in the shallow water.' If he allows himself to be content with the commonplace, he will be looked upon by others as a good servant, but 'never as the master who can draw to himself the faith and dreams of mankind'.

Behind these words lies a tradition of thought about leadership that goes at least as far back as Napoleon. In an interview with the *New York Times* in 1965, de Gaulle was reported to have declared, 'Men are of no importance, what counts is who commands.' As a young officer in the First World War, he had served under Marshal Ferdinand Foch, generalissimo of all the armies on the Western Front. A great exemplar of the Napoleonic tradition of leadership, Foch had written of the military commander. 'To think and to will, to possess intelligence and energy will not suffice for him; he must possess also "imperative fire", the gift of communicating his own supreme energy to the masses of men who are, so to speak, his weapon.'

This tradition is echoed in de Gaulle's short book on leadership, *The Edge of the Sword*, written originally as a series of lectures at the French War College and then published in 1932 (when de Gaulle was a forty-one-year-old army officer little known beyond the army). In it, he defined three key leadership qualities. To chart the right course, a leader needs *intelligence* and *instinct*; to get people to follow him along that path, he needs *authority*.

De Gaulle noted that leaders have always understood the importance of instinct or intuition. Instinct, he wrote, enables the leader to 'strike deeply into the order of things'. It is the natural analytical ability to see the essentials of a problem or situation. 'Our intelligence can furnish us with the theoretic, general abstract knowledge of what is, but only instinct can give the practical, particular and concrete *feel* of it.' Only when a leader makes proper use of both intelligence or reason and instinct or intuition, will his

decisions have the hallmark of prescience. Prescience –
knowing which way to lead – is an essential element of
good leadership.

It is not enough to know the uphill path, however, if no
one will follow. In his lectures, de Gaulle stressed that a
leader 'must be able to create a spirit of confidence in those
under him. He must be able to assert his authority.'

'He has a look upon his face that I would fain call master.'
'What is that?'
'Authority.'

Shakespeare, *King Lear*

Authority, de Gaulle believed, stems from prestige. For
him, prestige is largely a matter of feeling, suggestion and
impression, and it depends primarily on the possession of
an elementary gift, a natural aptitude which defies analysis.
It is a rare gift, one that 'certain men have, one might
almost say from birth, the quality of exuding authority, as
though it were a liquid, though it is impossible to say
precisely of what it consists'.

De Gaulle's recipe for creating or preserving this prestige
(or charisma, as it would be called now) was a modern
version of the old Persian formula of establishing a proper
distance between ruler and ruled. In *The Edge of the Sword*,
he wrote about the creation of an all-important *mystique*
surrounding the leader:

First and foremost, there can be no prestige without mystery, for
familiarity breeds contempt. All religions have their tabernacles,
and no man is a hero to his valet. In the designs, the demeanour,

and the mental operations of a leader there must always be a 'something' which others cannot altogether fathom, which puzzles them, stirs them, and rivets their attention . . . Aloofness, character and the personification of quietness, these qualities it is that surround with prestige those who are prepared to carry a burden that is too heavy for lesser mortals.

The price they have to pay for leadership is unceasing self-discipline, the constant taking of risks, and a perpetual inner struggle . . . whence that vague sense of melancholy which hangs about the skirts of majesty.

PRESIDENT RICHARD NIXON'S RECOLLECTIONS OF DE GAULLE

'I vividly recall de Gaulle's striking presence when he came to Washington for President Kennedy's funeral in November 1963. Mrs Nixon and I watched the funeral procession from a window of our suite in the Mayflower Hotel. The great and near-great from all over the world were walking behind the casket. De Gaulle was a big man physically, but he seemed to tower over the rest in dignity, stature and charisma as well as in height.

'Whenever I met de Gaulle, whether publicly or privately, he displayed an enormous, even stately dignity. His resolute bearing gave him a certain air of aloofness . . . He had a certain ease of manner when dealing with another head of state, whom he considered an equal, but he was never informal, even with his closest friends.

'As a national figure, de Gaulle attracted a fiercely loyal cadre of supporters, but he remained aloof from them, reflecting his own dictum that a leader can have 'no authority without prestige, nor prestige unless he keeps his distance'. In his office in the Elysée Palace, de Gaulle had two phones on a table near his desk. But they never rang. He considered the telephone as an intolerable nuisance of the modern world, and not even his closest advisers dared to call him directly . . . In the grandeur of Versailles, de Gaulle looked completely at home. He did not try to put on airs, but an aura of majesty seemed to envelop him.'

From Richard Nixon, *Leaders* (1982)

In Cabinet meetings, de Gaulle did not engage in long discussions. He would listen carefully to his ministers, taking notes on what they said. If he wanted to exchange views with a minister, he usually requested a private meeting. After being fully briefed, he made the big decisions himself, retiring into solitude in order to do so. He placed much stress upon a leader's need to have time to think, and he insisted on reserving several hours of his day for uninterrupted thought.

To maintain his personal *mystique*, de Gaulle avoided friendship with any of his colleagues. They addressed him with nothing less formal than '*Mon Général*'. It has even been alleged that de Gaulle deliberately transferred his personal staff after a certain period in order to reduce the risk that they would become too familiar with him. Although he did not indulge in small talk in the context of his work, at banquets or dinner-parties he was invariably a courteous host or guest. But his warm emotions were reserved for his family, and he kept them well hidden.

Field Marshal Viscount Montgomery, in his book *The Path of Leadership* (1961), wrote of de Gaulle: 'Some will say that his manner is cold and that he lacks the personality to be an outstanding natural leader. On the surface he may appear thus, giving the impression that he lacks a sense of humour and has few real and personal friends. The point is that he is shy and doesn't open up too easily. But he has a warm and generous heart, and this very soon becomes evident once you get to know him ... He has those qualities of leadership which I admire so greatly – calmness in the crisis, decision, the ability to withdraw and have time to think.'

If de Gaulle possessed charisma it had eluded the British. Hence Montgomery's attempt to portray de Gaulle to his compatriots in a good light. But the personal magic that is charisma is tied to language and culture. For most of the French nation, de Gaulle was undoubtedly a great leader. In the Algerian crisis, for example, the French followed de Gaulle because in the hour of great need he seemed 'the only possible man' or 'the only one who can save France'. His subsequent performance won him deep respect and substantial popularity, but he was never adored in a quasi-religious way. During that crisis, he appeared on television – dressed in his general's uniform – in order to reassert his authority. With a calm, self-assured manner he asked the nation for its support. As he wrote later, he had to appear 'animated and spontaneous enough to seize and hold attention' without compromising himself by 'excessive gestures and misplaced grimaces.' His broadcast ended with the deeply emotional appeal: 'French people, French people, help me, help me!'

'Others made greater contributions than de Gaulle, but few had his strength of character,' wrote Richard Nixon in *Leaders* (1984), in words that make a good summary of de Gaulle as leader. 'He was a stubborn, wilful, supremely self-confident man of enormous ego and yet at the same time enormous selflessness. He was demanding not for himself but for France. He lived simply but dreamed grandly. He acted a part, playing a role he himself created in a way that would fit only one actor. Even more, he fashioned *himself* so that he could play it. He created de Gaulle, the public person, to play the role of de Gaulle, personification of France.' A strange, shy, aloof man, but a great French leader.

ADOLF HITLER

Hitler was not in fact a German. He was born in Austria, when it was part of the dual monarchy of Austria-Hungary, Germany's principal ally in the First World War. Like Napoleon, he became the leader of a great nation which was not his own by birth.

Germany as a united nation was much younger than France. Indeed it was Napoleon who first united Western Germany in the Confederation of the Rhine (1806), and introduced to it the ideas and reforms of the French Revolution, an influence which subsequently spread eastwards to Russia. In spite of persecution, the ideas of democracy and national unity spread, and inspired the unsuccessful revolutions of 1848. The growth of industry helped to make national unity an economic necessity. Under Bismarck's leadership, after victorious wars with Austria and France, Prussia established its hegemony over a united Germany. Political, industrial and colonial rivalries with Britain, France and Russia all combined to produce the First World War. In 1918 a revolution overthrew the monarchy. The Socialists seized power and established the democratic Weimar republic. A sustained economic crisis brought Germany close to revolution and, in the reaction, the National Socialist German Workers Party manoeuvred itself into power. Adolf Hitler, as leader of the Nazis and already effective national ruler in 1933, became officially Head of State in the following year, with the title of *Führer*.

The German Minister of Propaganda, Dr Josef Goebbels, stage-managed Hitler's appearances and speeches in order to create the image of the *Führer* as a powerful leader who exemplified all the German virtues. Goebbels has the dubious honour of being the first and most successful of a long line of public relations experts who have addressed themselves to the task of invoking a charismatic response to their clients who seek the highest political offices.

MACHIAVELLI AND LEADERSHIP

Machiavelli's theme was power: how to attain it and how to hold it. By power he meant the subjection of people to the will of the ruler. Machiavelli subscribed to the ancient Roman saying: 'Let them hate as long as they fear.' Seneca had denounced that proverb as a vile, detestable, deadly sentiment. The English tradition sided with Seneca; Machiavelli did not. 'It is far better to be feared than loved,' he wrote. 'The bond of love is one which men, wretched creatures that they are, break when it is to their advantage to do so; but fear is strengthened by a dread of punishment which is always effective.'

His historical statement – an Italy riven with internecine warfare and dominated by its powerful neighbours – largely explains his desire for a strong, masterful dictator of tyranny, the teacher of subtle and ruthless methods of how to enslave a free people. In *The Prince* (1513) he wrote, 'Men ought to be well treated or utterly crushed since they can avenge small injuries but not great ones.' That was the flavour of Machiavelli.

A ruler should free himself from moral restraints, however privately he might regret the necessity for doing so. He should not, of course, practise the wanton cruelty of Nero, but nothing must stay his hand from the actions that must be taken to achieve his task. Necessity, not morality, should be his sole guide. 'A prince who wants to hold his own,' he wrote, 'must know how to do wrong when necessary.'

Machiavelli taught that princes or governors need not actually possess the qualities or virtues associated with leadership, as long as they seem to have them. 'It is unnecessary for a prince to have all the virtues, but very necessary to appear to have them.' But humility was one virtue that a prince need not even simulate, because it had no place in statecraft. What mattered in a dictator was strength, will-power, valour, high spirit, technique and efficiency.

Hitler did have a talent for leadership, which enabled him to climb on the pinnacle of power in his country. So there was substance behind the image. Moreover, he believed in the myth of his own superhuman powers as a leader, especially in the military field. He also acquired a certain awesome presence. For Hitler took pains to look and sound the part. He may well have read or heard about the concept of the 'charismatic' leader, as defined by Max Weber. Hitler quite deliberately sought to arouse a response of awe and devotion by exerting his inner powers upon people. His blue eyes, slightly protruding, seemed radiant to the Germans under his sway. Many who met him were unable to withstand his gaze; knowing this, Hitler looked people straight in the eye without blinking. His sonorous voice, punctuated by energetic gestures and mounting to a shouting crescendo, had a mesmeric effect on vast German crowds. The party rallies did much to create the phenomenon of charisma: they were theatres where audience and performer worked together to create a form of magic. To those who met Hitler it seemed almost impossible to communicate to others his personal impact upon them. 'Such could be its strength that it sometimes seemed a kind of psychological force radiating from him like a magnetic field,' wrote one. 'It could be so intense as to be almost physically tangible.'

Albert Speer, Hitler's architect and later his Minister of Production, named his master's greatest strength as his uncanny ability to know men.

> He knew men's secret vices and desires, he knew what they thought to be their virtues, he knew their hidden ambitions and the motives which lay behind their loves and their hates, he knew where they could be flattered, where they were gullible, where they were strong and where they were weak; he knew all this . . . by instinct and feeling, an intuition which in such matters never led him astray.

This faculty gave him an extraordinary power over others (including Speer himself). Far from engendering a fellow feeling, Hitler's perceptiveness left him with a supreme contempt for his fellow men.

After showing some flair as a generalissimo in the early days of the Second World War, Hitler was soon completely out of his depth. Despite his occasional intuitions, coupled with a phenomenal memory for statistics and a good knowledge of military hardware, he lacked the Greek quality of *phronesis* which the English called prudence. He was deficient in practical wisdom or transcendent common sense. Field Marshal Manstein, one of the best of Germany's professional soldiers, who was always hostile to Hitler, did concede that he had 'a certain eye for operational possibilities', which he said was frequently found among laymen. Manstein qualified this judgement by adding that it was an eye dimmed by a tendency to overestimate the technological resources at hand and by an inadequate assessment of possible results.

Nor would Hitler listen, another fatal weakness in leadership. The contrast with Franklin D. Roosevelt, who became Commander-in-Chief of America's forces by virtue of being President, with no military experience, is especially striking. It shows how a little knowledge combined with a big faith in one's own intuitive powers can be a highly dangerous thing. For Hitler had served in the trenches during the First World War, rising to a non-commissioned officer rank. Churchill, on the other hand, who had more of a military background, always accepted the advice of his Chiefs-of-Staff in the end, if he failed to bring them around to his own way of thinking.

Towards the end of the war, an atmosphere developed around Hitler which was described shortly after the catastrophe by a senior General Staff officer. He had experienced it while briefing Hitler during March and April 1945, and found it repulsive. He wrote:

My impression – and as I determined in my conversations with others, by no means mine alone – was that a person was not merely spiritually crushed by this atmosphere of servility, nervousness, and untruthfulness, but that one could even sense it as a sort of physical sickness. Nothing was genuine there except the fear. There was fear of all shades and degrees.– from being afraid of somehow provoking the displeasure of the *Führer* or annoying him by some ill-advised comment, to naked fear for life itself in view of the impending end of the drama.

The fear felt in Hitler's presence is understandable. Like Napoleon, he could explode with anger. Signalled by finger-snapping, his rages were terrifying. They were also symptoms of Hitler's irrationality. General Guderian, who saw Hitler face to face after Stalingrad for the first time in fourteen months, reported that at this period 'he easily lost his temper and raged, and was then unpredictable.'

To those who opposed him, Hitler could be merciless. He believed that no officer had the right to disobey an order emanating directly or indirectly from him. One corps commander who did so was court-martialled and later shot. Some senior officers did find a way of dealing with him. Field Marshal Model, for example, had the advantage of enjoying Hitler's confidence and was therefore in a better position to stand up to him. He avoided making too many requests; he either came up with forceful proposals or simply reported what he had already done. Hitler's courtiers, too, found ways of manipulating their master. According to Speer, Hitler did not see through their subtle manipulation of his opinions.

He had apparently no nose for methodical deceit. Among the masters of that art were Goering, Goebbels, Bormann and, within limits, Himmler. Since those who spoke out in candid terms on the important questions usually could not make Hitler change his mind, these cunning men who knew how to manage Hitler naturally increased their power. But Hitler tended more and more to hold fast and rigidly to whatever standpoint he had first taken, no matter what objections or alternatives might be urged upon him. He showed an ever-stronger tendency to dismiss reports that did not fit into his picture; and when he could no longer ignore them, he attributed unacceptable defeats to the inadequacy of those carrying out his orders, whether local field commanders, officers at the theatre-command level, or members of the General Staff, whose basic attitude he increasingly distrusted.

Hitler died in the supremely arrogant belief that the German people had failed him: they had not proved worthy of his greatness. They had brought *Götterdammerung* upon their own heads. He was a victim of their betrayal, whom history would one day acknowledge for the genius he knew he was.

'Mistake is an honourable thing in those following great leaders,' wrote the Roman teacher of rhetoric Quintilian in the first century AD. When it was all over, men like Alfred Speer and General Jodl came near to justifying their behaviour by a version of that idea. They could still feel Hitler's hold upon them after death, despite all that reason and common sense now told them. They talked about themselves as if they were subjects awakening from hypnosis, apprehensive and guilty about what had happened while they were under the spell. In varying degrees of intensity, except for a hard-core of unrepentant Nazis, the German nation collectively experienced those same feelings.

Plainly Hitler was not a great leader. He accomplished nothing but the total defeat of his people, the destruction of their homes and untold misery to countless other human beings. Hitler's talent as an orator and his ability to inspire many German hearts are not in question. But charismatic powers can be used for either good or evil ends. Setting aside his charisma, Hitler's weaknesses as a leader outweigh his strengths, so that even in the more technical or functional sense of the word 'good', he fell short of the requirements of a good leader. Above all, Hitler's case tells us that there is no greatness in leadership without moral integrity and the pursuit of ends that history or God will judge as good. In that context, Hitler's story does have a significant lesson for all those who aspire to lead.

MAHATMA GANDHI

Mahatma Gandhi exercised leadership through his personal example and influence rather than through power. But would his style of leadership have worked in the West? Gandhi's example, even more than those of Lincoln, de Gaulle and Hitler, reveals the extent to which leadership is bound up with culture.

For a long time the word 'culture' was used mainly as a synonym for Western civilization – the secular process of human development. In England it acquired definite class associations. But in the late eighteenth century the German writer Johann Herder challenged this view. 'Nothing is more indeterminate than this word,' he wrote, 'and nothing more deceptive than its application to all nations and periods.' Herder attacked the comfortable assumption that the self-development of humanity had moved in a unilinear progression to flower in the European culture around him. Indeed, he attacked the European assumption of cultural superiority.

> Men of all the quarters of the globe, who have perished over the ages, you have not lived solely to manure the earth with your ashes, so that at the end of time your prosperity should be made

happy by European culture. The very thought of a superior European culture is a blatant insult to the majesty of Nature.

It is then necessary, he concluded, to talk of 'cultures' in the plural: the specific and variable cultures of different natures and periods, and even the sub-cultures (as we call them) of different social groups within the nation.

In India, the equivalent of *leader* is the word *neta*. In its positive sense it is used for a person who commands respect and even awe and has charismatic qualities about him. Because of the misdeeds and misdemeanours of some of the political leaders in the post-independence era, the word has also come to be used as a taunt for those who pose as leaders but are not accepted as such. In India, the test of leadership lies in personal example, inspirational image and acceptance of the leader's qualities and attributes by the followers.

When asked, Indians tend to name Gandhi as the great leader in their nation's history. Mohandas Gandhi was born in Portbander, on India's North West Coast. In 1887, at the age of eighteen, he was sent to London, where he stayed for three years studying law. Working as a lawyer in South Africa, he experienced active racial discrimination. He led a political and religious campaign against South Africa's racist laws and was imprisoned in 1908. Returning to India in 1919, he used 'civil disobedience' to attack the caste system.

This fragile-looking man, ridiculed by some but revered by millions, advocated a simple, non-violent way of life. In 1932 he started a 'fast unto death' to demand rights for the lowest of the Indian castes – the 'Untouchables'. Later, as a member of the Indian National Congress, Gandhi was arrested in 1942 for his part in the campaign to remove India from the British Empire. Home Rule was eventually granted in 1947. During the transfer of power from the British, Gandhi toured India trying to build peace between Hindu and Muslim. At the age of seventy-nine he fasted for five days to try to prevent war between them. On 30 January, 1948, on his way to a prayer meeting, Gandhi was shot and killed by a fanatical Hindu, and thus ended a life dedicated to peace and the abolition of violence.

Such is the bare outline of his story. Through his asceticism – Mahatma means literally 'Great Soul' – and his popularity with the masses of poorer Indians, born out of his complete identification with their lifestyle and aspirations, Gandhi acquired an immense influence. He was the only one among the top leaders who adopted the dress and lifestyle of the poor masses and risked being called 'the naked Fakir' during his visit to England. This is an example which was not emulated by any of his colleagues, who appeared to show a certain degree of ambivalence towards poverty and the lifestyle of those in authority.

The image that Gandhi presented – a frail, barefooted man dressed in a *dhoti* of hand-spun cotton – may have seemed totally outside the English experience of leadership. But it echoed in one forgotten strand in the Western tradition. For Jesus had also walked barefoot (if early Arab sources are to be believed), wearing an undyed woollen robe, and practising both celibacy and a degree of asceticism.

India places spiritual life on a higher plane than material progress or even existence. Gandhi epitomized that quality of India more than any other political leader before or since. In order to lead India, he knew he must disinfect himself of ego and become as nothing. Deep in the Indian soul, too, lay a fundamental concern with right and wrong. The cultural forms in which those contrasting values are explored and deified appeared strange to the English, for the moral tradition was embedded in the mythological doings of the pantheon of Hindu gods: *Brahma* and his associates *Vishnu*, the preserver, and *Shiva*, the destroyer and regenerator.

At the heart of the Indian experience lay the concept of spiritual quest for truth, a seeking after a state of being which is higher than the present plane of existence. Because he so manifestly followed that way, Gandhi achieved his massive popularity. His life was a spiritual quest, he maintained, and political activity came from it as a second-ary mode of expression. His emphasis on right and wrong in the moral sense, in what the secularized British held to be political matters, struck a deep chord in the Indian villages. For the Indian villager also saw life in the context of an eternal struggle between good and evil.

Gandhi's quest for spiritual truth in religions other than his own, notably in the Gospels, was entirely in keeping with the eclectic tradition of Hinduism and also the primacy of the spiritual search for truth. But his search for a universal God, transcending the religions and sects of the world, also had political implications. Both before and after Independence, the most pressing issue for India was the division between those of the Hindu and Muslim religious faiths. Gandhi's search for a common God might have provided a source of unity, for in drawing near to God people draw near to each other.

Above all, Gandhi wanted to see India preserved as a unity. Like Lincoln, he saw bloodshed as inevitable: if so, let it be within India rather than between divided nations on the sub-continent. Gandhi's critics may well be right in their charge that in this respect he was naive and unrealistic. Gandhi is also open to the criticism that he did not attempt to win over the Muslim leader, Muhammad Ali Jinnah, to his vision of India before his attitude had hardened beyond change. By the time Gandhi bestirred himself, the British, under Mountbatten's camouflage screen of charm, were beginning to wash their hands of India. Partition gave them a face-saving exit from the subcontinent.

As a political leader Gandhi was not great. His greatness lies more in his spiritual and moral leadership of India. His strength came from his closeness to the people. Gandhi's identification with the villagers of India led him to campaign for a restoration of traditional values. In order to stem the population drift in the already overcrowded and poverty-stricken cities, such as Calcutta and Bombay, he sought to call a halt to industrialization. The British had imported Indian cotton, milled it and sold back their manufactures to the Indians. As part of his rural economic programme, Gandhi advocated that the villagers should keep their raw cotton and spin it themselves. As a natural leader, he led by example – spinning for at least an hour every day.

An attractive warmth pervaded Gandhi's attitude to the Untouchables, those Indians so lowly that they had no place in even the lowest of the four main caste groups that together made up the ladder of incarnation. Gandhi gave these Untouchables a name – *Harijans*, God's people. With a clear eye, he not only saw that the caste system was the key threat in India's unity and harmony, but he took what symbolic action he could to bring that message home. Of course one man, however influential, could not alter such an integral feature of Indian social life. Perhaps the inroads of Western technology, business and secularist thought may succeed (at least in the large cities) where Gandhi failed – but in India nothing is assured.

People travelled miles to see Gandhi. In India, even looking upon a holy man from afar is believed to give the

THE GIFT OF EQUALITY

'He who treats as equals those who are far below him in strength really makes them a gift of the equality of human beings, of which fate had deprived them . . .'

Simone Weil

beholder a share in his *darshan* – his inner spiritual integrity or power. People wanted to touch Gandhi, too, in order to have contact with this integrity, just as the throngs reached out hands to Jesus in order to touch him. With Gandhi, as with Jesus, people touched the feet or hem of the garment, for by doing so they gave a sign that they had humbled themselves as near to the ground as possible.

Many who were friends or disciples of *Bapu* (father), or otherwise knew him well, still have about them the aura of this charming and friendly man, and embody the stoic self-discipline he inspired. Many of them still spin their own yarn on the *charkha* every day as Gandhi taught them to do, an example of his lingering message of self-sufficiency.

Gandhi's successor, Jawarharlal Nehru, was not of the same mould. While he had his own charisma, he was an essentially westernized politician without Gandhi's extra-ordinary *rapport* with the grassroots of India, nor his moral edge. Prime Minister Indira Gandhi (despite the name she and Gandhi were not related) knew Gandhi well. Some of her political strength came from that fact. She appreciated the need to keep in touch. India needs leaders who can combine the values of the old with the best of the new. Such political leaders will be travellers on the spiritual path that Gandhi followed.

NELSON MANDELA

A great nation in a great crisis . . . South Africa found in Nelson Mandela a statesman of real stature, one aptly named after that English leader of genius already portrayed in this book. His story is one of outstanding moral courage against seemingly impossible odds, of determination to destroy the evil of apartheid, and – above all – of tireless efforts to bring about reconciliation in his homeland.

Nelson Mandela reveals many of the qualities that go to make a leader, such as confidence in humanity – 'I am fundamentally an optimist' – patience and tolerance, a strong sense of justice, and an unswerving loyalty to his colleagues. But there are two qualities he personifies: *strength of mind* and *magnanimity*.

MANDELA'S EARLY LIFE

The man who has become such an inspirational figure was born in 1918, the eldest son of a Xhosa chief (the Xhosas are the next biggest tribe to the Zulus) in what is now the nominally independent homeland called Transkei. After training as a lawyer, he joined the African National Congress in 1944 and was a leader of the Congress's non-violent campaigns against apartheid during the 1950s.

After police killed sixty-nine unarmed black protesters at Sharpeville in 1960, Mandela and other Congress leaders abandoned increasingly their hopes for peaceful change. In 1961 they formed the Congress's military wing, Umkhonto we Sizwe (The Spear of the Nation).

Mandela evaded arrest, earning the nickname 'The Black

Pimpernel', until August 1962, when he was jailed for five years for incitement and leaving the country illegally. In 1963 he was tried again, along with other underground leaders, and in 1964 was jailed for life for sabotage, which he openly admitted.

At his trial, Mandela spoke of 'the ideal of a democratic and free society in which all persons live together in harmony and with equal opportunities. It is an ideal which I hope to live for and to achieve, but if need be an ideal for which I am prepared to die.'

As Mandela began his long sojourn in the harsh outpost of the South African prison system, Robben Island, he resolved that he would not allow this experience to remove from him his essential dignity as a person:

In and of itself, that assured that I would survive, for any man or institution that tries to rob me of my dignity will lose because I will not part with it at any price or under any pressure. I never seriously considered the possibility that I would not emerge from prison one day. I never thought that a life sentence truly meant life and that I would die behind bars. Perhaps I was denying this prospect because it was too unpleasant to contemplate. But I always knew that someday I would once again feel the grass under my feet and walk in the sunshine as a free man.

James Gregory, Mandela's jailer for twenty years, has written a book about his prisoner who became a friend. Soon after his arrival he had his first dramatic encounter with Mandela, then working in slave labour conditions in the searing light and heat of the Robben Island lime quarry, scene of many a fearful atrocity. Prisoners were beaten and abused and had dogs set on them. It was here that Gregory saw Mandela, standing tall, 'his ramrod back and broad shoulders prominent' in his prison shorts and sandals, amidst a group of prisoners, his whole body, says Gregory, a statement that 'I am a leader. You will not intimidate me.' Mandela greeted Gregory with a firm good morning and 'Welcome to Robben Island' and Gregory, before he knew it, slipped into the Zulu greeting he had not used since childhood, a mark of respect which left Mandela stunned.

Gradually the two men became friends. When Mandela's son Thembi was killed in a road traffic accident, Gregory, then a young man, lent him what support he could. At exactly the same age and almost twenty years later, Gregory's son was killed in a car crash, and Mandela appears to have saved Gregory from despair and even suicide by talking to him daily for weeks. Saying farewell to this prison warder whom he had known for twenty-three years, Mandela embraced him with tears in his eyes. 'The wonderful hours we spent together during the last two decades end together,' he wrote in a note, 'but you will always be in my thoughts.'

After his release from prison – 'these long, lonely, wasted years' as he wrote – Mandela showed the rare quality of *magnanimity*, which from the Latin means literally *greatness of spirit*. For the Greeks and Romans it was the sure sign of a great leader. Stemming from a well-founded high regard for oneself, *magnanimity* manifests itself as generosity of spirit and equanimity in the face of trouble or adversity.

A magnanimous leader such as Nelson Mandela lacks any kind of pettiness and rises above even justified resentment. Consider what he endured. His children were traumatically affected by those years, his first wife Evelyn was unprepared to accept his allegiance to the ANC, he was unable to pay his last respects to his mother or his son. Add to that the government's relentless persecution of his family. He says: 'To see your family, your children, being persecuted when you are absolutely helpless in jail, that is one of the most painful experiences I have had . . . Your wife being hounded from job to job, your children being taken out of Coloured schools, police breaking into your house at midnight and even assaulting your wife.'

Yet not once does he express bitterness towards the white community for his grim ordeal, only against the system they imposed. How typical that upon his release from prison, he called for the blacks to exhibit generosity of spirit; and on the day of the Election (27 April 1994) he spoke of the need to give the white minority 'confidence and security'.

Even when Mandela met Percy Yutar, the lawyer who led the prosecution in the trial that ended with his sentence to prison all those years ago, he smiled and placed his arm around the slender shoulders of his one-time adversary, now 84 years old, saying what had happened was now truly in the past. After this meeting Mr Yutar described the President as a 'saintly man'. And Mandela invited his jailer James Gregory and his family as guests of honour to his presidential inauguration. His natural authority and charisma are evident to all those who meet him, and he possesses the gift of a winning smile. He remains courteous and attentive to individuals, whatever their age or status. He retains the common touch, greeting workers and heads of state with the same warm civility and punctilious manners.

It is such generosity of spirit that makes Nelson Mandela one of the world's most significant moral leaders since Gandhi. His moral stature stands out even more in an age so often deprived of political morality.

His greatest achievement has been to create through majestic leadership a climate in which the new South Africa can collect itself for the journey that lies ahead.

KEY POINTS

- To be a great leader in the historical sense there are three requirements: a great nation, a great necessity and a man or woman of great natural leadership ability.

- There are very different styles of leadership, related to individual personalities, nations and cultures. They can be equally effective in giving a strong direction for people to follow.

- As the lives of Abraham Lincoln and Charles de Gaulle show, a great leader is one who has the spirit and dignity of character which are equal to the greatness of the office.

- But some approaches – such as that adopted by Hitler – are fatally flawed. Morally unscrupulous leaders, who manage people essentially by fear and mislead them to corrupt and destructive ends, will eventually forfeit the trust of all but a few fanatically devoted followers. 'Trust being lost,' wrote the Roman historian Livy, 'all the social intercourse of men is brought to naught.'

- Gandhi's example reminds us of the importance of a leader staying close to the people and representing their greatness of spirit. Humility, in the sense of treating men and women as equals, belongs to the essence of great leadership.

- Nelson Mandela has shown the world a lofty and courageous spirit, a nobility of feeling and generosity of mind. Such a spirit enables a leader to bear trouble calmly, to disdain meanness and revenge, and to make sacrifices for worthy ends. It can also alter the mood of a nation.

POINTS TO PONDER

☐ 'Rome showed itself to be truly great, and hence worthy of great leaders,' wrote Plutarch in his biography of Cato the Elder. Nations and organizations often forget that greatness lies within themselves as much as in their leaders. Great teams and great organizations deserve excellent leaders – and often find them. Never blame your troubles on lack of leadership: put your own house in order so that you become worthy of the best leaders available.

☐ Some nations, in times of difficulty, are fortunate to find the great leaders they deserve; others are not. In the future, nations and organizations will have to invest more time and thought in exploring ways in which to grow leaders of calibre to face the demands of the twenty-first century. How do you think that nations can improve their stock of political and social leaders? What is your organization doing to grow or develop leaders for tomorrow?

12

LEADERS FOR TOMORROW

'Those having torches will pass them on to others.'
Plato

An almost universal sense of the need for good leaders has appeared within recent years. There are now many educational and training programmes specifically designed to develop leaders for today and tomorrow. Why has this come about?

The chief reason is a steady and deep shift in values, like a movement of the continental plates, a seismic change which underlies all our national cultures, shaking some more than others. The higher value placed upon the individual, fed from classical and biblical sources, has led to much more emphasis on education. Men and women are assumed to be born, in all the important aspects, free and equal. We, as individuals, are seen as ends in ourselves, not merely as means to other ends. This unique value of each person is increasingly taken for granted, and egalitarianism has been in the ascendant for some time.

Does not this affirmation of our essential personal equality lessen the opportunity and need for leadership? On the contrary, the truth has become increasingly clear that a democratic society does need good leadership. For leaders enable free and equal people to be effective in doing what needs to be done. That principle applies to *every* organization and institution within a democratic society. 'Those who are near will not hide their ability,' wrote a Taoist author, Hsun-Tzu, 'and those who are distant will not grumble at their toil ... that is what is called being a leader and teacher of men.'

THE TRIBAL LEGACY

The thirty or so large tribes which the Romans found in Britain had their own tradition of leadership, which they shared with their cousins on the mainland of North-Western Europe. The Roman historian Tacitus has left us some clear glimpses of how they organized themselves. 'About minor matters, the chiefs consult among themselves; about greater matters, all consult. But even those things which are kept for the general opinion are fully considered by the chiefs,' he wrote. The tribes had no fixed times for their general assemblies, and two or three days could be lost in calling all the men together. They came to the meetings fully armed. After the priests called for silence, the first to speak in debate would be the king, a chieftain or some other wise elder. Vote was by voice and acclamation.

Tribes throughout the world in human history have shared that freedom from unnecessary hierarchy, that sense of equality and deference to good leadership. In her account of her travels in *Bedouin Tribes of the Euphrates*, for instance, the Victorian writer Lady Anne Blunt described the Bedouin tribe as 'the purest form of democracy to be found in the world'. A later authority on the Bedouin, Wilfred Thesiger, described the role of the tribal chief thus:

> A Bedu sheikh has no paid retainers on whom he can rely to carry out his orders. He is merely the first among equals in a society where every man is intensely independent and quick to resent any hint of autocracy. His authority depends in consequence on the force of his own personality and his skill in handling men.
>
> *Arabian Sands* (1959)

An early version of the legend of King Arthur has his 'miraculous table' being made on his order by a crafty Cornish carpenter. Unlike the traditional baronial hall, with a high table on a platform, the Round Table seated all its company on the same level. There was no head of table, and so no quarrels over precedence; mutual respect and reciprocal generosity were engendered. It symbolized the English tribal tradition of a leader as 'first among equals'.

But can leaders be trained? The common-sense conclusion of this book is that leadership potential can be developed, but it does have to be there in the first place. Most people have some degree of aptitude for getting things done with people. In this respect learning to lead and learning to swim are analogous. Most people can be taught to swim, but few will reach Olympic standards and become great swimmers.

Lord Slim may have sounded as if he was exaggerating when he said in words earlier quoted: 'There is nobody who cannot vastly improve his or her powers of leadership by a little thought and practice.' But young people in particular need that voice of encouragement from one of the great leaders of our times. For many of us do have hidden potential for leadership which too often only emerges in times of crisis, such as wars. Yet the problems and opportunities of our troubled peace call for leadership on an unprecedented scale.

LEADERSHIP MENTORS

The word 'mentor' is derived from Greek mythology. When the hero Odysseus left Ithaca, he entrusted his son Telemachus to an old friend on the island named Mentor. The goddess Athena took Mentor's shape on more than one occasion, to help Telemachus in the difficulties that befell Ithaca during his father's absence. Under Mentor's inspired tutelage the untried youth eventually became a seasoned leader.

Telemachus appeared at first in the story as a good and dutiful son, but lacking in spark or drive: he was timid and unenterprising. Later, at the behest of Athena working through Mentor, he ordered his mother's domineering suitors to depart. When they refused, guided by Mentor he resolved to sail to the mainland and report the calamitous turn of events to his father. As the story unfolds Telemachus demonstrates ever more resolve, energy and resourcefulness. When Telemachus eventually joins Odysseus upon the latter's return to Ithaca, he acts as an intelligent and enterprising helper. He astonishes his mother Penelope, for example, by taking command in the house and leading the fight against the over-mighty suitors.

This Greek myth does illustrate a truth about leadership. Leaders are inspiring. In order to become so they need to be inspired themselves. Mentors are those who both inspire us with a vision of leadership and consciously aid our individual development as leaders. They do so as much by their example as by their words.

Leadership is probably more caught than taught. The example of a few good leaders ignites in us the spirit of leadership, and we in turn have the responsibility of passing on the torch to those who are ready to receive it. But the leaders of tomorrow will need a personal greatness as leaders which does not characterize many leaders today. Hence this book, which is in part an appeal from history over the heads of this generation to the leaders of tomorrow, showing the way to a new excellence in leadership.

NOT FOLLOWERS BUT COMPANIONS

Leadership as a concept, however, has one questionable assumption, caught like a fly in amber, within the image behind it. A leader seems to imply a follower. The basic metaphor of leadership – a leader on a track or journey going ahead and showing others the way – does give us a picture of followers. Indeed, a leader has been defined as 'a person who creates followers'. Now sheep are programmed to follow, which is why they are so easy to lead. Men and women are inclined to follow, too, but being rational, they ought always to exercise their reason or judgement before doing so. Alexander the Great found that he could not lead his Greeks against their better judgement. Discriminating and determined colleagues are as important as good leaders.

Educated, intelligent, highly technically competent people today are not likely to see themselves as followers. When the Germans allowed themselves to become a nation of followers, with a demagogue as their misleader, they did so with disastrous results. Good leaders today will tend to see people as colleagues, companions or partners, not followers. As one progresses through levels of leadership, of

THE LEADER AS FIRST COMPANION

John Hunt, now Lord Hunt, led the British expedition that first climbed Everest in 1953. These words are from a talk he gave in 1959, entitled 'Leadership in the Modern Age'.

'Firstly, I will give you my definition of leadership, as applied to someone to whom other people are entrusted. To me, it is best described as the art of inspiring others to give of their best, and the courage to use this art. That is what leadership means to me: it demands that the leader operates from inside his group, not from above it; that in setting a good example, he does not steal the initiative of the others; in other words that he takes his full share — but no more than his share — of the job in hand. This implies a willingness not merely to decentralize, or apportion the burden, but an ability to persuade each other member of the group that his is an equally essential job, and that each has his own liberty as well as responsibility to develop that part as a whole.

'Good leadership derives from a right attitude to the job of leading; that this is only one of the jobs to be done. A leader has been well described as a "first companion". Then, of course, it is the art of blending the efforts of everyone concerned to produce a combined result.'

course, many of those colleagues will be leaders in their own right. Apart from the Taoist teachings, there are examples in the Western tradition of how leaders can transform subordinates or followers, giving them a sense of being co-equal partners in the common enterprise. 'No longer do I call you servants, for the servant (or slave) does not know what his master is doing,' said Jesus to his disciples, 'but I have called you friends, for all . . . I have made known to you.' Nelson saw his captains as a 'band of brothers' and treated them as such. True leaders want equals, not subordinates.

AN INVITATION TO GREATNESS

'Be not afraid of greatness,' wrote Shakespeare. Greatness in leadership is possible to many more people now than in Shakespeare's day. Historical greatness in politics, of course, is restricted to few men and women, because it depends not only upon a person's gift for leadership but also upon his or her headship of a great nation or group of nations in a time of great necessity. But more politicians will become world leaders, if not great statesmen, as they learn to transcend party and national interest, taking a much broader view of what is good for the world and developing the leadership skills needed to move in that direction. 'The leadership of the privileged has passed away; but it has not been succeeded by that of the eminent,' wrote Winston Churchill in *Great Contemporaries* (1937). 'Nevertheless, the world is moving on; and moving so fast that few have time to ask – whither?' In a period when politicians have become even more dominated by short-term issues, Churchill's words are still apposite.

NOT RULERS BUT LEADERS

The celebrated Dutch historian John Huizinga concluded his chapter on 'The Spirit of the Netherlands', in *Dutch Civilization in the Seventeenth Century* (1968), with these words:

Authority, yes, provided it is understood aright – authority based not on brute force but on the subordination of authority itself to the highest law and bound by legal principles that draw their inspiration from it.

Leadership, gladly, provided our leaders are guides and not dictators. We do not wish to be led like Breughel's blind or like a bear on a chain. Our leaders must be those who submit to a higher wisdom, to wisdom that sets its sights beyond the limits of national and state interest, just as the helmsman steers by the stars.

To keep trust, to point the way, to care, to direct – those are the ancient virtues by whose presence St Augustine distinguished the true political task from the evil appetites for power and domination. Political thinking aware of the commands of justice and the limits of human power must always come back to the old images of the steersman who, knowing his own human frailty, holds the oar steady in the storm, of the fallible shepherd who humbly tends his flock. A poet put it into the mouth of him, but for whose labour there would have been no Dutch nation and no Dutch state:

> 'Your shepherd never sleepeth albeit
> you have strayed'*

* From the national anthem.

One man who personified the leadership needed in tomorrow's politicians was Dag Hammarskjöld, Secretary General of the United Nations. Son of a Swedish prime minister, he became the world's leading civil servant in 1953 and held that job until his death in a plane crash in 1958 while attempting to solve the crisis in the Congo. After his death a book of his reflections was published under the title of *Markings*. That word translates the

Swedish phrase *Väg märken*, the waymarks or stone cairns that are found beside mountain paths. One of Dag Hammarskjöld's 'markings' underlines a message that has emerged as one of the central themes of this book. Speaking to himself when alone one evening, he wrote: 'Your position never gives you the right to command. It only imposes on you the duty of so living your life that others can receive your orders without being humiliated.'

Other leaders, at all levels and in all fields, can and should aspire to that ideal. For it is the only kind of leadership that will really work over a long period of time among free and equal people.

Thus greatness now is more a matter of quality rather than degree. It is possible to be a great leader as a supervisor or hospital sister, as the head of a university department or as a school teacher, as the chief executive of a company or as the director of a government department. Such greatness in the 'ordinary' roles of leadership is what helps to constitute a great nation in the spiritual and moral sense of that word.

In peace, as in war, there are now many situations that call for personal greatness. The first step towards it is always the willingness to take responsibility. 'The price of greatness is responsibility,' wrote Winston Churchill. Position is really secondary. True, people who occupy the major roles or positions of leadership *ought* to lead and be trained to lead, but it is possible for those in much humbler positions – or even those with none – to achieve a degree of excellence in leadership and teamwork. Lord Hunt, of Everest fame, made that very point in the talk already quoted: 'In its true sense, leadership should mean giving a lead by example, even without a position of authority. True leadership is simply an expression of human greatness. Some of the finest examples of this aspect of leadership are displayed by men who have no high position or reputation at stake, but with much to lose in security, in comradeship and convenience, who stand up for what they know, from their conscience, to be right.'

Our greatness lies in our ability to transcend ourselves in the service of that which has greater value to us than ourselves. There is not a single man or woman who has not had great moments, who has not risen to rare occasions. It is true that we need situations which call out the best in us as leaders, but all leaders can prepare themselves for such a time. Nor will opportunities be lacking. For as Walt Whitman wrote: 'It is provided in the essence of things, that from any fruition of success, no matter what, shall come forth something to make a greater struggle necessary.'

KEY POINTS

- A leader should be able to place himself or herself on an equal footing with the others involved, relying upon their authority of knowledge and personality to gain respect. Such a stance does require considerable inner confidence; people will soon sense if it is there. They will soon sense, too, if a leader can show them the way forwards and lead them on their journey.

- Leadership exists on different levels – team, operational, strategic, national and global. The philosophy of leadership in this book applies to *all* those levels. It transcends colour, race, gender, time and space. Why? Because underlying human nature is more or less the same.

- Leadership comes into its own when people are free and equal. Leaders create not followers but partners in the common enterprise.

- 'Smith is not a born leader yet,' one manager read on his annual report. Yet given some natural aptitude for leadership – much more widely distributed than was once supposed – everyone can develop leadership ability. You have no excuse! But tomorrow calls for a new standard of quality of leadership within you, one only glimpsed in times past in the very best of natural leaders. Now the world calls for many more of such great leaders. Will you be among their number?

- The author Graham Greene was once asked if he considered himself to be a great novelist. 'Not great,' he replied, 'but one of the best.' It may be that personal greatness in leadership may elude most leaders, dependent as it is upon situations which evoke it as well as one's gifts as a leader. But you can and should aspire to being 'one of the best'.

- Real excellence goes hand in hand with humility, that unlikely leadership virtue. Humility includes both seeing the truth about oneself and also being open to learning more about good leadership. It suggests, too, that necessary sense of greatness in others. For in John Buchan's words:

The task of leadership is not to put greatness into humanity, but to elicit it, for the greatness is there already.

FURTHER READING

Aristotle, *The Politics* and *Ethics*, Penguin Classics, 1981 and 1976.

Asser, *Life of King Alfred*, Penguin Classics, 1983.

Barnard, C. I., *The Functions of the Executive*, Harvard University Press, 1938.

Barnett, C., *Bonaparte*, George Allen and Unwin, 1978.

Blondel, J., *Political Leadership: Towards a General Analysis*, Sage, 1981.

Bosworth, A. B., *Conquest and Empire: The Reign of Alexander the Great*, Cambridge, 1988.

Burns, J. MacGregor, *Leadership*, Harper & Row, 1978.

Carlyle, T., *On Heroes, Hero-Worship and the Heroic in History*, 1841, Oxford University Press ed., 1904.

Carpenter, H., *Jesus*, Oxford University Press, 1980.

Crozier, B., *De Gaulle*, Eyre Methuen.

De Gaulle, C., *The Edge of the Sword*, Greenwood press, 1932.

Emmet, D. M., *Function, Purpose and Powers*, Macmillan, 1958.

Fest, J. C., *Hitler*, Penguin, 1977.

Greenleaf, R. K., *Servant Leadership: A Journey into the Nature of Legitimate Power and Greatness*, Punlist Press, 1977.

Gregory, J., *Goodbye Bafana: Nelson Mandela, My Prisoner, My Friend*, Headline.

Hamilton, N., *Monty: Master of the Battlefield 1942–1944*, Hamish Hamilton, 1983.

Hammarskjöld, D., *Markings*, Faber, 1964.

Harvey-Jones, J., *Making It Happen: Reflections on Leadership*, Collins, 1988.

Heider, J., *The Tao of Leadership*, Wildwood House, 1986.

Hsun Tzu, *The Art of War*, ed. J. Clavell, Hodder & Stoughton, 1981.

Huntford, R., *Scott and Amundsen*, Hodder & Stoughton, 1979.

Huntford, R., *Shackleton*, Hodder & Stoughton, 1985.

Jay, A., *Management and Machiavelli*, Hodder & Stoughton, 1967.

Kennedy, L., *Nelson and His Captains*, Collins, 1975.

Lane-Fox, R., *Alexander the Great*, Allen Lane, 1973.

Lawrence, A. W. (ed.), *T. E. Lawrence by his Friends*, Jonathan Cape, 1937.

Lewin, R., *Slim the Standard Bearer*, Leo Cooper, 1976.

Mandela, N., *Long Walk to Freedom*, Little, Brown, 1994.

Mant, A., *Leaders We Deserve*, Martin Robertson, 1983.

Montgomery, B. L., *The Path to Leadership*, Collins, 1961.

Needham, J., *Science and Civilisation in China*, Vol. 2, Cambridge University Press, 1956.

Nixon, R., *Leaders*, Sidgwick & Jackson, 1982.

Oman, C., *Nelson*, Hodder & Stoughton, 1947.

Plutarch, *The Rise and Fall of Athens, Makers of Rome, Fall of the Roman Republic*, Penguin Classics, 1960, 1965 and 1972.

Pollard, S., *The Genesis of Modern Management*, Edward Arnold, 1965.

Raab, F., *The English Face of Machiavelli*, Routledge & Kegan Paul, 1964.

Schram, P. E., *Hitler: The Man and the Military Leader*, Allen Lane, 1972.

Scott, J. M., *Gino Watkins*, Hodder & Stoughton, 1935.

Slim, W., *Defeat into Victory*, Cassell, 1956.

Stewart, D., *T. E. Lawrence*, Hamish Hamilton, 1977.

Tead, O., *The Art of Leadership*, McGraw-Hill, 1935.

Tendulkar, D.G., *Mahatma*, Greenleaf Books, 1983.

Thucydides, *History of the Peloponnesian War*, Penguin Classics, 1954.

Tinker, H., *Men Who Overturned Empires: Fighters, Dreamers and Schemers*, Macmillan, 1988.

Thomson, R., *After I was Sixty*, Hamish Hamilton, 1975.

Warner, O., *A Portrait of Lord Nelson*, Chatto and Windus, 1958.

Watt, E.D., *Authority*, Croom Helm, 1982.

Watts, A., *Tao: The Watercourse Way*, Jonathan Cape, 1976.

Willner, A. R., *The Spellbinders: Charismatic Political Leadership*, Yale University Press, 1984.

Xenophon, *Memorabilia* and *Oeconomicus*, ed. E. C. Marchant and O. J. Todd, 'Xenophon in Seven Volumes', Vol. IV, Harvard University Press and Heinemann, 1923.

Xenophon, *The Persian Expedition* and *A History of My Times*, Penguin Classics, 1972 and 1979.

INDEX

Abercrombie, General Sir Ralph, 103
Absolute rule, 56, 61–3
Adams, Abigail, 85, 208
Agamemnon, 12
Agamemnon HMS, 93, 101
Alamein, Battle of (1942), 157–60
Alanbrooke, Field Marshal Alan
    Brooke, Viscount, 132
Alexander the Great,
  calmness in battle, 58
  charisma of, 57–61
  common touch, 61
  death of, 65
  hero and demi-god, 53, 56, 57,
    61–5, 210
  leadership, 41, 43–50, 58–61,
    244
  self-importance, 58–61
Alfred, King, 210
Antisthenes, 29–30
Appearance, *see* Physical
    characteristics of leaders
Aquino, Cora, 180
Aristophanes, 11
Aristotle, 81, 113
Arran (Flavius Arrianus), 44–5, 61
Arrogance, 71, 117
Artaxerxes II, 16
Artemisia, 182

Arthur, King, 242
Ashley, Laura, 197
Attila the Hun, 55–6
Attlee, Clement,
  on Cabinet government, 122–4
  leading decision-making, 111
  and management through
    leadership, 172
Authority, 16, 52, 215–17

Babylon, 63, 65
Ball, Sir Alexander, 97
Bandaranaike, Sirimavo, 180
Bevan, Aneurin, 123
Bevin, Ernest, 122
Bhutto, Benazir, 180
Bolivar, Simon, 210
Bonham-Carter, Lady Violet, 86
Boone, Daniel, 43
Boudicca, 182–3
Brunel, Isambard Kingdom, 166–7
Bullying, 19
Business skills,
  common attributes of leaders,
    30–32
  and military leadership, 146, 151
  transferability of, 29–32, 40
  see also Management
Butler, Josephine, 193

Cabinet government, 122–4, 204, 219

Callaghan, James (Lord Callaghan), 198–90

Captain of the ship (parable), 11–12

Carduci tribe, 22–4

Carlyle, Thomas, 165, 168

Carrel, Alexis, 124

Ceaucescu, Nicolae, 57

Change,
  bringing about, 163
  Industrial Revolution and, 165–9
  key points, 178
  managing, 177
  points to ponder, 179
  technological, 164, 165–6

Charisma, 51–68
  Alexander the Great's, 57–61
  de Gaulle's, 217–18
  evil, 66
  evocation and invocation, 54–6
  Hitler's, 223–4
  key points, 66–7
  meaning of, 52
  Napoleon's, 63–4
  self-forgetful love, 68
  tied to language and culture, 220

ch'i (effortless effort), 73

Chinese philosophy, 72–8

Chirisophus, 22–4

Christianity,
  disciples as leaders, 79–81
  'the Way', 72
  see also Jesus Christ

Chuang Tzu, 74

Churchill, Sir Winston, 41, 86, 205, 209, 210
  acceptance of expert advice, 225
  humility, 119
  humour, 134–5
  on leadership, 246
  persuasive powers, 116
  progress-chasing, 118

Civil War (English), 189–90

Clarendon, Edward Hyde, 1st Earl of, 75–6

Clearchus, 16–17, 18–20, 25, 115

Cleitus, 59

Coenus, 60

Collier, John, 139

Collingwood, Admiral Cuthbert, Baron, 105

Communication, 99–100, 132
  clarity in giving orders, 140
  effective, 140–42
  of energy, 156
  key points, 161
  necessity for leader, 139
  points to ponder, 162
  putting people in picture, 160
  two-way, 140–41, 161
  see also Inspiration: Listening; Morale

Companions of leaders, 244–6

Conrad, Joseph, 108

Culture, 228

Cunaxa, Battle of (401 BC), 16, 18

Cyrus the Great, 35, 57, 63

Cyrus the Younger, 16, 20

Dayan, Moshe, 126

de Gaulle, Charles, 208, 214–21
  authority of, 215–17, 220
  charisma, 217
  clear purpose, 214–15
  grandeur, 215
  on leadership, 216–17
  Montgomery on, 219–20
  Nixon on, 218–19

Decision-making, 111–38
  board of directors, 111
  in Cabinet, 122–4
  calmness under pressure, 111, 131–4
  common sense, 115
  decisiveness, 115, 121–2
  flair, 126–7
  humour, 134–6

immagination, 128–31
implementing decisions, 117–22
intuition, 124–8
judgement, 121
key points, 136–7
motivation, 115–16
persuasion, 116
points to ponder, 138
progress-chasing, 117–18
prudence, 112–13
reasoned argument, 116–17
responsibility for, 118–21
succinctness in argument, 123
summing up, 123
time to think, 112–17, 219
by women, 195–6
Deioces, 62
Delegation, 134
Demosthenes, 115, 140
Diades, 47
Dionysodurus, 12–13
Discipline, 18–19
Drake, Sir Francis, 185–6

Eden, Sir Anthony (Earl of Avon), 134
Education,
for leadership, 38–9, 41, 240–44
rulers' need for, 17
see also Knowledge
Effortless effort (ch'i), 73
Einstein, Albert, 125
Eisenhower, General Dwight D., 116, 119–20
Elizabeth I, Queen, 184–8, 210
Elyot, Sir Thomas, 102
Employment legislation, 167–9
Encouragement, 25
Equality, 233
Evocation, 54–6
Experience, 127–9

Factory Acts, 167–8
Fear, 15, 19, 132

Flair, 126–7
Francis, Saint, 52
Frederick II, 'the Great', King of Prussia, 18
Functional leadership, 7

Gandhi, Indira, 180, 233
Gandhi, Mahatma, 208, 228–33
background, 229
humility of, 230–31
moral leadership, 232
spirituality of, 231, 233
Gedrosian Desert, 44–6
George III, King, 107
Getty, J. Paul, 126
Gilbert, Martin, 134–5
Gordon, General Charles George, 41
Gorgias of Leontini, 20
Grahame, Kenneth, 131
Greatness, 83–6, 209–11
invitation to, 246–9
responsibility, the price of, 248
Greece and the Greeks,
army
Alexander's leadership, 44–8
authority of generals, 37–8
cavalry, 14–15
discipline, 18–19
disunity in, 64–5
election of generals, 12–13, 28
hoplites, 9, 16
spirit of unity, 47
staff officers, 46
Ten Thousand, 16, 21–4
closeness between leader and
followers, 62, 67
decision-making, 114–15
election to offices, 28–9
gods, 53–4
hero-worship, 53–4
lack of humility, 81
leadership myths, 243
Spartan wars, 114–15
wariness of absolute monarchs, 56

Greene, Graham, 250
Gregory, James, 235–6
Groups,
  needs
    achieving common task, 32–3
    individual skills, 32–3
    maintaining team, 32–3
  power of, 84
  sensing opinions of, 130
  see also Decision-making: Teams

Hamilton, Emma, Lady, 93, 107
Hammarskjöld, Dag, 86, 247–8
Hampden, John, 75–6
Hannibal, 135–6
Harvey-Jones, Sir John, 177, 195
Heath, Sir Edward, 200
Henry, Patrick, 85
Hephaestion, 47
Heracles, 59
Herder, Johann, 228–9
Hermocrates, 141–2
Hero-worship, 53–4, 61–5
Herodotus, 47, 56, 62, 182
Hitler, Adolf, 221–8
  charisma, 66, 223–4
  corrupt rule, 208
  despising experts, 124
  intuition, 124
  lack of judgement, 224–5
  perceptiveness, 224
  refusal to listen to experts, 124,
    225–7
  rise to power, 221–2
  subordinates' fear of, 225–6
  unpredictability, 226
  weaknesses of, 227–8
Ho Chi Minh, 210
Homer, 12, 47
Hood, Samuel Hood, Viscount, 94
Hoover, Herbert, 57
Hospice movement, 195
Howe, Admiral Richard, Earl, 100
Hsun Tzu, 82, 140

Huizinga, John, 246–7
Humility,
  accepting blame, 119–20
  Christian and *Tao* ideal of, 74–8,
    81
  of good leaders, 78–81
  Lao Tzu on, 74–8
  privilege of leadership, 83
  self-centredness, absence of, 83–4
  sharing hardships, 45–8, 70–71,
    81–2, 87–8, 129–30
  substitution of one pride for
    another, 85–6
  test of greatness, 83
  see also Service and leadership
Humour, 134–6
Hunt, John, Baron, 245
Hypasis, River, 60

Imagination, 128–31
Individuals, caring for, 48, 155–6
Inspiration,
  emotion and motive, 145
  getting the best from people, 245
  inspiring others, 142–5
  key points, 161
  morale, 148–60
  points to ponder, 162
  self-belief and, 152–3
  using energy of the people, 143
  in Second World War, 146–60
  see also Communication: Morale
Integrity, 187
Intuition, 124–8
Invocation, 54–6

Japanese management techniques,
  87–8
Jesus Christ,
  on humble style of leadership,
    79–81, 81, 245–6
  humility of, 77
  meekness advocated, 74–5
  servant-leader, 69

see also Christianity
Joan of Arc, Saint, 183, 215
Jones, Jim, 52–3
Joseph, Sir Keith, 200
Judgement, *see* Decision-making
Julius Caesar, 41, 71, 143–5

Keats, Admiral Sir Richard, 99
Kenyatta, Jomo, 210
Knowledge,
   authority flows from man who
     knows, 16, 98–9, 181
   desire for educated rulers, 17
   and experience, 127–9
   key points, 25
   and leadership, 14–17
   learning process, 6
   points to ponder, 25–7
   professional competence, 15
Kurdistan, 21–4

Lao Tzu,
   on humility, 76, 81
   on leadership, 78
   teaching of, 72–4
   see also Taoism
Laomedon, 47
Lathom House, 189
Lawrence, T.E., 129–30
Leach, Bernard, 86
Leadership,
   bullying leaders, 18–19
   caring for individuals, 48
   confidence breeding carelessness,
     15–16
   and discipline, 18–19
   education for, 38–9, 41, 240–44
   form of service to humanity, 32
   functions, 34–5
   key points, 49
   knowledge, importance of, 14–15,
     see also Knowledge
   'leader' derivation of, 43–4
   leaders born or made?, 38–9

   leaders known to subordinates,
     174–5
   leading by example, 22–4, 166–7,
     228
   management through, 35–8,
     172–7
   mentors, 243
   military, *see* Military leadership
   mystique of, 217–19
   need for, 240
   not followers but companions,
     244–6
   physical characteristics of leaders,
     18, 54, 57, 94
   points to ponder, 25–7, 41–2
   qualities required, 25–7, 34–5
   sharing hardships, 45–8, 70–71,
     81–2, 87–8, 129–30
   showing the way, 44
   situational approach, 25
   skills, 28–42
     key points, 39–41
   Socrates on, 11
   styles of, *see* Styles of leadership
   subtlety in, 186–7
   supplying needs of others, 32–3
   theory of, 41–2
   unscrupulous leaders, 54
   Western tradition of, 181–8
   see also Women as leaders
Lee, General Robert E., 133–4
Lewin, Ronald, 156–7
Lincoln, Abraham, 208, 210, 211–13
Listening,
   importance of, for leaders, 75, 121
   and questions, 141
   to unwelcome truths, 205
   see also Communication
Locker, Captain William, 99
Luck, 60

Macedonians, 47, 59
Machiavelli, 186–7, 222–3

Macmillan, Harold (Lord Stockton), 134
MacNeice, Louis, 168–9
Management,
  being known by subordinates, 174–5
  Captains of Industry, 165–6
  factory legislation, 167–8
  key points, 178
  leadership in, 35–8
  man-management, 34–8
  nineteenth-century despotism, 165–9
  points to ponder, 179
  social conscience, 169
  through leadership, 172–7
  women as leader–managers, 195–7
  Xenophon on, 36
  see also Business skills
Mandela, Nelson, 234–8
  early life, 234–5
  imprisonment, 235–6
  magnanimity, 236–7
Manstein, Field Marshal Fritz von, 225
Marduk cult, 63
Marius, 70–71
Mark Anthony, 53
Marlborough, John Churchill, 1st Duke of, 133
Marriage, see Women as leaders
Medes, 57, 62
Meir, Golda, 125–6, 180
Military leadership,
  attributes of successful general, 13
  coolness in action, 133–4
  election of generals in Athens, 28–9
  example under fire, 105–6
  Hsun Tzu on, 82
  inspiring troops, 14, 23–4
  leading by example, 22–4
  love and respect of men, 35–6
  more than tactics needed, 13

  not based on discipline alone, 19
  officer/man relationship, 20–21
  personal qualities of good generals, 18–20, 25–7
  privilege of leadership, 83
  relevance to business, 30–31, 146, 151, 172–7
  selflessness, 74
  sharing hardships, 70–71, 81–2, 129–30
  supplying men's needs, 32, 155
  teamwork on battlefield, 47
  see also Greece and the Greeks; Morale; Nelson, Admiral Horatio
Milton, John, 188–9
Model, Field Marshal Walther, 226
Montgomery, Field Marshal Bernard, 26, 146, 219–20
Morale,
  foundations of, 148–9
  knowledge that authority cares, 155
  meaning of, 148
  mutual confidence, 157–8
  of those in lowly positions, 150
  see also Communication: Military leadership
Motivation, 115–16
Motley, John, 210
Mountbatten, Lord Louis, 154
Mulberry Harbours, 118
Mystique of leadership, 217–19

Napoleon Bonaparte, 63–4, 221
Needs,
  and Christian ethic, 80–81
  common, in all areas of human work, 36
  of groups, see Groups
  human, and leadership functions, 32–5
  Nelson's care for others, 102–3
Nehru, Jawarharlal, 233

Nelson, Admiral Horatio, Viscount,
91–110
  acquisition of naval knowledge,
    98–9
  appearance, 94–5
  care for others, 102–3
  command of *Agamemnon*, 93
  communicator, 99–100
  despatches, 93–4
  discipline, 101, 104
  early life, 92–3
  human failings, 107–8
  inspiring confidence in others, 91,
    100
  key points, 109
  leadership qualities, 91, 108
  legacy of, 107–8
  legend of, 93–7
  meeting with Wellington, 95–6
  naval engagements, 93, 98–9,
    101–7
  Nelson touch, 100
  patriotism, 92
  physical courage, 98
  points to ponder, 110
  popular hero, 93
  promoting harmony, 100–101
  public relations fostered, 93–4
  relationship with crew, 101
  trust in subordinates, 100, 104–5
  vanity and modesty of, 94–7
Nicholas, Paul, 105–6
Nicomachides, 29–32, 40
Nightingale, Florence, 192–3
Nile, Battle of (1798), 93, 95, 97,
  101–2, 103–4
Nixon, Richard, 218–19, 220
Nkrumah, Kwame, 210

Obedience,
  duty of those being obeyed, 103
  given to knowledgeable leader,
    14–17

  unconditional, and lack of civil
    liberties, 56
  willing or grudging, 17
Odysseus, 243
Onassis, Aristotle, 210
Oratory, 75, 140
Ovid, 108
Owen, Robert, 168

Pankhurst, Emmeline, 193–4
Paul, Saint, 68, 183
People's Temple Sect, 52–3
Peres, Shimon, 113
Pericles, 15, 41, 113, 114
Perón, Isabelita, 180
Persian Empire, 16, 20, 21–4, 59,
  61–3, 81
Philip of Macedon, 46
Philosophy of leadership, 7, 41–2
phronesis, 112–13, 224
Physical characteristics of leaders, 18,
  54, 57, 94
Plato, 11, 17, 240
Plutarch, 41, 55, 70, 135–6, 143
Praise, 20–21
Proxenus, 20–21
Pym, John, 75

Qualities of leadership, 34–5
Quintilian, 227

Railway building, 166–7
Reagan, Ronald, 113, 209
Responsibility, 248
Roddick, Anita, 196–7
Roman Empire,
  army, 18, 144–5
  humility of leaders, 69–71
  revolt of slaves, 81
  tribal legacy, 241–2
Roosevelt, Theodore, 120
Royal Navy, 18, 31, *see also* Nelson,
  Admiral Horatio
Ruskin, John, 83

Sadat, Mohammed Anwar al, 113
St Vincent, Admiral John Jervis,
    Earl, 91, 94, 101
Samuel, 57
Saul, King, 57
Saunders, Dame Cicely, 195
Second World War,
  and de Gaulle, 214–21
  Montgomery before Alemein,
    157–60
  Slim's Far East campaign, 148–57
  see also Hitler, Adolf
Selecting right person for job, 30–31
Sense of direction, 43
Sertorius, 55
Service and leadership, 69–90
  Greeks' lack of humility, 81
  key points, 88–9
  points to ponder, 89–90
  see also Humility
Situational approach, 25
Slavery, 81
Slim, Field Marshal William,
    Viscount, 26, 28, 146–57
  and management through
    leadership, 172–7
Smiles, Samuel, 165
Socrates,
  on authority of knowledge, 14–17
  and conduct of life, 10–11
  death, 11
  humility of, 81
  on leadership, 11, 74
  philosophical teaching, 9–10
  'The Thinker', 12
  on transferability of leadership
    skills, 29–32
  on women as leaders, 181
  writings on, 11
Sohn, Rudolf, 53
Soteridas, 23–4
Spartacus, 81
Spartan army, 9, 29, 62
Speer, Albert, 224, 227

Steffens, Lincoln, 120–21
Stephenson, George, 165
Stirling, W.F., 130
Styles of leadership, 208–39
  greatness, 209–11
  key points, 238
  points to ponder, 239
Subtlety, 186–7
Success, 60
Suckling, Captain Maurice, 92, 99
Suffragettes, 193–4
Sykes, John, 98

Tacitus, 111, 131, 183
Tantalus, 56
Taoism,
  humility of great leaders, 74–8
  meaning of *Tao*, 72–4
  Tao of leadership, 74–8
  water, significance of, 73, 77
te (power or virtue), 73
Tead, Ordway, 121–2
Teams,
  building and maintaining, 43
  individual satisfaction in, 67
  weak teams with strong leaders, 84
  see also Groups
Technology, 165–7
Telemachus, 243
Tennyson, Alfred, Lord, 164
Thatcher, Margaret (Baroness
    Thatcher), 180, 198–205
  achievements of, 205
  courage of, 200
  election as party leader, 198–200
  femininity, 201
  lack of team spirit, 201–3
  on leadership, 202
  personal dominance, 201, 203–5
  strong leader and weak teams, 84
  Whitelaw on, 203–4
Thesiger, Wilfred, 242
Thomson, Roy, 112, 127–8

Three circles model, 7
Thucydides, 114–15, 141
Time to think, 112–17, 219
Tissaphernes, 23–4
Tomorrow's leaders, 240–50
Trade Unions, 168, 198
Trafalgar, Battle of (1805), 98,
    99–100, 104–7
Transferability of leadership skills,
    29–32, 40
Tribal legacy, 241–2
Trusting subordinates, 100, 104–5,
    132
Tu Mu, 82
Tyre, 58

Venizelos, Eleutherios, 210
Vietnam war, 18
Vision, 1421
Voltaire, François de, 133

Waller, Lady Anne, 190
Wardour Castle, 189
Washington, George, 84–5, 210
Watkins, Gino, 170–72
Weber, Max, 51–3, 223
Wellington, Arthur Wellesley, Duke
    of, 95–7
Western tradition of leadership,
    181–8
Whitelaw, William, 201–5
William III, King (Prince of
    Orange), 94, 101, 210
Wilson, Harold, 198
Women as leaders,
    in ancient times, 181–3
    in Christian church, 183–4
    feminist movement, 183–4

key points, 205–6
knowledge the key, 181
leader-managers, 195–7
in marriage, 188–91
obstacles to women, 180–81
points to ponder, 207
social reformers, 192–5
women's suffrage, 193–4
Woolf, Virginia, 180
Words, power of, 64
Wu Ch'i, 82
Wu wei (principle of not forcing
    things), 73

Xenophon, 63, 65, 69, 81, 103, 141
    birth, 9
    cavalry commander, 9, 14, 16
    commander of Ten Thousand, 24
    elected general, 19–20
    on good generals, 25–7
    on leadership
        ability to supply men's needs,
            32–4
        educating leaders, 38–9
        functional leadership, 7
        knowledge required, 11–12
        physical qualities, 35
    as military leader, 21–4
    philosophical instruction from
        Socrates, 9–10
    on types of obedience, 17–18
    works
        Cyropaedia, 25–6, 35
        Memorabilia, 11
        Oeconomicus (The Economy), 36
        Persian Expedition, 16

Yutar, Percy, 237